TRAFFIC STOP
© 2006 BY TARA WENTZ

ISBN 10: 1-933113-73-1
ISBN 13: 978-1-933113-73-9

First Printing: 2006

This Trade Paperback Is Published By
Intaglio Publications
Melbourne, FL USA
WWW.INTAGLIOPUB.COM

CREDITS
EXECUTIVE EDITOR: RUTA SKUJINS
COVER DESIGN BY SHERI (GRAPHICARTIST2020@HOTMAIL.COM)

Traffic Stop

By
Tara Wentz

DEDICATION

To Chris & Conner: The two loves of my life who gave up
their time with me in order for my dream to come true. I love
you both very much!

To my Mom: You have been the single-most constant in my
life. Thank you for being so supportive and for always being
there. I love you!

ACKNOWLEDGMENTS

Arlene: Thank you for your faith in me from the beginning.

Linda: I live for the lessons, Master Po! ~Little Grasshopper~

Joley: You always believed. Love you, my friend.

My beta readers: You have my heartfelt thanks!

Candena: Thanks for the help, little sis!

Detective Brent Curtis: For his patience. Thank you!

Officer Diane E. : For all the little details. Thank you!

Lori L. Lake & Radclyffe: For all the advice and encouragement.

Kathy Smith: For opening the door.

Sheri/Robin: My publisher-Thank you for giving me the chance to fulfill a dream. Also for the constant encouragement and open ear when I needed it.

Ruta: My editor, for making my story even better and not killing me in the process. <G>

Last, but not least, I owe more than I can say to Tara Young for going above and beyond on so many levels. Thank you just doesn't seem like enough, but...Thank you!

Chapter One

R yan Thomas leaned against the Jeep, watching the numbers roll as the gas filled her tank. It was an unseasonably warm day, making her glad that she wore her long, dark hair up in a ponytail. The gentle breeze was barely enough to ruffle the bangs on her forehead. She had removed her shirt, leaving her clad in dark uniform pants and a white T-shirt that clung loosely to her lean body. She walked across the parking lot, dodging the occasional pothole in the cracked pavement, her eyes moving idly across the parked vehicles. Ryan entered the convenience store and smiled at the clerk as she walked back to get something to drink. She opened the cooler door, feeling the rush of moist air on her arms and face, and grabbed a Diet Pepsi. The door closed, bumping the bottle, and knocking it from Ryan's hand. As she knelt to pick it up, she heard frantic yelling coming from the front of the store.

"Everyone down. Now. Now! Move it, or I'll blow your fuckin' heads off!"

"Damn," Ryan mumbled to herself. "I don't need this now."

She remained as still as possible, trying to recall how many other people were in the store when she entered. There were three, maybe four total that she could remember. Ryan cautiously peered around the display in front of her. She could see the back of a man standing in front of the counter. He was maybe five-foot-ten, skinny, and scruffy looking. He was pacing back and forth in front of the counter. When he turned slightly in her direction, she could see the pistol, a .38 that he was waving at the clerk behind the register.

The man tossed a small duffel on the counter and shouted, "Put all the money in the damn bag! C'mon! Do it!"

The boy behind the counter hesitated for a moment then yelped when the frenzied man fired the gun into the wall behind him. The boy cowered and wrapped his arms protectively over his head.

"Put the fucking money in the bag! I'm not going to say it again!"

"Okay, okay, just please don't shoot me," the boy said, half crying. As he started shoving bills into the bag, Ryan pulled her weapon from its holster around her ankle, then looked at the soda bottle in her other hand. Smiling at the plan that came to mind, she looked around the corner again to see the perp's back still facing her. Staying as close to the floor as possible, Ryan made her way to the next aisle and slowly rounded the corner. She saw a woman lying on the floor looking back at her. She placed a finger over her lips, cautioning her to remain silent. The woman nodded and put her head back down. Ryan reached the end of the aisle and looked up at the mirror above the doors. She saw that the robber was still pointing his gun at the clerk. She knew she would have to make her move soon, or the guy would see her in the mirror, too. Ryan saw that the weapon was in the man's left hand. She was certain that if her plan worked, and the gun accidentally discharged, no one would be in the line of fire.

Grasping the bottle tightly in her fist, she took a deep breath. *Please let this work!* Ryan rose and hurled the drink toward the man's gun hand. As the bottle hit its mark and sent the pistol skittering across the floor, she jumped from the aisle with her weapon trained on his chest.

"Freeze! Police!" Ryan yelled. "Put your hands where I can see them!"

Raising his hands, the robber stood there with a look of shock on his face. Ryan approached slowly, without taking her eyes off the would-be thief, and flashed the badge in her wallet.

"I'm Sergeant Ryan Thomas, call 911 now." As she heard the clerk place the call, Ryan moved closer to the suspect.

"Get down on your knees," Ryan said, motioning with her gun. The man dropped down, and she continued, "Now, lie face down with your fingers locked behind your head."

After he did as she asked, Ryan kicked his legs apart and crouched to pat him down. She pulled a switchblade from his back pocket and stood.

"Is everyone all right?" Ryan asked.

The few customers in the store assured her they were all right and talked quietly among themselves while she waited for backup to arrive.

Ryan knew it wouldn't be too much longer when she heard the sirens. The screeching tires outside the store attested to their arrival. Ryan heard car doors slam, and stepped back to the counter, keeping an eye on the man. She could see the officers approaching cautiously. Ryan waved, letting them know it was safe to proceed.

Officer Estes entered the convenience store grinning and shaking his head. "Sarge, you just can't stay away from trouble, can you?" Kneeling down, he cuffed the man and pulled him to his feet. As the other officer read him his rights and led him out, Ryan gave Estes her report on the attempted robbery. After getting statements from the other witnesses, Estes walked over to where she was standing.

"Nice job, Sarge. I think we got everything we need." Leaning closer and lowering his voice, "You really are the proverbial shit magnet, aren't you?"

Estes watched her smirk. Rumors flew about how trouble followed Ryan, and how she was always getting into some sort of predicament because of it, and now he knew it to be true. "See you tomorrow?"

Nodding her head, Ryan said, "You bet."

Ryan watched them leave and then looked around for her Diet Pepsi. Spotting it, she walked over, picked it up, and placed it on the counter. She glanced at the boy's nametag. "Sure you're going to be okay, Kyle?"

Kyle was shaking, but nodded.

"How much?" Ryan asked, gesturing toward the bottle of soda.

Kyle stammered, "T-take it; it's the least I can d-do."

Ryan smiled, understanding his nervousness. "Thanks, but if it's all the same to you, I'd rather pay."

Kyle rang up the gas and soda, and Ryan placed the money on the counter. Walking toward the door, she glanced back at him and, with a wink, pushed the door open and walked to her Jeep.

Ryan was supposed to meet Jake, her partner on the force for the past three years, at one of the bars that had recently opened downtown. Jake was impatiently pacing in the parking lot when she arrived.

"Where the hell have you been?" Jake asked, pulling her door open.

Ryan slid from the Jeep and waited for him to close the door before answering. "You aren't going to believe it..." she trailed off, seeing Jake raise a single eyebrow at her.

"Okay, maybe you will," Ryan laughed.

As they entered the bar and sat down, Ryan described what had happened with the attempted robbery at the convenience store. After giving her some ribbing about trouble following her, Jake patted her on the back for her quick thinking.

"If it were anybody else I wouldn't have believed it, but you... I believe," Jake chuckled.

Ryan grinned sheepishly.

Ryan bent her head close to Jake's as she tried to block out the beat of the music and the glare of the countless beer signs illuminating the walls. Not much of a dancer herself, she was more content to watch others gyrate and sway, but usually to a tune that she was at least able to enjoy.

A tap on Ryan's shoulder brought her head around. She looked up into dark eyes framed by long, fiery red hair. Lipstick-caked lips twisted into a cocky smirk as the woman leaned closer, practically shoving her breasts into Ryan's face.

"Hi, Ryan."

"Hello, Lisa."

"I haven't seen you around lately."

Ryan glanced at Jake before returning her gaze to Lisa. "I've been busy with work."

"You know what they say about all work and no play," Lisa said, running a long, painted fingernail down Ryan's upper arm. Ryan leaned away from her touch and clasped her hands tightly on the table. She sat quietly until Lisa spoke again.

"Would you like to dance?"

"No, thank you. You have a great night though," Ryan replied, dismissing her by turning back to Jake. She really didn't want to be rude, but Lisa never knew when to take no for an answer. She was a regular at many of the bars in town and made a habit of taking a different girl home each night. Ryan had never been one of them but not because of Lisa's lack of effort. She had no desire to be anyone's one night stand, and especially not Lisa's.

When Jake called Ryan's name to get her attention, she jerked from her silent musings to respond, "What?"

"When was the last time you went out on an actual date?"

Jake was relentless where the subject of her private life was concerned. He seemed to think he knew Ryan better than she knew herself. While on the verge of believing he was right, there was no way in hell she would ever admit that to him. Ryan worked a lot of overtime since her breakup with Stacey because it was easier than thinking of what to do with her time off.

"Are you ever gonna let this drop?" Ryan asked as she leaned back in her chair and sighed.

"You know the only reason I say anything is because I care. I don't like seeing you work so hard. You're way too young to do this to yourself. Tim and I worry about you."

"Jake..." Ryan paused briefly. "What exactly do you think I'm doing?"

"You know damn well what I'm talking about, Ryan."

Jake rested both arms on the table and looked into her eyes for a moment before continuing. "You know...you're right," he said, throwing his hands out. They had had this conversation more times than Jake could remember and always with the same results.

"Why do I even bother? You don't seem to care, so why should I?" Leaning back and crossing his arms over his chest, he stared at her as if begging for some kind of response.

Ryan lowered her eyes to her hands; she knew she needed to make things right with him. After all, he *was* right, and she knew he was only looking out for her.

"Look, I appreciate what you're doing. I know that you and Tim care about me, but I'm fine, really."

Jake gazed at her pensively before answering. "We just want you to have what we have; you deserve to be happy."

"Yeah, I want what you have, too. Well…not exactly, but you know what I mean," Ryan said with a laugh.

"Just think of yourself once in awhile, will ya?"

Ryan rolled her eyes and responded, "Okay, okay! Now, can we get out of here? This music is horrible." Standing at his nod, she added, "Oh, by the way, you're buying."

Jake laughed as he threw some bills on the table and wrapped his arm around her shoulders before heading out of the bar.

"You're right; that music is horrible," Jake said.

With a raised eyebrow, Ryan asked pointedly, "Then why on earth did we come here in the first place?"

Jake dropped his arm from her shoulder to hold the door open, and she stepped out and waited for him to respond. As the door closed, cutting off the music, he turned to Ryan with a sheepish smile.

"Well, um, Tim sort of mentioned this place the other night, so I thought I'd check it out before we came here."

"I should have known you had an ulterior motive when you asked me here," she said with a groan and a shake of her head. "How is Tim anyhow?"

"Tim is good, real good," he said, grinning. "When are you coming over for dinner?" Jake entwined his arm with Ryan's and grasped her hand before crossing the street to the parking lot.

"Soon, Jakey, as soon as I have some time off. Tell Tim I said hello and send my love."

"It had better be soon," he chastised.

Stopping beside their cars, Jake wrapped his long arms around Ryan and hugged her gently. He kissed her temple and pulled back to look at her. "Please be careful driving home, and I'll see you tomorrow, okay?"

"Okay, and Jake, thanks for caring."

Smiling, he cupped her chin and said, "Anytime, kiddo."

Jake turned to make his way to his car and Ryan hollered, "You be careful, too! Later, gator."

Ryan climbed into her Jeep and paused for a moment, watching as Jake pulled into traffic. She buckled her seat belt and pulled out behind him. Jake was a good friend and a great guy. He'd been on the force just two years longer than Ryan, and she couldn't have asked for a better partner. He always told her that she was the little sister he never had.

Jake and Tim had dated for just five months before moving in together. That was almost six years ago. At six-foot-three, two hundred and twenty pounds, with huge muscles and rugged good looks, Jake made an impressive appearance. As long as Ryan had known him, Jake had always taken very good care of his body and mind. He was also the gentlest man she had ever known, aside from her father. Between Jake and Tim, not one day went by without one of them calling her just to "check in," as they both put it. Ryan had wondered on many occasions if her mother had some kind of conspiracy going with them.

Ryan flicked on her turn signal and glanced in the mirror before turning down her street.

She knew that very few were aware that Jake was gay. He had commented on several occasions that he wasn't sure how well it would be received at the precinct. Rather than take a chance, he preferred to keep his private life separate from his professional one.

Ryan pulled into the garage, gathered her things, and made her way into the house. In the kitchen, she tossed her keys on the table and considered what to eat for dinner. As she did every night, she ate without tasting her food, and shuffled through the mail without really reading it. She dropped the mail back onto the table and stood up, smothering a yawn behind one hand.

The pulsating rhythm of the music at the bar had given her a niggling headache that was waiting to explode. Ryan grabbed a bottle of water from the fridge, found a couple of aspirin in a cabinet, and swallowed them with a gulp of water. She leaned back against the counter and took a few more sips. Usually she enjoyed the silence in the house, but some nights it made her feel really lonely; tonight was one of those nights. She sighed, recapped the bottle, and put it back in the fridge. Finally, before shutting out the lights and heading to the bedroom, she went through the routine of securing her home. It was so second nature that most nights she was barely aware of doing it.

Ryan slipped her work clothes off and pulled on a T-shirt and boxers. She brushed her teeth, clicked off the light, and crawled under the covers. The chill of the cool sheets made her shiver. There was a time when she would have welcomed that chill, knowing that shortly someone would be along to warm up the sheets—and her.

Goddamn you, Stacey! No! Stop that, Ryan. We are not going there tonight. Just roll over and go to sleep.

For once, Ryan listened to her inner self.

"Dr. Drexler, wait up a second. I have those reports you wanted to sign off on before leaving," Marcy called down the hall.

Tobi Drexler leaned her head back and closed her eyes. She was a radiologist with a specialty in ultrasound, and today she had lost count of the number of cases she had dictated. The ache and burning in her eyes hinted that it was time to go home.

"Ugh. This day is never going to end, Marcy. Just when I think I'm home free, someone else stops me," she said, turning toward her secretary and friend. Marcy grinned and handed her the reports.

"Tobi, I know you're tired and ready to get out of here, but can you honestly say that, come tomorrow, you'd have been happy with me if those were still sitting on your desk?"

Tobi glared for a few seconds before sighing. "No, I would not have been happy. I'm sorry for being so short with you. I'm just really tired, and a date with my tub sounds like heaven right about now."

"Well, just glance over these few reports and sign them, then you can get out of here. I promise not to hold you up any longer," her secretary replied while patting Tobi's shoulder in sympathy.

16

Tobi set her briefcase and jacket down on the counter and glanced through the first report before signing it. While looking over the second, she spotted a mistake that she normally would not make.

"How on earth does that dictation system confuse bladder with blabber?"

Marcy shrugged her shoulders as Tobi rolled her eyes and made the necessary correction before going on to the next report. Finally finished, she handed the reports back to Marcy.

"I'm going now; cover for me till I make it to the garage," Tobi said as she walked toward the stairwell.

"Get out of here, you goof! I'll see you tomorrow. Sleep well."

"Thanks. Oh," Tobi said, stopping in mid-stride. "Did you by chance water those two plants for me?"

"I got them, shorty."

"Hey, I'm not short, you're just an Amazon."

Laughing, Marcy replied, "What are you, all of five-foot-four?"

"I'm five-foot-six, thank you very much!"

"Whatever," Marcy said. "Listen, are you feeling okay? That sparkle in your baby blues has been missing lately."

"I'm fine," Tobi responded abruptly. Marcy didn't speak, but Tobi knew she was waiting for more of an explanation. "Really, I'm okay, but thank you for asking."

Marcy quietly studied Tobi before nodding. "All right. Go on then, get on out of here. I'll see you later."

"Good night." Tobi smiled tiredly as she waved and pushed through the stairwell door.

Tobi's heels clicked on the pavement as she walked toward her car. She keyed the remote to unlock the car doors and gave an audible sigh as she slid in and sank into the plush seat.

Finally, there is nothing that can stop me now. Eat dinner, take a nice hot bath, and crawl into bed for some uninterrupted hours of sleep. And all in that order, too.

Tobi changed into comfy clothes and browsed through the refrigerator, deciding on a chicken salad. She curled up in a corner of the sofa and ate while watching the evening news. After getting her fill of shootings, stabbings, and car accidents, she clicked the television off, put her bowl in the dishwasher, and headed into the bathroom for a nice long soak. Tobi turned the water on as hot as she could stand it, and then dropped in some bath beads. She slipped out of her clothing and gingerly stepped into the tub. The long day, combined with the anxiety over her own doctor's appointment tomorrow, pushed Tobi beyond exhaustion. She ran a finger lightly over the small, fresh, pink scar across her left breast. Her doctor had recommended she have a biopsy on a lump she had found just over a week ago. Tomorrow she would find out the results. She slid down until her chin was barely out of the water.

"Mmmm, heaven," Tobi mumbled as she closed her eyes and let the water work away some of the kinks.

She awoke with a start and sat up, sloshing water onto the tiled floor. "That was really dumb, Tobi." She opened the drain and stepped from the tub. After slipping into her bathrobe, she applied some moisturizer to her face and then shut the lights out. She loved the feeling of the thick, soft carpet squishing between her toes as she walked into the bedroom. Tobi let the robe slide from her body and fall to the floor before climbing into bed. She pulled the covers up over her bare shoulders and, with a soft sigh, closed her eyes to let Mr. Sandman carry her away.

Ryan's thoughts churned over and over in her head as her fingers tapped lightly on the steering wheel. She knew she had a ton of things she could be doing with her upcoming weekend off, but none of them seemed appealing. It was only Friday, 11 A.M., and already she wished it were Monday, 6 A.M. Over the past two years Ryan had found herself volunteering for shifts just to avoid the weekends, but she knew she couldn't keep up that pace. She already had enough people taking notice and telling her that she needed to get on with her life. "Go out, have fun," they said. *What exactly does that mean again?* Spotting a car up ahead, Ryan sighed. Ah, just what she needed, something to save her from herself.

"Jake, how many times have we traveled this same road?"

"Over the last three years? I'd say at least twice a day, almost every day. You do the math," he replied.

"And how many times have we had to stop and move along cars that were pulled over on the shoulder, even when they knew they were not supposed to stop along this strip?"

"At least twice a week. What's with all the questions?"

"Just curious; it looks like we are about to move another one."

As Ryan pulled the cruiser behind the blue Audi, she noticed a small decal on the bottom left corner of the rear window. Taking a closer look, she realized it was a black lower case Greek letter lambda in a pink box. She smiled to herself and glanced through the rear window. It appeared the driver was either leaning into or over the steering wheel.

"I'm gonna check this out. Stand by on the radio in case we need to call for medical assistance."

"Will do, Ryan."

Ryan stepped from the car and placed her hand lightly on her weapon. She walked cautiously to the driver's side window and tapped gently so as not to startle the driver. She could feel her heart pounding within her chest when one of the most beautiful women she had ever seen lifted her head and looked up at her. *My God. She's stunning!* The driver's fine hair was almost white-blond and long. It was the type of hair that Ryan itched to run her fingers through. Ryan couldn't see the woman's eyes because she was wearing sunglasses; she could, however, see that the woman had been crying.

"Ma'am, is everything okay? You know, you're not supposed to stop on this shoulder."

"Um, yes I'm fine. I...uh...well...I just needed to pull over a minute to collect myself. I'm sorry; I'll be on my way." Tobi surveyed the dark uniform covering the officer's lean torso, taking in lightly tanned and muscled arms. Her gaze wandered up a delicate neck and strong jaw, to soft, pink lips before continuing up to blue-gray eyes with long, thick eyelashes. She had just noted wisps of dark hair curling over small ears when she realized the officer was speaking to her. "I'm sorry, what did you say?"

"I said are you sure you're okay to drive? I don't mean to pry, but you seem very upset."

"It's just been one of those days, and I just..." the blonde

19

woman sighed. "I'm sorry, really, I'll just go."

What Ryan should have done at this point was let her go with a warning to drive carefully, the standard "cop send-off," but she could still see the tears on the woman's cheeks, and she wanted to reach through the window and brush them away. Instead, Ryan did something she couldn't even explain to herself. She leaned an arm on top of the car and bent down so their eyes were level.

"Listen, I know this is highly irregular, but I'm a pretty good listener if you need to talk."

"Thanks for the offer," she paused to glance at Ryan's badge before continuing, "Sergeant Thomas, but I'm really okay."

"All right then, if you're sure," Ryan replied, straightening up. "Please be careful."

Ryan watched as the woman started to roll the window up, then turned to walk away.

"Sergeant Thomas?"

Ryan turned back as she heard the woman call out her name. "Yes?"

At that moment the blonde slid off her sunglasses, and Ryan felt as if she was punched in the gut. The woman had the most incredible blue eyes; it was like looking at a summer sky after an afternoon sun shower.

"Thank you for...well, just thanks."

Ryan smiled gently at her. "You're welcome."

Tobi rolled the window up and glanced in the mirror before pulling out into traffic. She looked in the rearview mirror and watched as the attractive cop got back in her cruiser, spoke briefly to her partner, and then pulled back into traffic herself. As she drove, Tobi thought about her test results and decided that she was going to start living her life rather than merely existing. She couldn't remember the last time she had gone out with someone other than herself.

Ryan and Jake entered the station and headed to their mailboxes. This time of day was always busy as everyone was trying to finish up their reports before shift change. Ryan flipped through various memos while walking over to a desk.

"Thomas!"

Ryan looked up to see the desk clerk pointing at the phone in his hand and holding up two fingers indicating she had a call on line two. Sitting down in the chair, she reached for the phone.

"Sergeant Thomas, may I help you?"

"Hello, Sergeant Thomas. Um, this is going to sound insane, but I'm the woman who was pulled over on the side of the road earlier today..."

Ryan sat up in her chair. "Yes, I remember you. What can I do for you?"

Tobi nervously wrapped the phone cord around her hand before continuing. "Well, talking would be just what I need. That is, of course, if you still don't mind listening." *Please say you don't mind. I would really like to get to know you better.*

"The offer is most definitely still open."

Jake sat on the edge of Ryan's desk pretending to read through his memos, but actually hoping to hear more of the one-sided conversation.

"Great. How long before your shift is over?"

Ryan peered at her watch. "My shift ends in about a half hour." Ryan glanced at Jake just in time to see his eyebrows rise. Feeling the heat of a blush coming on, she turned her back, which garnered her a few chuckles from him.

Tobi was thrilled that the officer was still interested and took a deep breath to calm her shaking nerves. "Would you like to get together for dinner—say about sixish? There's a nice little Italian restaurant on the corner of 18th and Main that is really good."

"That would be perfect," the officer replied.

"Well then, Sergeant Thomas—"

"It's Ryan."

"Well...Ryan, I'll see you around six. By the way, I'm Tobi, Tobi Drexler."

"It's very nice to meet you, Tobi. I'll see you later then."

Ryan said goodbye, then looked at Jake and could tell by the smile on his face that he was not going to let her alone about this one.

"Not one word, Jake," Ryan said, pointing her finger at him.

Tara Wentz

Chapter Two

R yan stepped from the shower and grabbed her towel. She was extremely nervous about meeting Tobi; she hadn't felt comfortable enough to date in a long time. Ryan had been devastated when Stacey left. As she stood naked and chilled, towel in hand, she thought back to the day she'd walked through the door of their bedroom and saw two half-packed suitcases on the bed.

"What's going on, Stacey?" she asked when Stacey walked out of the closet.

"What does it look like? I'm leaving. Surely, you didn't think this would last forever?" Stacey said, throwing clothes into the suitcase.

Ryan did, in fact, think it was forever. Their moving in together signified a commitment in her book, not to mention the trip planned for the weekend during which Ryan was going to present her with a ring.

"Why?" Ryan asked, grabbing the shirt from Stacey's hands.

Stacey put her hands on her hips and glared at Ryan. "How can you act as if you didn't know this was coming? Did you honestly think I'd be happy being a cop's wife?"

Ryan's mouth dried up and dropped open. "But…how can you do this? Don't I mean anything to you?"

Stacey closed the suitcases and lifted them from the bed. "You were just a distraction, nothing more." She brushed past Ryan and down the stairs. It was only then that Ryan heard a knocking on the front door. Ryan's whole body was shaking as she turned on her heel to follow Stacey.

Stacey reached the door and Ryan's pulse raced as she desperately fought for something else to say that might change Stacey's mind.

"Stacey! Wait…please!" Ryan pleaded, stumbling down the last step.

"Goodbye, Ryan."

Although those were the last words Stacey spoke to her, it was the laughter Ryan heard as the door closed that lingered in her mind and did the most damage. It was all a big joke to Stacey. Ryan had felt like such an idiot. She never got the impression that things were going downhill, or she would not have purchased the diamond ring or rehearsed what she was going to say. Stacey's betrayal left her feeling hurt, angry, and guarded, even after two years. Just thinking of the day Stacey left made her sick to her stomach. She had sworn not to let herself be taken for a fool again. And yet, here she was, shivering and staring at herself in the mirror, getting ready to go out to dinner with someone she hardly knew. Already she feared any sort of attachment at all.

Still, there was something about Tobi. She had seemed so vulnerable earlier, but it took guts to phone the station and ask her out. Also, Ryan had been lonely long enough. Jake's constant harping hit home at last. She needed to connect with someone. She hoped it would be Tobi.

Ryan finished drying off and glanced back in the mirror. Her face was gaunt and pale and her shaggy bangs were more than due for a cutting. She couldn't even remember the last time it had been trimmed. Her dark brown hair was well past her shoulders at this point, and it had always been straight. She could never do a thing with it, which was why she pulled it back most of the time. Bluish-gray eyes stared back at her, and she could see small laugh lines at the edges, making her wonder if she looked older than her thirty-four years. Her best friend Lauren always said that her dimples and smile were to die for; Ryan usually brushed it off, never one to be particularly self-aware.

So why are you noticing these things about yourself now?
Does it hurt to just look?
Is that all this is? Or are you hoping a certain blonde will notice as well?
Maybe.
Mmm hmm...

Ryan shrugged her shoulders and tossed the towel on the hamper as she walked into the bedroom to get ready. She wasn't certain if she should dress casual or dress up, so she decided to go for something in between—khaki pants and a red button-down shirt with loafers. She ran a brush through her hair one last time, sprayed on cologne, and headed out the door.

Ryan entered the restaurant and noticed Tobi almost immediately, despite the dim lighting. She was wearing a blue dress that looked absolutely amazing on her. The short sleeves showed off well-toned arms, and the color brought out the blue of her eyes. She stood up as Ryan arrived at the table, and Ryan realized she had no idea how tall Tobi was, since she had not seen her standing. She was only a few inches shorter than Ryan's five-foot-nine, and was thin but athletic looking.

"Hi, Ryan, I hope this table is okay," she said.

"This is great. Thanks for inviting me." Ryan knew she was staring but couldn't seem to tear her eyes away.

They sat down and glanced through the menu, the waitress appearing almost immediately to take the drink and dinner orders. After she stepped away, Ryan decided to jump right in and ask Tobi about her day.

"So, do you still want to talk about this afternoon?"

"You know, it really wasn't for a bad reason that I was crying. It could have been, but it wasn't." She sighed, glancing away before turning back to Ryan. "Are you sure you want to hear all this?"

"Tobi, I don't say things I don't mean."

Tobi hesitated briefly before nodding her head.

"Three years ago, I lost my mother to breast cancer. Since then, I've been very good about keeping on top of my health. A little more than a week ago, I found a lump, and it really scared me." She paused and looked at Ryan with liquid-filled eyes.

Ryan wanted to know why Tobi was upset, but upon seeing the tears in her eyes all Ryan could think of was the need to comfort her.

"I went in for a biopsy, and today I got the test results back. Luckily, it was just a benign tumor. I was so relieved because I kept imagining the worst. I guess it all just hit me. "

Ryan impulsively reached over and took Tobi's hand, her thumb lightly caressing the soft skin.

"I can't even imagine how you must have felt," Ryan said softly. "I...well, I'm really glad that things turned out all right."

"Thanks," Tobi said with a gentle smile. "Your concern this afternoon was so sweet and really helped. I was pretty overwhelmed. Just thinking about it all made me really miss my mom."

"Well then, I'm glad I came by when I did," Ryan said, thinking how just a few minutes earlier or later, and she would have missed the chance to meet this intriguing woman. "And I'm especially happy that we're here now."

"So am I." Tobi gave a little shake of her head, as if dismissing the lingering sadness. In a lighter tone, she said, "So, tell me something about you."

Ryan started to speak but hesitated as the waitress appeared with their food. "Careful, these plates are hot," she said. Glancing first at Tobi, then Ryan, she asked, "Do you need anything else?"

"I think I'm good," replied Tobi.

Ryan nodded, saying, "Me, too."

The waitress smiled and headed to her next table. Ryan waited a moment before picking the conversation back up again.

"What would you like to know?" Ryan asked.

What wouldn't *I like to know, is the question! If she keeps looking so intently at me with those beautiful eyes, I am never going to spit it out. Relax, Tobi; pretend she's just another patient you're talking to.*

"Anything, just tell me anything," Tobi finally managed.

"Well, I was born on a cold, dark, and stormy night." Ryan grinned before continuing. "Seriously though, I'm not sure there is much to tell. I'm just a regular person, living a pretty simple life. I have a house out toward the edge of town, and I drive a Jeep that gets me where I need to go." She stopped briefly to take a bite before continuing. "I don't need a five-course meal every time I sit down to eat, but I appreciate a good meal with good company on occasion," she said. Ryan smiled when she noticed the faint blush on Tobi's cheeks.

"I really just try to enjoy spending time with the people I love and care about. That's pretty important for me. When I do go out it's usually with my best friend, Lauren; my partner, Jake, and his significant other; or with my family. I'm one of five children and the youngest. I'm also the only girl, so you can imagine what growing up was like," she said, with a bright smile. "Even though my brothers are a bit overprotective and overbearing at times, I wouldn't change a thing. I love them dearly. How about you?"

"Let's see, I'm thirty-three, and I have a younger sister. We're pretty close as well; a lot closer since Mom passed away. She doesn't live in town, so I don't get to see her as often as I'd like. My dad lives in the next town over, about forty minutes away. He and I generally try to get together once a week for dinner." Tobi took a sip of her drink before asking, "What about your parents?"

"My father was killed in the line of duty two years ago. He was a fire marshal. He usually supervised and didn't go into burning buildings. However, they had a pretty terrible fire that had consumed three homes already, and he heard screaming. He shouted at some of his men, and they went to see where it was coming from. It was a couple of kids on the top floor of another house." Blinking rapidly to keep the tears from welling up, Ryan swallowed hard and continued, "He went in to help save them and fell through the floor. He died instantly from a broken neck."

"Oh, Ryan, I'm so sorry. How horrible!"

"It's okay, really. I've had some time to come to terms with everything, and I know that he died doing what he loved. My mother had a tough time with it...she was angry for a bit, but she wouldn't have expected anything different from him. If not for him, those children would have died," Ryan said, her pride for her father showing clearly in her expression.

"Helping people in distress seems to run in your family then, huh?" Tobi replied with a grin.

"I would never put myself in the same group as my father, if you want to know the truth. I have to admit that I really idolized him. He was the strongest, most loyal person I've ever had the privilege to know. When I was growing up, he would stand behind me no matter what. He corrected me if I was wrong, but he always did it when it was just he and I. He let other people know that he was proud of me."

"He sounds like an amazing man."

"He was. I even got his name, which probably made us closer. His middle name was Ryan," she said with a proud smile.

"Then it must make you feel pretty special to be carrying his name."

Ryan nodded before responding, "Don't get me wrong. I love my mom, and she's a wonderfully sweet woman and very proud of her children; it's just that I guess I was really a daddy's girl. I think that sometimes my mom wished her little girl liked to cook and dress up and do all the fun girl things, but I also know that she loves me just as I am. Hey, I thought we were here so you could talk," Ryan said, laughing.

"I'm talking. It's just that I'm really enjoying listening as well. What do you like to do in your free time?"

"Oh, I don't know. I like to run, bike, and hike. I love to camp and fish. I love to watch football. I also enjoy reading and just relaxing to soft music on the stereo. See, here I go again. What do you like to do?" Ryan asked, leaning forward to rest her elbow on the table and her chin in the palm of her hand.

"Let's see, I also like to run and ride my bike. I like to camp and hike. I'm okay with fishing as long as someone else baits the hook," Tobi said, laughing. "I don't understand football very much, but that doesn't mean I don't like it. I'm great at checkers, and I really like to read, and listen to music. I just enjoy having fun. I don't care what I'm doing as long as I'm having fun doing it. Does that make sense?"

"It makes perfect sense. Checkers, huh? Care to take me on sometime?" Ryan inquired.

"Any time, any place," Tobi said, grinning. *Ryan is so easy to talk to. Her eyes are so expressive; tonight they look like tumultuous clouds swirling in a thunderstorm. And those eyelashes, could they be any longer?*

"I'll keep that in mind." Ryan watched the grin slowly leave Tobi's face and could tell that she was working up to asking something else, so she waited before saying anything more.

"Um, Ryan ..." Tobi paused, looking away briefly and shifting noticeably in her seat. She glanced back up into Ryan's eyes, and took a deep breath before continuing. "Are you seeing anyone right now?"

Somewhat surprised and a little uneasy about the question, Ryan was slow to answer.

"No, I'm not. It's been a couple of years since my last relationship."

"What happened, if you don't mind me asking?"

Ryan glanced up to see that Tobi was still looking at her, and she knew by the look that Tobi was not just being nice. She was genuinely curious, and Ryan found that she didn't want to keep anything from her.

"Her name was Stacey, and we had been together for almost two years. She suddenly decided to end our relationship, and I'm still not sure why. I really thought we'd be together forever, but Stacey had other ideas. She had a hard time accepting my job, I guess. I was totally blind-sided by her leaving." At this point, Ryan wasn't sure how much she should say. After shifting the napkin in her lap and fiddling with her fork, she focused her attention back on Tobi's face. Ryan could see quiet understanding in her eyes, and knew she could tell her anything. Still, she felt she'd said enough.

Tobi felt the shutters come down and sat back a little to give Ryan more time and space.

"I don't trust easily, but I'm learning to overcome that. I—" Ryan stopped abruptly. She was frustrated with how hard it was to tell Tobi her feelings. Placing her hands on the table and leaning forward slightly, Ryan said half laughingly, half warily, "I have no idea why I'm telling you all this. There's just something about you that makes me feel so comfortable."

"Hey, it's fine. I feel comfortable with you, too," Tobi said with a smile. "I know we just met, but I can promise that I would never purposefully do anything to hurt you. As for your job, well, I have to like some aspect of it or we never would have met."

Ryan looked into her eyes and could only hope that what she saw was sincere interest. As Tobi stared back, Ryan wondered what Tobi could see in her eyes— were they revealing her fear and insecurity?

"So, speaking of jobs, you know what I do, but I have yet to find out what you do," Ryan said, mentally shaking off the effects of Tobi's intense gaze.

"Ah, well, I'm a radiologist over at Truman University Medical Center. I've been there just a little over two years now."

"That sounds like an interesting field. Do you enjoy it?"

"I love it. There are some mundane parts to it, but overall, each day brings along something new and exciting."

"Sounds a lot like my job," Ryan said with a smile.

"The only downside is that I do have to take call. That can make things a little hectic, and sometimes I forget to allow myself to have a life outside the hospital walls." Tobi hesitated before continuing.

"I'm really enjoying our dinner together. You're so easy to talk to. I've missed that lately. Life gets so busy, and there's no time to get to know people."

"I understand completely. I've been concentrating on my job, ignoring—or maybe excluding—the personal side of things. God knows there's more to life than punching a clock." Ryan took a deep breath. "Tobi, I've enjoyed myself this evening, and I would very much like to spend some time with you again."

Tobi gave one of those heart-stopping smiles that, had Ryan been standing, would have made her go weak in the knees. Her belly fluttered and all she could do was smile back. Through the rest of dinner, Ryan thought she caught Tobi stealing glances at her as often as she did at Tobi. When the meal was over, Ryan realized she wasn't ready for the night to end.

"My place is just around the corner if you'd like to come up for a cup of coffee," Tobi said, as if reading the cop's mind.

"That would be great," Ryan said, smiling. "Lead the way, Doctor."

Ryan followed Tobi to a newly built townhouse. As Ryan got out of her Jeep, Tobi walked over to meet her.

"Nice," Tobi said, rubbing her palm across the top of the Jeep. "It suits you." Then she gave Ryan such a sweet smile it made her mouth go dry. It was more than just a physical response. Every time Tobi smiled it made Ryan forget what she was doing. This woman had gotten under her skin, and she had no idea how that had happened so quickly.

"Thanks," Ryan stammered.

Ryan turned and followed her up the steps and through the door into her home. She looked at her surroundings and waited as Tobi closed the door.

"Your home is beautiful, Tobi. I really like your taste ...uh, you know, in furniture and decor."

Laughing, Tobi said, "Thanks. It's taken a while to get it how I want it, but it's finally home. Let me get that coffee. Can you start a fire? Everything you need is just to the side there. I know it's been kind of warm outside, but it's cooled off so much, I think it would feel nice."

"I think I can handle that."

As Ryan turned to start the fire, Tobi walked up to her and placed her hands lightly on Ryan's shoulders. Ryan knew her eyes had gone wide as Tobi smiled and leaned in just close enough to place her lips on Ryan's. She kissed her gently, letting her tongue skip across Ryan's lower lip before pulling away.

"Sorry, I've wanted to do that all night. I'll go get the coffee," Tobi said as she turned. "By the way, Ryan, I like your taste, too," she quipped over her shoulder as she disappeared into the kitchen.

She left Ryan standing there with her mouth hanging open, her heart thumping wildly, and her body yearning for so much more. Ryan's blood ran hot and her legs trembled.

"God damn," Ryan muttered, somewhat bewildered. She shook herself out of her stupor and turned to get the fire started...in the fireplace.

Leaning against the closed kitchen door, Tobi slowly raised her hand to her lips. *What the hell just happened? I only meant for it to be a simple, teasing kiss. I wonder if she felt the spark, too.*

When Tobi came back in with two mugs of coffee, she was struck by how beautiful Ryan looked in the firelight. As Ryan rose from her crouched position, Tobi smiled and held the cup out to her. They sat beside each other on the couch and began talking. Ryan really could have listened to her all night, but two hours later, she realized she should get going and let Tobi get some sleep. Ryan was reluctant to leave the warmth that had enveloped her. It was more than just the sparks and heat coming from the fireplace.

"I've had a really nice time tonight," Ryan said, glancing at her watch. "I guess I should let you get some rest."

Tobi stood up and reached for her briefcase. "Here, this is my card," she said as she wrote something on the back. "I also wrote my home number on there. It has my beeper number and office numbers on the front. Please feel free to call anytime, okay?"

Ryan took the card and glanced down at the numbers before placing it in her pocket.

"I'll walk you to the door," Tobi said.

"You'll have to check your call schedule. Maybe we can get together again soon. We could see a movie or something if you'd like."

"That sounds like a great idea. Give me a call tomorrow afternoon and we can plan something. Would that be okay?"

Ryan stopped at the door and turned. "That would be more than okay."

"Please be careful driving home," Tobi said, softly.

"I will. Thank you for a wonderful evening," Ryan said as she leaned down to give Tobi a soft kiss on the lips. Straightening up, Ryan was relieved to see the little smile on Tobi's face.

Traffic Stop

"Goodnight, Ryan."
"Sleep well, Dr. Drexler."

33

Tara Wentz

Traffic Stop

Chapter Three

Ryan looked at the card in her hand, lightly rubbing her thumb over the embossed letters. *Tobi Drexler, M.D.* She still couldn't get over Tobi being a doctor. It was the last thing she had expected, and it took her breath away for a minute. Tobi just seemed so down to earth. Ryan was used to dealing with the ones who weren't. She had been into the Emergency Room many times for various reasons with some of the people she had arrested. The doctors there were either too busy, on a major ego trip, angry as hell, or all of the above.

Over the last month, she and Tobi had gone out at least twice a week and talked on the phone almost every night. They were taking things slow, which Ryan thought made both of them feel more at ease. Ryan enjoyed the sensual kisses they shared and looked forward to the time they spent together. She had long since memorized the numbers on the card, so she really didn't need it any longer, but couldn't bring herself to stop carrying it. It was a small reminder that Tobi was real and they were indeed dating.

Ryan had learned from Tobi's secretary that Tobi generally stayed in her office during lunch hours, so she decided to surprise her by bringing lunch. She walked down the hospital corridor searching for the suite number that matched the one on Tobi's business card. Ryan slipped the card back in her pocket and entered the office to find herself standing in a small room with a couple of chairs, a cabinet with various business cards and some plants on it, and a woman on the phone behind a large desk. The secretary waved Ryan over and asked her caller to hold before placing her palm over the phone. "Hi, I'm Marcy; can I help you with something?"

"Hi, I'm Ryan...Ryan Thomas. I'm here to see Tob...I mean Dr. Drexler," Ryan replied nervously. *Why am I so nervous? I know why, it's because I want Tobi to feel special and I'm afraid I won't succeed.*

"Ah, it's nice to finally meet you. She's just doing some paperwork; go on back. It's the last door on the right," Marcy said with a smile.

"Thanks," Ryan whispered.

Marcy winked and continued her phone conversation as Ryan turned down the hall. Marcy was not what she had expected. The woman had shoulder-length dark hair and big brown eyes. She appeared to be a little older than Ryan and was very attractive. She looked nothing like the matronly image Ryan had of what a secretary typically looked like. Chuckling, Ryan decided she needed to change her stereotypical thinking.

Ryan stopped just outside the door Marcy indicated and could see that Tobi's back was to her. She raised her hand to knock, but stopped when she realized Tobi was talking. Not wanting to interrupt, she waited until the doctor was finished.

"...Impression: Number One: Tender left ovary demonstrating a probable hemorrhagic cyst measuring up to 2.3 centimeters in greatest diameter. Number Two: There is heterogeneity of the myometrium with no focal myometrial mass detected. End."

Tobi set the hand-held device down and wrote something on a chart, so Ryan figured it was a good time to knock. When she tapped on the door, Tobi turned her chair around, noticed Ryan, and her lips curled into a smile.

"What a sight for sore eyes you are." Glancing down at the bags in Ryan's hand, she asked, "What have you got there?"

36

"I thought you might be a little hungry. Chinese?" Ryan questioned, raising the bags slightly.

"What a wonderful surprise," Tobi said, while sniffing the containers. "Mmm, I love Chinese."

"You know what they say, protect and serve," Ryan said with a chuckle. "I got the serve part right, didn't I?"

Laughing, Tobi motioned for her to sit down. "You are such a goofball. So, are we still on for tonight?"

Ryan handed one of the containers to her and sat down before replying, "Yep, I'm all yours. What did you want to do?"

"They have this marathon of scary movies on that I thought might be fun to watch. We could make some popcorn and turn the lights off. What do you think?"

"Sounds like a plan, Stan. What time do you want me to come over?"

Stan? Sometimes she says the craziest things. Tobi pursed her lips before saying, "How about six? That will give us time to eat dinner before the movies start." Looking over at Ryan, she couldn't help but smile when she noticed some sauce on Ryan's lip.

"What?" Ryan asked, raising an eyebrow at her.

"You've got some sauce on your lip there. Do you need some help with that?" *Oh, my God! Did I just say that out loud?*

From the startled look on Tobi's face, Ryan could guess what Tobi had been thinking.

"You did just say that out loud, and what if I do need some help?"

Ryan, seeing Tobi blush an even deeper shade of red, couldn't keep a straight face any longer and laughed out loud.

Tobi thought Ryan's laughter sounded wonderful, but decided she was carrying on a little too long. She reached over with an index finger and took the sauce off Ryan's lip. Then, smiling wickedly, Tobi drew her finger between her lips and slowly sucked the sauce from it.

Ryan's jaw went slack, and her pulse rate doubled as she watched Tobi's small, pink lips remove the last remnants of sauce from her finger. She was still staring at her lips when Tobi started laughing. She looked up into eyes twinkling with mirth. *I wonder if she'd still be laughing if I pinned her to that chair and kissed her senseless?* The thought of sharing that much passion made Ryan wet, but at the same time scared her to death. *The body is willing, but the heart isn't ready.*

Ryan cocked her head and grinned. "That was evil, Tobi."

"Yeah, well, that was just payback for your little comment," Tobi said triumphantly.

Ryan smiled as she stood up to throw away her container and discard the bags. She turned around to tell Tobi that she needed to go, and almost ran her over. "Whoa, what are you doing?"

"Oh, just thought I would make sure you didn't need any help with that," she said sweetly.

Stammering, Ryan replied, "Okay, well, I don't think I need any help, but thank you all the same."

Ohhh, what is this? Now I have her blushing? Rising up on tiptoe, Tobi leaned into Ryan and felt hands go around her waist. She kissed Ryan's chin first, then her lips. She felt Ryan's tongue move across her lower lip and beg for entrance to her mouth. Tobi parted her lips slightly and felt Ryan's tongue graze hers. Just as the kiss was about to deepen, Tobi heard a throat clearing. Jumping apart, they glanced at the door.

"Um, hello, Marcy. Ryan, this is Marcy, my secretary. Marcy, this is Ryan, my umm …"

"Friend, and we've met," replied Ryan.

Smiling gratefully at Ryan, Tobi turned back toward Marcy. "Lunch over already?"

"I knocked, but I guess you didn't hear me. Sorry to interrupt, but you are needed in Ultrasound Room One," the grinning secretary said.

"Okay, thanks," Tobi said, turning back to Ryan. "I need to go for now, but I'll see you tonight?"

"Okay. Have a great afternoon. I'll see you later." With a nod to the secretary, Ryan made her way back to the main hall. *I'll have to remember to ask Tobi how much teasing she had to endure when I see her tonight.*

Tobi walked briskly to the Ultrasound department and entered the technologists' viewing room. She was immediately concerned when she saw the tense look on the technologist's face.

"Kathy, what's wrong?" Tobi asked the sonographer as she stepped closer to the view boxes.

"I don't know what's going on, Dr. Drexler," Kathy started. She pushed a couple films up for the doctor to review and pointed to what she was concerned about. "When I started this woman's exam the baby's heartbeat was just fine. I came out to check the films and decided to do a couple more. When I resumed scanning I could not auscultate a heartbeat at all."

"Hmm. Okay, well, let's go take a look."

Tobi tapped lightly on the door to the exam room before she and Kathy entered.

"Hello, Mrs. Hyde. I'm Dr. Drexler."

"What are you doing here and when can I go? I'm tired of you people poking and prodding me."

The woman was visibly upset. Tobi noticed her eyes darting around the room as if looking for the closest way out. Her breathing was also very rapid and shallow.

"I'm just going to take a quick look here and then we'll get you on your way."

Tobi stepped closer to the machine, took the transducer in hand, and applied some gel to the woman's stomach.

"Have you had any problems with your pregnancy, Mrs. Hyde?"

"I already answered all these questions when I first came in. Why are you asking me them again?" the woman asked, glaring at Tobi.

"It's just routine, ma'am," Tobi replied. She was trying very hard to be polite to this woman, but it wasn't easy.

Before she could resume scanning the woman knocked Tobi's hand away and rolled up and off the table.

"I'm done with this, and I'm done with you. Let me the fuck out of here! He won't understand anyhow!"

Tobi stood in shock as the woman started swinging her arms and screaming at the top of her lungs.

"Ma'am, please," Tobi started, holding a hand up to get the woman to listen to her. "Calm down and we'll—"

"Shut up! I told you I'm done. None of it matters anyhow. Just get out of my way!"

Tobi glanced nervously at Kathy before edging a little closer to the woman. "We'll step out and let you get dressed. Okay?"

The woman seemed to calm down a fraction, but Tobi was not convinced that she wouldn't bolt the minute the door was opened. Kathy stepped back through the door and Tobi was going to follow when the woman groaned. Tobi felt helpless as she watched the woman's eyes flutter and then close before she dropped to the floor.

Tobi rushed to the woman's side and immediately felt for a pulse. There was saliva dripping from the woman's mouth. "Kathy, she's becoming anoxic. Hand me that airway!"

Kathy grabbed the airway taped to the cabinet and handed it to Tobi. She also got the oxygen tubing set up so it would be ready when Tobi needed it.

Tobi was attempting to get the airway in the woman's mouth when her jaw clamped closed and her body contracted in a seizure. "Dammit!"

The woman's body went limp and Tobi felt for a pulse once again. "Kathy, call a code and get the crash cart in here. Now!"

Kathy ran from the room while Tobi tried to get the woman's airway open. Tobi could feel the sweat accumulating between her shoulder blades as she repositioned the woman's head. There was no pulse, and no air moving from the woman's lungs.

The side door burst open as the code team entered the room. Tobi briefly relayed what had happened, and stepped back so they could take over.

Ryan pulled up in front of Tobi's house and noticed that there were not many lights on. Matter of fact, there was only one. She made her way up the steps to the front door. Before she had the chance to knock, the door opened, and there stood Tobi. She looked like she had been crying.

"Tobi, what's wrong?" Ryan asked, trying not to show the alarm she felt.

"Come on in, Ryan."

Ryan followed her into the living room, dropped her jacket on the closest chair, and sat down beside her. She wasn't sure if she should say anything or just wait until Tobi was ready to talk. Ryan watched her take a sip from a mug and followed her trembling hand as she placed the mug back on the table. When she looked back up at Tobi's face, she could see tears welling in her eyes again.

"You're starting to scare me, Tobi, what's wrong?" Ryan asked and took her hand.

"Earlier today, after you left, I had a case that really went south. Actually, it was the one that Marcy came and got me for while you were still there. I don't like to discuss patients, but I really need to talk to somebody about this," she said as the tears flowed more freely.

"Ssshhh, I understand," Ryan said as she slid closer and wrapped her arms around the distraught woman. "Go on whenever you're ready. I'm right here."

Laying her head on Ryan's shoulder, Tobi couldn't believe how lucky she was to have this woman in her life. Right now, Tobi really needed a friend, and Ryan was being that and more. Snuggling deeper into the warmth of Ryan's body, Tobi described what had happened.

When she finished, Ryan sat quietly before saying anything. "Wow, I'm so sorry that happened."

Tobi took a deep breath. "Kathy said the woman was like a whole different person from the one she started scanning. She really scared me. I was trying to talk to her and get her to calm down, but that only seemed to upset her more."

By this time, Tobi had sat up and was looking at Ryan while continuing with what had happened. Ryan could see that Tobi was confused by the earlier incident and couldn't understand why the woman at the hospital was so upset.

"Do you think she had taken something while Kathy was out of the room?"

Tobi took Ryan's hand in hers before responding. "I really don't know, but I think so." Glancing down, Tobi ran a finger over the soft skin on the back of Ryan's hand. She sighed, and meeting

Ryan's eyes said, "If she did, it was either then or just before she came to the department, and it just happened to hit at that point. They managed to revive her, but for how long is anyone's guess." Tobi looked away and then met Ryan's gaze again. "Ryan, it was almost as if she wanted this to happen. She said it didn't matter, as if she wasn't going to keep the baby anyhow. I don't know how to explain it, but I really don't think she wanted this baby."

"Maybe she didn't, honey. Was someone with her?"

How is it that one simple endearment from her makes me feel so much better?

Ryan watched the emotions cross Tobi's features. She had no idea that *she* was the reason Tobi's thoughts had turned inward. "Tobi?"

"Oh, sorry," Tobi said, startled from her reverie. "No, her husband was not there. One of the things she said, though, is that he wouldn't understand; understand 'what' is the question I want answered. Anyhow, I'm going to check on her tomorrow; I hope she makes it through the night. It just really upset me, Ryan. I can't imagine doing something like that to my body, knowing I was carrying a child, knowing that it was affecting more than just my own life."

"I agree. It seems like such a waste. I'm really sorry that you had to go through that. It must have been so terrifying and confusing."

"It was. Thanks…again," Tobi said with a smile in her tone.

"Again?" Ryan asked.

"Yes, again. Once again, you were there to listen to me when I needed it the most. What did I ever do without you?" she said while looking into Ryan's eyes.

Leaning down, Ryan placed a gentle kiss on her lips and murmured, "What, indeed."

Tobi poked her in the side and turned to face her while sitting up a little straighter.

"Ryan, I need to explain something so you won't think I'm just overreacting to what happened today."

"I don't think you overreacted…"

"Wait, just let me explain, okay?"

Ryan nodded her head in agreement as Tobi thought about what to say. Not exactly what, but how.

"When I was in college, my best friend, Terry, became pregnant. The father refused to take any type of responsibility, and her family was so conventional about everything that she was terrified to tell them. She was upset and crying one minute, and the next, she was angry and irrational." Tobi stopped as her gaze focused on something beyond the window. She took a deep breath and looked back to Ryan before continuing. "We talked for hours about what she should do. I kept telling her that things would be all right, that we'd find a way to deal with this. We decided that I would go with her, and we'd talk to the crisis counselor at school to see what kind of options she had."

Tobi squeezed Ryan's hands, saying, "I really thought she felt better about things when we finally went to bed. The next morning, I knocked on her door to see if she was ready. When she didn't answer, I went in to check on her. She was curled up on her bed; I thought she was asleep. I kneeled on the bed to wake her up and saw three prescription medicine bottles. Ryan, I have no idea how many pills she actually took." Tobi paused while reflecting back to that morning. She would never forget how still and cold Terry's body felt. This was her best friend, someone she had loved like a sister. Shaking her head, she looked back at Ryan, and what she saw in her eyes and body language was a quiet understanding. Ryan pulled Tobi close and held her, knowing from the look of guilt in her eyes the toll this was taking on her.

"I felt like there should have been something more I could've done. It hurt terribly knowing that she felt so alone, so isolated, and so dejected about things that she found suicide to be her only option. I ached for the things she would never know, and the child that would never be. That's what upset me, Ryan. It wasn't really that woman's situation, but my impression of her seeming so alone and lost. I know that she is most likely not going to make it, and that just brings to the surface all those old memories of Terry."

"I can certainly understand why you were upset, and for the record, I don't believe that you were overreacting. This just tells me that you're a sensitive and compassionate person."

"God, you're so sweet. That means a lot. Thanks."

They sat quietly for a few minutes until Tobi's growling stomach interrupted.

"Are you ready to eat now? My empty stomach just reminded me that I invited you to dinner and it's well past that time," Tobi asked.

"I'm ready whenever you are."

"Good, because I'm starving!" Tobi said as she stood up.

When are you not starving? Ryan thought, smiling to herself. She hopped off the couch and followed Tobi into the kitchen.

As the final credits rolled on the movie, Ryan glanced at her watch and saw that it was after midnight. Ryan knew she should get going, but she was really enjoying the evening and hated to see it end. She was glad that Tobi was able to relax and enjoy the movie, even though the events earlier in the day were not pleasant. At some point during the last movie, they had both shifted on the couch so that Tobi was leaning against Ryan's side; Ryan had her arm across Tobi's shoulders and Tobi's head on her chest.

"Tobi?"

"Hmmm?" she mumbled into Ryan's chest.

"I was just checking to see if you were still awake."

"I'm awake, just very comfortable."

"Me, too. But it's late, I should get out of here so you can get to bed," Ryan replied as she lifted her arm off Tobi's shoulders. *I don't want to go.*

"I'll walk you to the door." *I don't want you to go.*

When Ryan slid to the edge of the couch to get up, Tobi put her hand on Ryan's thigh and waited for her reaction.

Ryan looked into Tobi's eyes and noticed that they had become a shade darker. The rush of heat from Tobi's touch made her stomach tighten and her heart thunder. She could feel Tobi shift closer to her. Tobi's scent had been driving her crazy all night, so clean and fresh with just a hint of something else that she couldn't describe.

How it happened, Ryan had no idea. One minute they were talking and the next they were only inches from each other. Ryan couldn't help but notice how inviting Tobi's lips were. They were so soft and just a touch moist. Ryan's tongue slipped out to dampen her own lips, and Tobi moaned softly. She saw the desire in Tobi's eyes, and any reservations Ryan might have had crumbled. She leaned forward, closing the last few inches between them, and gently kissed her lips. As Ryan leaned back to end the kiss, she felt Tobi's arms go around her neck. Tobi tugged her back and deepened the kiss. When her tongue danced across Ryan's lips and into her mouth, everything clicked. Ryan felt a sense of contentment that she'd never imagined possible. *Home.* She had never in her life felt like this before. Tobi pulled back and placed kisses on the side of Ryan's jaw, down her neck, and over her chin to her lips. She rose up on her knees to kiss Ryan's eyes, her nose then her lips again. It took everything in Ryan's power to stay still as her body screamed in need, wanting to devour Tobi right then and there. As the kiss slowly ended, Ryan reclined against the couch to catch her breath.

"Wait...I should go...I, I want this so much, but I..."

Tobi placed her fingers over Ryan's lips to stop her before saying, "I want this, too, but I want you to be comfortable. You're worth the wait, Ryan, and when it happens, it'll just happen."

Ryan needed Tobi to understand that she wanted more than just tonight. The feelings she had for Tobi were intense. It was different from anything she had ever experienced, which made Tobi feel all the more special to her.

Tobi hesitated briefly and sighed, "C'mon, I'll walk you to the door."

Standing on her porch, Ryan turned to look at her. Tobi leaned against the door jam and smiled. Ryan couldn't help but drift closer to place a sweet kiss on her soft lips.

"Good night, Tobi."

"Good night," Tobi said as she leaned into Ryan for one more kiss. She wrapped her arms around Ryan's neck, drawing her in tightly as she whispered in her ear, "Stay."

Tara Wentz

Chapter Four

S tay?" Ryan asked as she pulled back slightly to look into Tobi's eyes.

"I really don't want to be alone tonight. You can even sleep in the guest room if you'd feel more comfortable." Tobi hesitated before saying, "Please?"

Ryan watched the changing emotions cross Tobi's face and knew she couldn't say no. Truth was, she didn't want to say no. She knew that Tobi needed comforting. With that in mind, Ryan nodded her head and took Tobi's hand. "I'll stay," Ryan said as she closed the door and turned the locks.

Tobi studied her profile in the dim light. *Her every move is so graceful. I think I've fallen in love with her. Is it too soon to feel so strongly about her?* As Ryan turned back, Tobi was smiling.

"Ready?" Ryan asked.

"Ready," Tobi replied. "Where would you like to sleep?"

"Where would you like me to sleep?"

"I'd really like you next to me, if that's okay," Tobi said gingerly.

Ryan nodded, and said, "Okay." She smiled at Tobi and squeezed her hand reassuringly.

Turning out the lights, they walked to the bedroom. As they entered the room, Tobi turned to Ryan. "There's an extra toothbrush in the top drawer, and I'm sure I have a T-shirt that will fit you just fine." Tobi pulled out an oversized shirt, handed it to her and pointed to the bathroom. "You can go first."

"Thanks, I'll only be a minute."

When the bathroom door closed, Tobi stripped off her shirt and sweats and pulled on a nightshirt. Just as she pulled the hem down over her thighs, the bathroom door opened. Ryan looked at her with a raised eyebrow. Tobi glanced down at the T-shirt and couldn't help but chuckle.

"I guess that T-shirt isn't as big on you as it is on me. Will that be okay?"

"It'll be just fine, but next time, I think I'll bring my own," Ryan said, with a start realizing what she had just implied. If Tobi noticed, she didn't say a word. Instead, she moved to the bathroom as Ryan walked toward the bed.

"I'll be just a minute," she said. "Go ahead and get comfortable."

Tobi closed the door and leaned against it. *Next time? Yes! I hope she didn't think I picked that shirt intentionally...what a body!* Pulling herself from her thoughts and away from the door, she brushed her teeth and returned to the bedroom. She walked to the bed, noticing that Ryan was already under the covers on the right side. Ryan looked up and smiled hesitantly.

"Is this all right? I wasn't sure what side you normally sleep on."

"I sleep on the left, so this is perfect," Tobi said, climbing under the covers.

Tobi leaned over, turned off the light, and settled down with the blankets just below her chin. "Good night, Ryan."

"Night," Ryan said as she let her mind drift back over the time she spent with Tobi before and after the incident. Aside from that, it was a pretty good day.

Ryan figured Tobi would fall right to sleep, but her constant fidgeting said otherwise.

"Tobi?" Ryan whispered.

"Yeah?" Tobi responded.

Ryan was nervous about what she was going to offer, but knew Tobi needed some comforting. She opened her arms and said, "Come here."

Tobi didn't hesitate as she moved in next to Ryan. The warm heat emanating from Ryan seemed to soothe her nerves. With her head on Ryan's shoulder, she closed her eyes and felt her body relax as Ryan's arms tightened around her.

Ryan smiled as she felt the tension leave Tobi.

I wonder if it's too soon to tell her how I feel about this relationship. I don't want to see other people.

Like that is even happening.

Shut up, I'm thinking here. I don't want her to see other people, either.

Then you know what you need to do.

Didn't I just tell you to shut up? I know what I need to do, and I'm going to do it.

When?

Soon, okay? Very soon.

At some point during the night, Ryan awoke to hear Tobi whimpering and thrashing around in her sleep. She wasn't sure when Tobi had moved back to her own side of the bed, but she scooted next to her and peered over Tobi's shoulder to see that she had tears running down her cheeks. Ryan tried to wake her up by gently shaking her arm.

"Tobi? C'mon, honey, wake up. It's just a bad dream."

Tobi rolled onto her back and Ryan could see that it was taking some effort to pull out of the last remnants of the nightmare. Ryan pulled Tobi into her arms and held her close until the shivering and crying stopped.

"You okay?"

"Yes, I am. It was like I was reliving this afternoon with that woman all over again. Something is just not right with that whole picture. I'm sorry I woke you."

"Tobi, you have nothing to be sorry for. I'm glad I could be here for you."

"I'm glad you're here, too. I'll call and check on her first thing in the morning," Tobi said, glancing at the clock on the bedside table. "I guess it is morning," she said with a small but sigh. "I'll call when it's a more reasonable hour."

She snuggled closer to Ryan and relaxed in her warmth. Sighing, Tobi let herself drift back to sleep.

Ryan smiled when she felt Tobi relax in the circle of her arms. *I would protect her forever, if she'd let me. I hate seeing her upset. At least I was able to calm her fears and comfort her when she needed it.*

Placing a kiss on the top of Tobi's head, Ryan let her body relax, as well. As she listened to Tobi's deep breathing, she felt herself matching her breath for breath, and before she knew it, she also was drifting off to sleep.

Tobi let her hand roam over the warm, soft surface and sighed to herself with a small smile. Her bladder was telling her that it was time to get up, but the rest of her body refused to cooperate. Knowing she couldn't wait much longer, Tobi opened one eye and peered across her pillow, which happened to be Ryan's shoulder. To her surprise, she had not moved an inch after waking from the nightmare and reclaiming her spot next to Ryan. She was still spooned against Ryan's body, one leg thrown over hers, her arm across Ryan's waist and her hand seemingly having a life of its own where it rest against Ryan's breast. Raising her head slightly, she looked at Ryan's face, and, to her relief, Ryan was still asleep. She slowly pulled herself away and padded to the bathroom. Tobi glanced back before closing the door and smiled. *She looks absolutely adorable.* Ryan had one leg outside the covers, her right arm above her head, and her forehead resting against the crook of that arm.

Ryan rolled to her side and brought her hand to the space next to her, only to find it warm but empty. She opened her eyes and realized it was morning. Small shafts of light were making their way through the blinds, promising a sunny day. The weather had been so erratic lately, with very few days that were actually warm, but the sun always helped. Ryan's gaze roamed about the room before landing on the closed bathroom door. She heard the shower being turned off in the bathroom, and before she could avert her eyes the door opened. Standing there in nothing but a bath towel was Tobi. Ryan could see the curve of her smooth, creamy breasts where they disappeared behind the cotton barrier. Her hair was wrapped, as well, but a few escaping tendrils curled against her cheeks. Ryan watched as water droplets slid gently down Tobi's slender neck, making her suddenly very thirsty. The towel barely covered everything, and Ryan glimpsed the outline of a shapely hip before her eyes traveled slowly down her long, graceful legs. As she admired the view she could feel a tightening spasm in her belly. She belatedly sensed that Tobi had quit moving and looked up, falling into amused eyes. Realizing she was caught, Ryan could do nothing but raise an eyebrow and smile.

"I see you're awake," said Tobi, blushing profusely.

"I am at that, very awake," Ryan said, still grinning.

"I'll just take these clothes and get dressed. The bathroom is all yours," Tobi said, rolling her eyes at Ryan's flirtatious response. She rushed to make an exit before Ryan could see her blush any further. She swore she could actually hear Ryan snicker as she left the room. *I guess I don't have to wonder if she enjoyed what she saw.* Tobi stopped long enough in the hallway to throw her clothes on before heading to the kitchen to get breakfast started and the coffee brewing.

"Something sure smells good," Ryan said as she walked into the kitchen, startling Tobi who let out a little yelp of surprise. "Sorry," she said, grinning sheepishly.

"I didn't hear you walk in. You sure are quiet," Tobi said, smiling and turning back to the stove.

Ryan walked up behind her and wrapped her arms around Tobi's waist, inhaling her scent. She always smelled so good. Tobi leaned back against her, and Ryan tilted her head to the side to place a kiss on the top of her ear. Hearing her moan, Ryan leaned down farther to kiss the side of her neck. Tobi set the spatula on the counter and turned to wrap her arms around Ryan's waist. She raised her head and placed her lips upon Ryan's, her tongue peeking out to taste Ryan's lower lip. Without much more thought she tightened her arms, pulling Ryan in, and deepened the kiss. She felt Ryan's nipples harden against her, causing a pang of desire to rush through her body. The smell of bacon brought her back to her senses, but she lingered for a few seconds longer before breaking the kiss.

"Breakfast, sweetheart," Tobi said huskily.

"Right," Ryan said breathlessly.

She kept her arms around Ryan a little longer before giving her a gentle squeeze and turning back to the stove. "Coffee is ready if you want some."

"Thanks," Ryan said, pouring a cup. "Would you like some?"

"I fixed a cup already, but thanks. How did you sleep?"

"Like a baby. How are you feeling this morning?"

"Mmm, I'm okay." Tobi said while taking a sip of coffee. "I called the hospital while you were in the shower. Ryan, Sylvia Hyde, the pregnant woman, didn't make it."

Ryan sat in surprised silence. She had a strong desire to take this woman in her arms and just make everything go away. She had no idea what to say. She knew how Tobi felt about the woman.

"I'm sorry, honey."

"Me, too, I just wish I understood what happened. The baby was stillborn," she said with a hint of sadness in her voice. "They're going to do an autopsy, but based on her lab work, everything points to an overdose."

"I know you're anxious to find out the results." Sensing Tobi's need to change the subject, Ryan added, "Do you need any help over there?"

"Nope, all done," she said, as she turned with plates in her hand.

Tobi took a chair opposite Ryan at the table. With her hair still damp and her cheeks rosy from the shower, Ryan had an angelic look about her. She was such a beautiful woman, and as Tobi watched her butter a piece of toast, she realized how casual and normal waking up and having breakfast with her felt. It felt right.

"Ryan, I was wondering if you had any plans today. I know it's the weekend and you probably have things to do..."

"Actually, I really don't have much going on. I have some laundry that needs to be done, and tomorrow I'm supposed to go to Mom's for dinner, but that's it," she said, while munching on a piece of bacon.

"Would you like to spend the day together? We could go down to the beach for a walk, and maybe afterward, we could get some ice cream." At that, Ryan immediately perked up. "You like ice cream, huh?"

"Nooo, I don't like ice cream, Tobi, I absolutely love it! It's one of my weaknesses, if you must know," Ryan said with a gleaming smile.

"Any particular flavor or you just like them all?" Tobi asked, laughing.

"Mmm…Mint chocolate chip, but not the green kind. It has to be real mint chip."

"Ah, well, let's get a move on so we can hit the beach, and you can get your ice cream fix." Tobi took one last sip of coffee. "C'mon! Time's a wasting," she said, pulling Ryan to her feet.

Their walk on the beach turned into a playful romp as each tried to avoid the teasing edge of the cool water rushing at their feet. Almost three hours later, they stopped for the promised ice cream. Watching Ryan eat her dessert was more than enough entertainment for Tobi. Ryan was not kidding when she said she loved mint chocolate chip. There was a look of pure delight on her face with each bite. When Tobi reached over to wipe a smudge of ice cream off Ryan's chin, Ryan grinned wickedly as she grabbed Tobi's hand and sucked the offending ice cream off her finger.

Tobi inhaled a sharp breath and slowly let it out as Ryan just smiled, winked, and continued eating.

When they both finished, Ryan threw their napkins and papers in the trash and held her hand out for Tobi.

"So, tell me something, Tobi, why is it that you've never mentioned any long-term relationships?"

"Well, I had a few girlfriends through college, and medical school really didn't afford much time for me to sustain anything long-term. I was always so busy studying. It honestly wasn't as important to me as my career at the time."

"And after medical school?" Ryan asked as she navigated their walk from the pebbled beach to the tree-lined walkway.

"After medical school came residency. There was a woman I saw for about a year in that time frame, but it was just someone to spend time with, for me anyhow."

53

"What do you mean?"

"She wanted more of a commitment, and I couldn't give her that. I enjoyed being around her and doing things with her, but I didn't feel that "forever" chemistry."

"What happened?"

"We stopped seeing each other, and since then, I've just had the occasional date here and there. There hasn't been anyone special." *Until now.*

They walked along the concrete path a little farther before Tobi finally broke the silence.

"What about you, Ryan? Was there anyone before Stacey?"

"I had a few short-term relationships but nothing substantial."

"Did you and Lauren ever date?"

Ryan laughed easily before responding. "No, Lauren and I never dated. We've been best friends since middle school. However…"

"However?" Tobi asked.

"There was a night back in college when Lauren's girl of the moment stood her up. She was in a pissy mood, so we both stayed in that night. We had stashed some alcohol and pulled it out and started drinking. The more we drank, the more we talked, and the more we talked, the more we drank."

"And?" Tobi prodded.

"And we ended up kissing. What should have been a long passionate kiss turned out to be a long kiss that left us both with sour looks on our faces," Ryan said, laughing. "We decided then and there that kissing each other felt like kissing our own sister. I love Lauren, but there have never been any romantic feelings toward her."

Tobi smiled at the obvious affection Ryan felt for her best friend. They stopped walking and sat on an old wooden bench, watching as couples and families traipsed along the beach and walkway. Tobi could tell by the intense look on Ryan's face that she had something on her mind.

"Ryan, is there something you want to talk about?"

Ryan turned slightly to look at Tobi. Clearing her throat, she said, "Actually, there is something. I did a lot of thinking last night and…" Ryan saw the panicked look on her face and reached for Tobi's hand before continuing. "No, it's nothing bad, honest. It's just that...well, Tobi, I really like being with you."

"I like being with you, too," she said hesitantly.

"I'm sorry, I'm not expressing myself very well," Ryan said, glancing away.

Running her fingers down Ryan's cheek, Tobi turned her face so Ryan was looking directly into her eyes. "Ryan, just say what's on your mind. If you feel it, then say it."

"Since meeting you, I've been the happiest I can recall ever being. I love spending time with you. I want to know everything there is to know about you. I think about you all the time, and I don't know how you feel about this, but I have no desire to date other people, Tobi. I'd like to see where this goes," Ryan blurted while ducking her head to look at her hands.

Ryan's nervous rambling tore at Tobi's heart. She knew what admitting her feelings cost Ryan. She was giving Tobi her trust, and now it was up to Tobi to honor it and not hurt her. Tucking her hand under Ryan's chin, Tobi raised her head so she could see her eyes. What she saw made her smile. Ryan was chewing on her bottom lip, which the doctor had come to realize was a way for Ryan to deal with her nervousness.

"Ryan, I want that, too. There are so many layers and facets to you, and I'm selfish enough to admit that I want you all to myself." Pausing, Tobi glanced off at the trees. Knowing that Ryan needed to hear the words, she looked back, intent on expressing her feelings. "I will admit that I don't have a lot of experience with relationships. I've never had my trust and love steamrollered like you have. It's just never been the right girl. Without a doubt, what I feel for you is completely different from anything else I've ever felt."

"You have no idea how scared I was to talk to you about this. I wasn't sure if now was the right time," Ryan said, with an obvious slump of relief.

"I was scared, too; that's why I'm so glad you said it first," Tobi said with a nervous chuckle.

Ryan shook her head, surprised that Tobi accepted her declaration so readily. Now, Ryan felt confident enough to broach the other subject she wanted to discuss.

"How would you feel about going with me tomorrow to meet my mom?"

"Is that what you want?"

"I'd really like you to come. Two of my brothers will be there, as well," Ryan said hopefully.

"I'll make you a deal. If I can make you breakfast in the morning, I'll go to dinner at your mother's in the evening."

"What time do you get up on Sundays?" Ryan asked.

"I don't know, but you'll be there, so just wake me when you're hungry."

"That's your deal?"

"That's my deal," she said with a smirk.

Ryan tapped a finger to her chin and pretended to ponder the offer. When Tobi poked her in the stomach and stood to walk away, Ryan reflexively grabbed her arm, pulling Tobi back around.

"Sorry, um, it's a deal." Ryan stood and leaned in to seal it with a kiss.

Slowly pulling back from Ryan's lingering lips, Tobi looked at her with a pout, then out came that beautiful smile. Ryan tucked Tobi's hand in hers, and they resumed their walk.

Chapter Five

T here is nothing to be nervous about, Tobi, just relax," Ryan said, watching Tobi fidget in her seat as they pulled into her mom's driveway.

"I'm trying, but what if she doesn't like me?"

"What's not to like? Please, just trust me on this, okay? She'll love you."

Ryan walked around to Tobi's side of the car and opened the door. She gave Tobi a reassuring smile and held her hand as they walked to the front door. Ryan knocked lightly before entering. As they walked down the hall, they were met by an attractive older woman who was a little shorter than Ryan but taller than Tobi. Her hazel eyes were set off by fashionably styled salt and pepper hair.

"Hi, Mom," Ryan said, wrapping her arms around her for a hug.

"Hi, sweetie," she said before stepping back to look at Tobi.

"Mom, I'd like you to meet someone very special to me. This is Tobi, Tobi Drexler. Tobi, this is my mother."

"Hello, Mrs. Thomas, it's very nice to meet you," Tobi said as she extended her hand.

"Please, call me Grace, honey. Now, get over here and give me a hug. Any special friend of Ryan's gets more than just a handshake," Grace said as she engulfed Tobi in an embrace.

Ryan rolled her eyes behind her mother's back. Tobi grinned and returned the hug.

"Why don't you girls come on into the kitchen and get something to drink? Ryan, your brothers will be here shortly. They ran to grab a couple of things from the store for me."

Ryan took Tobi's hand as they walked into the kitchen. She motioned for Tobi to sit at the table and walked to the refrigerator.

"Tobi, what would you like? There's tea, lemonade, water, Kool-Aid, soda, beer, and milk."

"Hmm, is that all?" Tobi asked with a chuckle. "Tea would be great, thank you."

Ryan got a couple glasses down and turned toward her mother. "Mom, would you like anything?"

"No, dear, I have something. Thank you."

Ryan handed Tobi her glass and took a seat next to her. Smiling, she winked at Tobi before taking a drink.

"So, Tobi, when my daughter is not dragging you around all over the place, what is it that you do?"

"Mom, we haven't even been here five minutes yet!" Ryan exclaimed, almost spilling her drink.

Tobi, sensing Ryan's discomfort, placed her hand lightly over Ryan's and squeezed gently.

"I'm a radiologist down at Truman University Medical Center, Grace. For the record, though, I'm the one who has been dragging your daughter around," Tobi said, laughing.

Grace smiled at Tobi and took a seat next to Ryan at the table.

"Do you enjoy what you do, Tobi?"

"I do enjoy it, most of the time. It has its ups and downs like any job, I suppose."

"I'm sure it keeps you busy."

"With after-hour call, it does. Sometimes, I have to make an effort to recognize what's going on around me outside that place."

"It's good that you can stop to smell the roses sometimes, dear," Grace said with a pat to her hand. "Ryan here hasn't told me much about how you two met. How long ago was that?"

"It's been a little over a month. Ryan was actually on patrol when we met." Glancing over at Ryan, Tobi smiled.

With mock seriousness, Ryan's mother said, "Well, I hope she wasn't being mean to you."

Tobi shook her head, "No, I was pulled over on the side of the road, and she had stopped to make sure that everything was okay. She was very sweet."

At this, Ryan rolled her eyes. Tobi was having a hard time carrying on a conversation with Grace because she had never seen Ryan so exasperated before. It was really quite charming.

"Good. At least I taught her some manners," Grace said as she squeezed Ryan's arm. The look of adoration on Ryan's face revealed how smitten she was with Tobi.

Ryan heard a commotion at the front door and went to greet her brothers, leaving Tobi and her mother talking in the kitchen. Standing in the hall, she watched them come through the door and close it before saying anything.

"Hey there, 'Trick," Ryan said, as she walked over to give the big man a hug. Turning toward the taller blond man, she punched him lightly in the arm saying, "Hi, Mory."

"Hey there, RAT," the brothers greeted in unison, each wrapping an arm around her waist.

Elbowing them both, she turned around to see Grace and Tobi, with smiles on their faces, standing in the hall. She took Tobi's hand to introduce her.

"Tobi, I'd like you to meet my brothers, Patrick and Morgan. Guys, this is Tobi."

"Hi, Tobi, it's really nice to meet you," said Patrick, shaking Tobi's hand.

"Hello, Tobi. I have to admit that when Ryan told us about you, she failed to mention how beautiful you are," Morgan said as he leaned in to place a kiss upon Tobi's cheek. Ryan smiled happily at Morgan's sweet gesture, which took Tobi by surprise.

"It's really nice to meet you both. Ryan has told me a lot about you two," Tobi said with a blush. *Although she didn't mention how strongly you all resemble each other.* Tobi thought it had to be the eyes because they were all the same bluish-gray.

Even Morgan with his curly blond hair couldn't be mistaken for anyone but a Thomas family member.

"Okay, kids, dinner is about ready. Why don't we seat ourselves at the table?" Grace called.

Ryan turned toward the kitchen and saw Tobi raise her eyebrows and mouth "RAT?" Ryan narrowed her eyes and glared at her brothers' backs.

"Dinner smells wonderful, Mom," Morgan said, reaching around her to grab a piece of roast and popping it into his mouth.

Grace, backhanding him lightly in the stomach, said, "Why don't you put that on the table before you eat it all?"

Morgan leaned down to kiss Grace on the cheek, and as she smiled in return, he took the platter of meat to the table.

Glancing at the table covered with roast, potatoes, gravy, carrots, and green beans, Patrick said, "I see you fixed Morgan's favorites."

Ryan laughed before saying, "Stop your pouting, Patrick. If I recall, she fixed your favorites the last time we were here."

Grace set a basket of rolls on the table and patted Patrick on the back as he grumbled good-naturedly. Of her five children, these three were the closest, and a Sunday dinner never went by without the teasing.

"Let's eat," Grace said.

Tobi listened to the lighthearted banter that continued while plates were being fixed. She was hard-pressed to find a reason why she would ever feel uncomfortable around Ryan's family. Like Ryan, they were warm and welcoming. As she looked around the table, her eyes fell upon twinkling hazel ones. She smiled in return as Grace winked at her. Under the table, Tobi felt long fingers tangle within hers as she looked into Ryan's smiling face.

Dinner went surprisingly well, and Ryan was happy that Patrick and Morgan were on their best behavior and genuinely seemed to like Tobi. It wasn't until they were drinking coffee and eating dessert that she could have killed them both.

"Patrick, I noticed when you guys first got here that Ryan called you Trick, and Morgan, Mory. Is there a story behind that?" Tobi asked.

"See, when Ryan was little, she had trouble saying our full names; that's what they were shortened to so she could call us by name. After all these years, it's stuck," Patrick explained. "She never had trouble pronouncing Jack's or Raef's name, though, so they are just Jack and Raef."

"So when you called her 'RAT,' that was because...?" Tobi inquired.

Patrick and Morgan burst out laughing. Patrick looked to Morgan to explain.

"Well, that has something to do with Ryan's middle name..." Morgan started.

"Morgan," Ryan said in a threatening tone.

"Ryan, you don't scare me, so pipe down," Morgan said, chuckling.

Ryan sat back in her chair and pouted while Morgan continued with his explanation.

"Ryan's middle name is Althea, and when she was younger, we used to tease her about it. One day, she told us that she'd rather be called RAT, her initials, than ever be called Althea. From that day on, we have called her RAT," Morgan finished as he and Patrick burst out laughing at the look on Ryan's face.

Poor Ryan, Tobi thought to herself as she laughed with Ryan's brothers. She couldn't help but giggle and was relieved to see a slight smile edge the corners of Ryan's lips. Morgan leaned over and placed his arm across Ryan's shoulders and bent down to whisper something in her ear. Ryan started laughing and shoved him away to sit up.

"Ryan, you know we love you," said Patrick, still smirking.

"Yeah, yeah! I love you, too." Ryan glanced at her watch. "On that note, I think it's time for us to get going. Mom, dinner was delicious, as always," Ryan said, standing. They all walked to the door to say their goodbyes. Patrick and Morgan were giving Tobi a hug as Ryan embraced Grace.

"Thanks," Ryan whispered in her mother's ear. "I love you."

Grace rubbed her back as she said, "I love you, too, honey."

Giving both Patrick and Morgan a hug, Ryan waited for her mom to finish talking with Tobi.

"It was really nice to meet you, Tobi," Grace said while still holding Tobi's hands. "Please don't be a stranger, and feel free to come by anytime."

"Thank you, Grace, that means a lot."

On the drive home, Tobi was a little quiet. Ryan wasn't sure whether to ask her if everything was okay, so she said nothing. Fortunately, the silence didn't last long.

"Your family is very nice, Ryan. Thank you so much for sharing them with me."

"Yes, they are, and you are more than welcome. Thank you for going with me. Even if they did betray me, the little finks."

"So, Althea, huh?" she said. Ryan knew she was trying to contain a laugh.

"Don't even start. It was my aunt's name, and I was lucky enough to be the next child in line for the name to be passed down to."

"Was?"

"Yes. She passed away when I was very young. I really didn't get much of an opportunity to know her. She was my father's sister."

"In which case, you probably feel it's an honor to carry on her name."

"Precisely," Ryan said. She nodded and continued smiling. *How does she seem to know me so well in such a short time?*

"So it must make you feel really special to have your father's middle name and your aunt's name."

"It does. You know what else makes me feel special?" Ryan asked.

"What's that?" Tobi replied, turning slightly in her seat to face Ryan.

"You. It really means a lot to me that you came with me today. I could tell my family really likes you."

"You *are* special to me, and I really enjoyed myself this afternoon."

Ryan pulled into the driveway but left the engine running. With both of them working the next day, she knew it had to be an early night. Turning to face Tobi, she was surprised to see Tobi had already unfastened her seatbelt and turned all the way in her seat toward her.

"You know, I really wish this weekend didn't have to end, Ryan."

"I know. I'll call you tomorrow, though, if that's okay," Ryan said.

"That's more than okay. I look forward to it. Please drive carefully, and I'll see you tomorrow."

They gravitated toward one another, slowly narrowing the distance between them. Ryan hesitated briefly, giving Tobi a chance to make the first move. The moment of time that passed felt like forever. Ryan wasn't sure that Tobi was going to do anything until she felt Tobi's lips connect with hers. Tobi's hand slid up into her hair, pulling her closer. As Tobi brushed her lips, Ryan opened her mouth fully to deepen the kiss. Ryan's hands caressed Tobi's back and sides and pulled her even closer. Tobi's hand moved between them and gently cupped Ryan's breast making her nipples harden in response. Ryan fought hard to keep herself under control. All she wanted to do was give in to her need for Tobi, but now was not the time. She ended the kiss and rested her forehead against Tobi's. Ryan leaned back, opened her eyes, and caressed Tobi's cheek.

"Sweet dreams, Tobi."

Tobi climbed out of the Jeep and glanced back. "Good night, Ryan."

Ryan watched until Tobi's front door closed completely and a light switched on before pulling away. *Good night, my sweet Tobi.* She could still taste Tobi on her lips and knew that sleep would be eluding her tonight. Ryan's body was more than ready to proceed, but her head wouldn't follow. She knew that Tobi was nothing like Stacey, but she couldn't seem to keep that out of the back of her mind. Tobi seemingly understood because each time Ryan backed off, she never pushed for more. That wouldn't stop the burning ache that kissing Tobi caused, though, and Ryan knew it was time for a shower—and a cold one at that.

Tara Wentz

Traffic Stop

Chapter Six

Ryan usually looked forward to Mondays, but today she didn't. She hadn't wanted the weekend to end. The time she spent with Tobi only made her want to spend more time with her. *How is it that after such a short time, she can be so deeply ingrained in my system that I can't imagine her not being there?* It took everything she had not to call Tobi last night after they parted. She knew Tobi needed her sleep, as did Ryan. Only one more hour until break, then she would give her a call.

Startled from her meandering thoughts by the abrupt halt of the police cruiser, Ryan looked over at Jake to see what the problem was before glancing out the front windshield. She barely caught the taillights of the car that had pulled out in front of them as it zipped over into the next lane and in front of another car. Jake flipped the switch to initiate the lights and sirens. Ryan watched as he maneuvered them in behind the car. After a brief distance, the car pulled over to the side of the road. When Jake got out to approach the driver, Ryan picked up the radio to call in the license plate.

"Charlie Nine to Dispatch."

"Dispatch, go ahead, Charlie Nine."

Ryan gave the information and waited for a response. As Jake climbed back into the cruiser, he was grinning and shaking his head.

"What's so funny?"

"Her," he said, pointing to the car in front of them. "Do you believe she had the nerve to hold up her hand for me to wait because she was on her cell phone?"

Ryan shook her head in disgust, but before she could respond the radio crackled in response.

"Dispatch to Charlie Nine."

"Charlie Nine, go ahead."

"I'm showing a bench warrant on your party, Carsten, Tiffany A., date of birth five, ten of seventy-three, showing physical as white female, five-foot-two, red hair, brown eyes—break—"

"Go ahead."

"Outstanding tickets with multiple fines."

"Charlie Nine, copy."

Ryan followed Jake out of the cruiser to take the driver into custody.

"Ma'am, I need you to step out of the car," Jake said.

"Why?" the woman asked, defiantly.

"Just step out of the car and I'll explain everything."

The woman tossed her purse into the passenger seat and mumbled under her breath as she opened the car door.

"Now what is it that you want?" the woman asked, placing her hands on her hips. "I haven't got all day to play your games."

"Ma'am, I need you to turn around and place your hands on the hood of your car," Jake responded.

"Excuse me? I don't know who the fuck you think you're dealing with, but I don't have time for this."

Jake reached out and grasped the woman's arm as she attempted to get back into her car.

"Ma'am…" Jake started.

"Get your God damned hands off me, you filthy pig," the woman screamed as she turned and slapped at Jake's hands.

At this point, Ryan stepped in behind the woman in case Jake needed assistance.

"I'm going to ask you one more time, ma'am; shut up, turn around, and put your hands on the car."

The woman became irate and started swinging her arms. "Why you lousy mother—"

Ryan didn't hear the rest of what was said for when the woman started her assault a flailing arm caught Ryan in the mouth, splitting her lip wide open.

"Son of a bitch," Ryan gasped, spitting a mouthful of blood onto the ground.

Ryan and Jake reacted immediately by grabbing the woman's arms to restrain her and take her to the ground. Ryan kept a knee in the woman's back while Jake applied the cuffs. They lifted her to her feet and Jake led her to the cruiser while reading her rights.

"You have the right to remain silent. Anything you say...," Jake's voice trailed off as he put the woman inside the cruiser.

"Damn," Ryan said, palpating her tender lip with the tips of her fingers.

Maybe I won't get to call Tobi in an hour after all. Ryan sighed and then fingered the mic to call a tow truck to transport the woman's car to the impound lot.

Ryan sat on the desk and let Jake clean her split lip. She knew he was just biding his time to make some smart-ass comment.

"You know, Ryan, I don't ever recall a little five-foot-nothing getting the better of you."

"You know, Jake, I don't ever recall you needing help with a five-foot-nothing."

Laughing, Jake reached up and grasped her chin. "Now, hold still; this is probably going to sting a little."

Ryan gritted her teeth against the sharp pain and waited for Jake to finish. By the time he stepped back, the pain had dulled to a steady burn.

"Damn, what did you do? Put salt in the wound?" Ryan whined.

"Stop being such a baby. It should quit hurting in just a bit," he teased. "So, wanna tell me what had you so preoccupied today?"

Ryan waited until he put the first aid supplies away and sat in front of her before responding. She knew she could trust Jake.

"I'm really enjoying this…this whole thing that Tobi and I have. I've never met anyone like her. She's kind and compassionate; she's funny and silly…most of all, she likes me for who I am." Ryan stopped to take a breath and noticed that Jake was smiling affectionately.

"What?" she asked suspiciously.

"Nothing. It's just really nice to see you this happy again. I can tell that Tobi means a lot to you. She met your mom this past weekend, didn't she?"

"Yeah," Ryan said with a crooked grin. "Mom absolutely loved her. Even Patrick and Morgan were taken with her. I think I'm falling in love with her, Jake, and it scares the hell out of me."

Jake scooted forward in his chair and took Ryan's hand in his. "Don't be afraid. Just go with it and be happy. You deserve it," he said with a pat to her knee. "Now, let's get that report done so we can get out of here."

Ryan smiled at Jake. He always worried about her. When things were at their worst after Stacey left, he was the one who kicked her ass back into shape. He would not let her mope around. He and Tim both made complete nuisances of themselves and let her know that they wouldn't go away. They made Ryan top priority, and for that she would be eternally grateful.

It had been a grueling day so far, and to top things off, Tobi hadn't heard from Ryan at all. She knew Ryan had a demanding job; she just missed hearing her voice. Tobi had enjoyed the weekend they spent together. She didn't know what she had expected from Ryan's family, but they were great. Ryan's mother was so personable and friendly. From what she saw of Ryan and her brothers, Grace had to have been a saint to put up with them. Laying her pen down, Tobi stood up and walked to the window. She watched several leaves float past; the overcast skies made her realize that it wouldn't be long before it turned really cold outside. And now she had Ryan to keep her warm at night. *Where did that thought come from?*

Tobi was startled when the phone rang. She glanced at the clock and, realizing Marcy was already gone for the evening, stepped over to answer it. She hoped it was Ryan calling to make plans for the evening.

"Dr. Drexler."

Silence.

"Hello, this is Dr. Drexler. May I help you?"

Tobi could hear breathing on the other end.

"Hello?" she said again.

Placing the phone back in the cradle, Tobi stood there with her hand still on the receiver. *That was odd.* Tobi hoped that it wasn't an emergency. She gave a startled yelp when the phone rang again. She picked it up and raised it to her ear.

"Dr. Drexler," Tobi said cautiously.

More silence.

"This is Dr. Drexler speaking. Who is this?"

Again…nothing.

"I'm going to hang up if you are not going to talk." Waiting a full ten seconds, she made good on her threat. Before she had time to think about anything else, the phone rang again.

"Dr. Drexler!" she said, exasperated.

"Tobi?"

"Ryan," Tobi said, relieved.

"What's wrong?" Ryan asked, immediately alert.

"It's nothing really. I just had a couple of phone calls that threw me off."

"What do you mean? Threw you off how?"

"When I answered the phone, nobody said anything. I could hear someone breathing, but even when I threatened to hang up, they didn't say anything."

"Do you ever get accidental phone calls, being in the hospital and all, where people hang up without saying anything?"

"That does happen, but this person didn't hang up. It was almost like he or she was playing some kind of game with me."

Ryan was silent for a minute before saying anything.

"I'm off duty in about ten minutes. Why don't you wait there and I'll come get you? We can go get something to eat for dinner if you'd like."

"You don't have to do that, but I would like to see you, if you're sure you don't mind. Dinner sounds like a great idea."

"I'm positive. I'll see you in about twenty-five minutes, okay?"

"Okay."

After Ryan hung up, she sat quietly for a few minutes. The cop in Ryan wondered if these calls to Tobi were just random or if there was something behind them. Placing the report she had just finished in its folder, Ryan stood up and grabbed her jacket. She placed the folder in the "finished" wire rack, and with a wave to Jake, headed out the door. Truman University Medical Center was not that far, but all the stoplights made it seem farther. The only thought in her head was to get to Tobi and make sure she was okay.

Being a little protective, aren't we?

You again!

You say that like it's a bad thing.

What do you want?

Just thought I would point out that you are being protective.

And?

And—just that it's been awhile since you've felt this way about anyone.

Your point is?

My point is that you've already made a commitment to the relationship and Tobi.

I didn't make a commitment!

Didn't you? You're taking chances and giving things of yourself that you never thought you'd do again.

I don't have time for this; I need to get to Tobi.

Ryan scrambled out of the Jeep and made her way into the hospital and up to Tobi's office. She knocked on the door and jumped in surprise when it was yanked open and her arms were filled with a trembling woman.

"What's wrong? What happened?"

Ryan wrapped her arms around Tobi and walked them over to the couch in her office. Once seated, Tobi leaned back and took a deep breath before looking at Ryan.

"Right after we hung up, the phone rang again."

"The silent caller?"

"Yes, but this time, he talked."

Seeing her visibly shiver, Ryan pulled Tobi back into her arms before nudging her to continue. "Go on."

"He said, 'I know who you are, and very soon, you will know who I am,'" she said with a catch in her voice.

"Did you recognize his voice?"

"No."

"By your reaction, I take it that he didn't sound like a secret admirer."

"His voice was threatening. He sounded very angry."

"We should report this."

"Report it to whom? Report what? Don't you see, Ryan, he's done nothing yet that would require any kind of response."

"I know," Ryan replied, blowing out a breath of frustration. "I know. It's just…I just wasn't thinking there for a second. Sorry."

"Don't be, I understand."

Ryan could hear the fear in her voice. She knew Tobi was right, but she couldn't just stand by and not do anything. Before Ryan had a chance to think about what she was saying, she blurted out what was on her mind.

"I'll stay with you. Until we figure out what's going on, I'll stay at your house, and I can drive you to work."

"Ryan, I can't ask you to do that. We have no idea if this is really a threat or if anything will even happen. He just shook me up."

"You're not asking me to do it, and I'm not willing to chance that it's not a real threat." Ryan softened her tone before continuing. "Hey, I've just found you; I can't pretend that I don't have feelings for you, and I'd be lost if something happened to you," she pleaded, hoping Tobi would understand.

Leaning back in Ryan's arms, Tobi looked into her eyes and knew that the words she had just spoken came straight from her heart. Knowing how much Ryan cared for her brought tears to her eyes. Tobi stood up and placed her hands on Ryan's shoulders. Bending down, she gave Ryan a simple kiss to convey her heartfelt gratitude. She placed her palms against the smooth surface of Ryan's cheeks and for the first time noticed the cut on her lip.

"What happened to you?" Tobi asked, running her thumb lightly over Ryan's bottom lip.

"We had some problems with a suspect earlier. She took offense to the fact that she was under arrest. It's no big deal; I wasn't paying attention and got caught by a flailing fist."

"Does it hurt?"

"It's okay, really. It's just a little sore."

"I want you to promise me something, Ryan. I want you to promise me that you will take extra care of yourself out there because I'd be lost if anything ever happened to you."

Ryan stared into Tobi's eyes for a brief moment and finally answered, in almost a whisper, "I promise."

Tobi leaned down and placed a tender kiss against the cut on her lip. With a hand around the nape of Ryan's neck, Tobi pulled her head gently to her chest and wrapped her arms around her. Tobi held her tightly for a few minutes then let her hands slide down Ryan's arms before pulling her to her feet.

"C'mon, let's go get something to eat," Tobi said.

Ryan smiled and waited while she locked the door. As they walked side by side, Tobi reveled in the feelings of being loved and protected.

Piercing dark eyes locked on the two women as they entered the elevator. The closing doors swept across his line of vision, breaking his fixation on the women. "And now, I've found your weakness," he spat as he turned and walked away.

Chapter Seven

After stopping at Ryan's house so she could pick up some things, they grabbed some takeout before heading to Tobi's. They were both lost in their own thoughts, making the ride home a little subdued. Ryan knew Tobi had to be thinking about the "silent caller." Although she wasn't outwardly showing any fear, Ryan knew his calls had shaken her. Tobi maintained some kind of physical contact during the entire ride, whether it was her hand on Ryan's thigh or her fingers curled around hers.

Ryan pulled into the driveway, stepped out, and walked around to open Tobi's door. She grabbed her bag from the floorboard and threw the strap over her shoulder, then lifted the sack of food from Tobi's lap. Ryan waited for Tobi to climb down from the Jeep, but she sat there for a moment before looking into Ryan's eyes.

"You really are very sweet, Ryan."

Ryan smiled and blushed as she held out her free hand for Tobi. Making their way into the front foyer, Ryan put down the bags, closed the door, and turned the locks. She leaned her

73

forehead against the door as she felt the warmth of Tobi's hands on her back. Tobi's hands slid around her waist. A sigh escaped from Ryan when she felt the length of Tobi press against her. Ryan turned in Tobi's arms and kissed her on the forehead before looking into her eyes.

"You ready to eat some dinner?" Ryan asked softly.

"Yes. Actually, I'm starving."

Ryan picked up the bag of food, took Tobi's hand, and led her to the kitchen. Tobi grabbed a couple of plates while Ryan fixed them something to drink.

Tobi dished out the fish and fries along with a side of cole slaw. She set the plates on the small square table and took a seat. Ryan smiled as she handed Tobi her glass and sat down next to her.

"Mmm, this smells great. I don't think I've ever had their food before," Ryan said, taking a bite. "This is really good."

"It's one of my favorite places. They have the best fried fish."

As they ate dinner, Ryan carefully avoided mentioning the caller so as not to spoil the meal. After they finished eating, Ryan sent Tobi off to the living room while she cleaned up. She was postponing the inevitable, knowing it would not be pleasant for Tobi. There were questions that had to be asked, and Ryan was afraid they might offend her. Flicking the light off, she walked into the living room and sat on the couch, close to Tobi, but not touching. Ryan needed a clear head and being too close to Tobi would not allow that.

"Do you feel up to a few questions about earlier?"

Nodding her head, Tobi replied, "I knew the law enforcement side of you couldn't hold out for much longer. Ask away, Sergeant Thomas."

Ryan smiled gratefully and cleared her throat. "For starters, I'm going to ask the obvious. Is there anyone you are aware of who would have some kind of vendetta against you? Anyone who would have a reason for saying what he did?"

"I thought about that on the way home. In the more than two years that I've been at this university, I can't recall a time when I've had such a heated discussion with anyone that it would warrant any kind of revenge. That's not to say that I haven't had disagreements with colleagues, but those were professional and nothing of a personal nature."

"What about any patients? Was there anything beyond the professional realm of things?" Ryan knew this question would not be welcomed, and by the look on Tobi's face, she was right. *Please, baby, don't be angry.*

Tobi stood and paced a few feet away before turning. "Ryan, if you are suggesting in any way that I had a personal relationship with a patient, then you are wrong!"

"I had to ask," Ryan responded quietly. *Damn!*

Sighing dejectedly, Ryan leaned back against the couch and closed her eyes. She knew this was hard on Tobi, and she hated that she was the one making it harder. Ryan had hoped that Tobi would see the question for what it was, and not as a personal attack on her character. Ryan wondered how long the doctor was going to be angry, but she didn't have to wait long.

"I'm sorry," Tobi whispered, slipping onto the couch next to Ryan.

Taking Tobi's hand in hers, Ryan gently traced the outline of her hand before lacing her fingers within Tobi's. "So am I."

"Don't be sorry for doing your job. I shouldn't have snapped at you."

"Do you think you can answer one more question for me?"

"I'll answer any questions you have."

"On a professional level, have you had any complaints from a patient? Were there any disagreements on a diagnosis or an exam with a less-than-stellar prognosis? Is there anything that you can remember a patient becoming upset about?"

"Nothing," Tobi said, shaking her head. "Nothing comes to mind. It's not a perfect world, and there are bad things that happen to good people, but I've never had someone threaten me."

"If you think of anything, please tell me, okay?"

"I will. So…where do we go from here?"

"At this point, we just have to wait and see if he contacts you again. I know that seems like a cop out, but there really isn't anything more we can do until we have more to go on."

"No, I understand."

Tara Wentz

They both remained silent for some time. Tobi laid her head back and closed her eyes while Ryan propped her head in her hand and studied an unguarded Tobi. Her skin, Ryan knew, was so soft, and her features, to Ryan's eyes, were just so perfect. Blond eyebrows and eyelashes gave her face an almost serene, angelic look. *She is so incredibly beautiful. She could have absolutely anybody she wanted, so why me? How did I get so lucky?*

Ryan glanced at the clock and realized it was getting late and that they should call it a day. She bounced Tobi's hand lightly in hers and waited for Tobi to look in her direction. When she didn't, Ryan thought she was sleeping.

"Tobi?"

"Hmm?"

"I thought you had fallen asleep."

"No, I was just waiting for you to finish ogling me."

With a startled gasp, Ryan responded, "I was not ogling you."

"Okay, you were checking me out then," Tobi said, laughing.

"I most certainly was not checking you out." Tobi rolled her head toward Ryan and looked knowingly into her eyes. Realizing she was caught, Ryan grinned. "Maybe I was looking at you, but I was not ogling you or checking you out. I was just thinking about how beautiful you are and how lucky I am," she said, grasping her lower lip between her teeth.

Tobi rubbed her thumb across Ryan's lower lip. "I'm the lucky one. I didn't realize what I was missing in my life until the day I met you." Tobi's heart was bursting with emotion and this time she was pretty sure it was love. Love for this tough cop in her life. Love for Ryan.

Ryan leaned toward her and placed her lips on Tobi's as her eyes fluttered closed. She put her arms around Tobi and pulled her down so she was lying across Ryan's body. The full press of Tobi's body against her made Ryan's body tingle in anticipation. *Sweet Jesus she feels good against me!*

Tobi groaned in delight and intensified an already hungry kiss. She slid a thigh between Ryan's legs, pushing them open a little farther.

"Yes," Ryan panted and opened her eyes.

Tobi felt Ryan tremble and lifted her mouth away long enough to see arousal darken Ryan's eyes. *She is so, so beautiful.* Tobi leaned back down and claimed Ryan's lips in a mind-numbing passionate kiss.

Ryan couldn't stop her hips from pressing against Tobi. She pulled her mouth away and rested her hot, flushed cheek next to Tobi's. Feeling Tobi's moist lips nipping at her neck, she tilted her head back, silently urging Tobi lower.

Christ! I could die now and be happy! Ryan thought just before Tobi bit the sensitive skin at the base of her neck. A fierce yet pleasurable pain raced down her body, landing with an urgent crash on her clit.

"Oh, God, you have no idea what you are doing to me," Ryan said in a throaty whisper. She reached between their bodies and raked her palm across Tobi's breast, making her already awakening nipple even harder.

Tobi gasped and reflexively clenched her legs, trying to ease the heavy ache growing between her thighs. In the corner of her mind she knew they were moving a little too fast and that one of them, reluctantly, needed to slow things down. She was afraid that the strain of the day was pushing their emotions further than either of them was ready for.

"Ryan, wait," Tobi said hoarsely as she pulled away. "We need to stop. It's late, and we've both had a stressful day."

Ryan took a deep breath, let it out, and nodded in agreement.

Tobi traced Ryan's lip and winced. "I think I split your lip back open."

Ryan ran her tongue across her lip and could feel the faint sting of the open cut. Catching her breath, she sighed, "I'm quite certain this isn't the most romantic setting, either."

"No, it's not," Tobi said, laughing as she gazed at Ryan's feet dangling over the edge of the couch.

Tobi lifted her body from Ryan's and stood. She waited until Ryan was sitting up and then extended her hand to pull Ryan to her feet. Lights off and locks checked one last time, they made their way to bed.

After dropping Tobi off at work the next morning, Ryan drove to the precinct. She had an hour before her shift started, so she thought she might have a chance to talk to Jake. He always arrived early to use the gym, and she had no doubt that he would already be there. Ryan changed into shorts and a T-shirt, closed her locker, and went in search of him. Finding him in the weight room, she strolled over to where he was using the free weights. She leaned against the mirror to watch, and waited until he noticed her standing there.

"Hey there, kiddo. What are you doing here so early?"

"Can't a girl just come to work out?"

He looked at Ryan cynically before setting the weights down and giving her his full attention.

"What's wrong?" he asked.

"You know me too well, my dear friend. I need some insight on something."

"Go on."

"Last night, Tobi got a phone call in her office. The man called twice, both times not saying a word. On the third call, he told her, 'I know who you are, and very soon, you will know who I am.' It shook her up pretty bad. We talked it over and she couldn't find a reason for anybody to be calling her and saying that. I don't know what to think of this, Jake." Running her hand through her hair, she waited for him to respond. Ryan knew what he was going to say because she kept telling herself the same thing over and over.

"You know there is really nothing we can do until he makes another move. We have no way of knowing who this man is or what he wants."

"I know, I know," Ryan said, exasperated. Pacing in front of him, she said, "I just can't sit by and watch her get hurt. I just can't do it."

Jake placed his hand on her arm, and Ryan stopped.

"We'll do everything we can. If this wasn't a prank call then he'll make another move. Hopefully he'll be a little careless, and we can get some kind of lead to work from. Ryan, they all make mistakes sooner or later. Just hang in there. You need to be strong, if not for yourself, then for Tobi."

"Thanks, I knew I could count on you to help."

"Always, honey, and don't you forget that."

Jake wrapped his arm around her shoulders, and Ryan swatted him away. "You stink," she said, laughing.

"That's not what Tim says when I sweat," he said with a wink.

"That is way more information than I needed to know, Jake!"

"I'll see you in report, sweetheart."

Watching him walk away, Ryan contemplated their conversation. She knew he was right, and she really didn't have anything else to go on. So, until this man made another move, they would just have to sit and wait.

"Marcy, can you come here for a second?" Tobi called from her office.

"Did you need something, Tobi?"

"Do you know where those reports that I left on my desk last night went to? I was almost certain that I left them here on the corner."

"I didn't see any reports when I laid the mail on your desk this morning. Are you sure you didn't place them somewhere else?"

Tobi thought back to the past evening's events; her confusion and fear when she left the office kept her from being a hundred percent sure where anything was at this point. Not wanting to alarm Marcy, she decided to keep quiet about the phone calls.

"No, I'm not positive. If I can't find them, can you reprint them? I know it means extra work for you, and I'm sorry about that."

"It's not a problem, Tobi. Don't worry about it."

"Thanks. You're a godsend."

Marcy started to return to her desk but paused in the doorway. Tobi leaned back in her chair and waited for Marcy to voice what was on her mind.

Marcy closed the door and returned to the seat in front of Tobi's desk.

"So, want to tell me more about this gorgeous woman you've been seeing?"

Tossing her pen onto the desktop, Tobi grinned at Marcy before replying, "What exactly would you like to know?"

"Oh...how about everything, for starters?" she said with a wiggle of her eyebrows.

"Now, Marcy, a girl has to have her secrets. I can tell you this much, though: she is amazing. I've never met anyone like her. She's so smart and funny. She's really very sweet behind that tough cop persona."

Tobi's eyes lit up as they always did when she talked about Ryan, and it was something Marcy always noticed. Tobi was a different person with Ryan in her life.

"Didn't you go to her mother's recently?"

Tobi leaned back in her chair and smiled. "Yes. I met her mother, Grace, and two of her brothers. The other two live out of state. They are a warm and wonderful bunch. Just like Ryan, they are very easy to talk with, but very ornery. I can't imagine how Grace kept her sanity when they were all younger."

"What about her father?"

Tobi's expression turned somber as she responded. "He was killed in an accident a couple of years ago."

"Wow," Marcy said, sadly. "That's rough."

"Yeah, she really looked up to him. He was her hero."

Marcy let a few moments of respectful silence go by before she stood and placed her hand on the back of the chair. "She really sounds like a good person, Tobi. You've been so much happier lately, and you're not staying till all hours of the night anymore." She walked to the door, and then turned back, "Oh, don't forget the board meeting at four."

"Thanks for the reminder and, Marcy...thanks for being a friend."

"You are most welcome...on both accounts. Holler if you need anything."

Resting her forearms on the desk, Tobi thought about Ryan and then about her own conversation with Marcy. She was quickly realizing everything that Ryan meant to her. She couldn't imagine not having this amazing woman in her life. Tobi knew that the intimacy they had shared affected Ryan as much as her, but she wasn't sure that Ryan was ready for a more physical relationship. With the hurt Ryan had endured in the past, Tobi could only imagine what must be going through her mind. Tobi didn't want to push Ryan into making love if she wasn't ready for it. She knew that when the time was right, there would be no hesitation, and it would just happen. She wanted their first time together to be so very special. She wanted it to be slow, slow enough for her to explore every inch of Ryan with her hands and mouth; slow enough to make Ryan forget everything except her, slow enough to make Ryan tremble and beg. Tobi closed her eyes and drew a deep breath, trying to calm her own body's reaction to the images in her mind. Until Ryan was ready for more, Tobi would cherish every touch and smile. She grabbed her pen and set to work so that when the meeting was over, she could get out of there on time.

Tara Wentz

Traffic Stop

Chapter Eight

It had been almost two weeks since the incident with the
silent caller, and Tobi had not heard anything more from
him. Ryan wondered whether this was a one-time
occurrence or if he had a plan he was following. Either way, she
knew it was still bothering Tobi. She had confessed that each time
the phone rang in the office it startled her and put her on edge. The
only thing Ryan could do was to assure her that she would do
everything she could to protect her. Although Tobi told Ryan she
didn't have to keep staying with her every night, Ryan insisted
that she really wanted to stay, for her own peace of mind. If Ryan
went home, how could she possibly sleep at night wondering
whether or not that man was still plotting to harm Tobi in some
way? Tobi seemed just as relieved by her answer as Ryan was
about Tobi's letting her stay.

"C'mon, we're going to miss the beginning."

Startled out of her thoughts, Ryan saw Tobi grab the popcorn
and head toward the theater. She picked up the sodas and
followed. Ryan settled down next to her and handed Tobi her
drink. Tobi smiled and tilted the popcorn in Ryan's direction.

"Thanks. Do you know anything about this movie?"

"Mmm, not really," Tobi said, taking a sip. "Marcy said it was pretty good, though."

Ryan hesitated, her drink halfway to her mouth. She set it back in the cup holder. "Marcy said it was good?"

"Yeah, what's wrong with that?"

"Tobi, you told me that Marcy really only likes sappy love stories."

"Oh, Ryan, I'm sure she likes other movies. Now, shhh, it's starting."

A third of the way through the movie, Ryan realized this was, in fact, a sappy love story. However, she couldn't bring herself to mind since Tobi was holding her hand. Periodically, Tobi would run her palm up Ryan's forearm and back down, the soft strokes coaxing goosebumps to the surface. Ryan felt an overwhelming desire to take Tobi in her arms and kiss her until she gasped from sheer want and need. She wanted to unbutton Tobi's blouse and bask in her warm scent; slip her hand beneath the denim barrier and skim her fingers over wet folds to the hardened bundle of nerves begging for release. Ryan clasped her legs together, barely restraining a moan of pleasure. If she wasn't careful, she'd miss what the movie was all about.

Who are you kidding?

What are you doing here? Can't you see I'm trying to pay attention?

Trying being the key word.

I give up. What is it you want?

You know you'd go see whatever Tobi wanted to, and it doesn't matter if it's a sappy love story.

So?

So, what does that mean when you will sacrifice your likes for those of someone else?

It means I like her and want her to be happy. It really doesn't matter what we see as long as I get to spend time with her.

I see.

What exactly do you see?

Just that I think you, Ryan, are in love with Tobi.

Ryan glanced in her direction and was startled to see Tobi's eyes upon her. Tobi raised an eyebrow at her questioningly, and

Ryan just shook her head. Shrugging her shoulders, Tobi turned her attention back to the screen. Ryan knew Tobi saw the stunned expression on her face, but how could she possibly explain? *Would she understand the fear I have of what I feel for her?* For the rest of the movie, Ryan forced herself to pay attention.

As they exited the theater, they zipped their jackets and huddled close. The wind had picked up since they entered the building, and it smelled like rain was in the air.

"So, what did you think of the movie?" Tobi asked.

"It was good. Did you like it?"

"I liked it a lot. I'll tell Marcy that you said it was good," she said smugly.

Ryan rolled her eyes and opened the Jeep door. "Get in, you goof." As she waited for Tobi to settle in before closing the door, Ryan glanced across the row of cars to see a man watching Tobi's every move. She looked at Tobi, then back to where the man had been standing and saw he was gone. *What the hell was that all about?*

"Ryan?"

"Oh, sorry," she said, closing the door. Running around to the driver's side, Ryan hopped in, started the engine, and pulled away from the parking lot. They failed to notice the man watching from his beat-up van.

Tobi, while waiting for the elevator to arrive, thought back to the evening at the movies. Ryan was so good to go and watch a chick flick and not complain. What really got Tobi's curiosity going was the shocked, even almost fearful look on Ryan's face at one point during the movie. For the life of her, she couldn't figure out what Ryan had been thinking. It couldn't have been a reaction to the movie because it was a slow point, and nothing was going on. Ryan hadn't been acting any differently, except for the brief time in the parking lot when she was staring off into space. Tobi guessed she would just have to wait to find out what Ryan had been thinking, if she ever did.

She was snapped from her thoughts by the ding of the elevator. Tobi shifted the folders in her arms and moved in among the crowd to take a spot by the wall. As the elevator rose, she glanced through a couple of charts, knowing they were due back later that day. When she shifted the folders around, one slipped from the pile to land on the floor. Before she could pick it up, a tanned and rough-looking hand entered her line of vision and picked it up for her. Tobi looked at the man and extended her hand. "Thank you," she said while waiting for the folder. It took a few seconds for the man to put it in her hand, but when she tried to place it back in the stack, he had yet to release it. He seemed fixated on her hand, or rather the bracelet that encircled her wrist. As the elevator doors opened, Tobi tugged the folder from his fingers and exited into the hallway. She walked away from the elevator, but before she went too far, she peered over her shoulder and found the man staring at her. Lately Tobi felt like she was constantly being watched. She shivered slightly before continuing on to her office.

Ryan drummed her fingers lightly on the desk while waiting for the phone to be answered. Overall, it had been a pretty good day, except for being forced to listen to Jake's singing, that is. That man could not carry a tune in a bucket. However, it was good to see him in such a great mood. As much as she wanted to know why he was so happy, history reminded her not to ask. On the few occasions she did venture to ask, she had wished she hadn't. Jake was notorious for giving more details than Ryan ever wanted—or needed—to know.

"Dr. Drexler's office, Marcy speaking. How may I help you?"

"Hi Marcy, it's Ryan. Is Tobi available?"

"Well, hello there. Actually, she was in a meeting but should be back any time. Want me to page her?"

"No, that's okay. Just tell her that I should be getting out of here right on schedule, and I'll be there shortly."

"Will do...Ryan, for what it's worth, I haven't seen Tobi this happy in a very long time. I'm glad you've come into her life."

"Thanks, that means a lot. I'm glad she's come into my life, as well."

"Take care, Ryan. I'll talk to you later."

"You, too; bye, Marcy."

Ryan hung the phone up and leaned back in her chair with a smile. It was good to know that she was making Tobi so happy. As she swiveled her chair around, she caught sight of Jake's big feet propped up on the desk, hands clasped over his stomach, and his eyes fully upon her. And he had the biggest, dumbest smile on his face.

"What *is* up with you, Jake?" Ryan asked as she stood up and stretched.

"Oh...nothing."

"Uh-huh, like I believe that." Picking up her jacket, she knocked his feet off the desk as she walked past him and continued out the door. Ryan hopped into the Jeep and glanced in the mirror before backing out of the parking space. *Look at you, Ryan. No wonder Jake was teasing you so much. You can't quit smiling and seem to have a constant blush.* Ryan pulled out into traffic and headed to the hospital.

"Hey, Tobi, you just missed Ryan," Marcy said, placing the phone back in it's cradle.

"Missed her?" Tobi asked, glancing around.

"On the phone. She called about fifteen minutes ago. She said she's right on schedule, and she'll be by to get you shortly."

"You had me worried there for a second. I thought I was running late." Tobi entered her office and placed the charts on the corner of her desk. Hopefully, she would remember to return them in the morning. If not, Medical Records would surely hunt her down.

"Personally, I think she just wanted to hear your voice," Marcy said, leaning against the doorjamb.

Once seated, Tobi looked at Marcy and knew the smile on her face matched the one on her own.

"You think so, huh?"

"Definitely. That woman is absolutely gorgeous and seems to be completely devoted to you."

"Marcy, what on earth makes you say that?"

"Have you seen the way she looks at you? How about her daily calls, or the fact that she will do anything for you? If I weren't straight, I'd be fighting *you* for her!" *If that increasing*

Tara Wentz

smile on Tobi's face means what I think it means..."She's behind me, isn't she?"

As Tobi watched her turn around to face Ryan, she couldn't help but laugh at how red Marcy's face had become.

"Hi, Marcy," Ryan said with a wiggle of her fingers.

"Uh...hi, Ryan. I'll see you tomorrow, Tobi," she said, making a hasty exit.

As the door closed behind Marcy, Ryan looked at Tobi, and they burst out laughing. Walking to within inches of Ryan, Tobi mock glared. "Should I be worried?"

"Oh, no...I'm as loyal as a cocker spaniel; besides, she's straight, remember?" Ryan replied, desperately trying not to smile.

Tobi wrapped her arms around Ryan's waist and pulled her closer. "That's good because I would have fought for you." Tobi watched as Ryan's eyebrows rose in question. She looked seriously at Ryan, then said, "I would; you're worth it."

Tobi saw the small gulp Ryan took as the meaning of the words dawned on her. Ryan put her arms around Tobi's shoulders and hugged her, sighing as warm arms returned her embrace.

Feeling the air escape Ryan's lungs, Tobi waited for her to breathe in again before lifting her head and placing a kiss on Ryan's lips. Tobi released Ryan and grasped her hand.

"Let's get out of here. I want nothing more than you, me, food, and the TV."

"I'm glad to see that I come before food and the television," Ryan said with a chuckle.

As the elevator slowly made its way down, Tobi gave Ryan's hand a tender squeeze. When Ryan looked at her and smiled, Tobi couldn't help but agree with Marcy. "She was right, you know?" When Ryan raised an eyebrow she continued. "Marcy...she was right. You are absolutely gorgeous." Ryan shook her head and pulled Tobi out of the elevator. As they passed the gift shop, Tobi noticed the strange man from the elevator and slowed her step. His eyes met hers briefly before he turned his back to pay the cashier. The blonde doctor and her partner were gone before he could turn back around.

88

"Tobi, your meals just get better and better. Dinner was fantastic."

"Thank you. That was the one thing Mom made sure we knew how to do, and not just do, but do well. She was a great cook."

"Your mom sounds like she was a neat lady."

"She was. It makes me very happy to be able to share her memory with you; well, not just her memory, but everything. I want to share everything with you."

Ryan was not sure what she expected Tobi to say, but certainly not that. Tobi always laid her feelings right on the line, and she made it appear so easy, too. A part of Ryan wanted to just plunge headfirst into this and let everything else be damned; another part of her was scared to death. Right now, the scared part was winning out. Maybe soon she would be able to do more than just tell Tobi how she felt. Either by coincidence or sensitivity to Ryan's feelings, Tobi always seemed to know when to back off, especially when Ryan herself felt a little out of control.

Brushing a lock of hair behind Tobi's ear, Ryan smiled at her before running the backs of her fingers down her cheek. As Tobi closed her eyes and turned her face into Ryan's palm, Ryan felt tears well up in her eyes. She could only shut her eyes and rest her forehead against Tobi's. *How could this be? Just looking at her makes my heart ache.* Ryan hadn't realized her tears had spilled over until she felt thumbs gently wiping them from below her closed lids. When she opened them, Tobi was gazing fondly at her. As Ryan opened her mouth to say something, Tobi placed a finger against her lips and shook her head.

"Are you ready for bed?"

Clearing her throat, Ryan said, "Whenever you are."

Tobi held Ryan close to her, realizing that tonight was her night to do the comforting. She wasn't sure what spurred the tears in Ryan's eyes, but she could sense that she needed to be strong and give Ryan time without a lot of questions. With her head on Tobi's shoulder, Ryan curled her body around Tobi's and fell asleep almost instantly. She had one leg draped over Tobi's and an arm possessively across her stomach. Tobi placed her lips against the top of Ryan's head and kissed her gently. She wanted Ryan to know how important and special she was to her, so she mentally wrote herself a reminder to call her friend, Shelly, in the morning. It was time for a little surprise getaway. *I hope she likes surprises.* Tobi closed her eyes and let the thought of Ryan in her arms, and a day away with just the two of them, lull her to sleep.

Chapter Nine

While Tobi gathered her things and locked the office door, she couldn't help but think about the next day. Tobi wanted to do something special with Ryan and show her how much she enjoyed spending time with her. Also, she thought it would be nice to get away from things for the day, so they could both relax. Having made sure that Ryan had no plans for the weekend, Tobi told her she had something she wanted to do on Saturday, and wanted her to go along. Ryan was a little suspicious but agreed.

Shelly lived on a vast expanse of land that boasted several ponds and one huge lake. With fall arriving, it would be a little cooler, but the trees would be in a multitude of colors, and the ducks would still be on the lake.

She grinned when she recalled the conversation she'd had a few days earlier with Shelly.

"So, I was wondering if it would be okay to bring a friend out to ride the horses."

"A friend or a friend *friend?" Shelly asked.*

91

Tobi laughed. "Let's just say that she's a very special friend."
"Well, in that case…" Shelly started before chuckling herself.
"Tobi, you know that you never need to ask. I look forward to seeing you and your special friend."

The ding of the elevator brought a smiling Tobi back to the present. Just two more doors separated her from the person she desired to see the most.

Tobi exited the hospital, ran out to the Jeep, and climbed in. She saw the smile on Ryan's face and couldn't resist leaning in for a kiss.

"Mmm, what was that for?"

"Just because I missed you today, not to mention how darned cute you look in that uniform."

"You are such a sucker for a woman in uniform," Ryan laughed.

"Not any woman in uniform…just you. With or without the uniform, I think you're the most beautiful woman I've ever laid eyes on."

Seeing her blush and look away, Tobi decided to take pity on Ryan and change the subject. "So, what are we going to do for dinner, because as usual—"

"You're starving," Ryan said.

"Yes ma'am, so lead on, McGruff."

As Ryan crawled into bed and waited for Tobi to join her, she realized it all seemed so natural. Each night that passed, they became that much more comfortable with each other. Strangely enough, they already had a routine established, but maybe it only seemed odd because Ryan was not sure that she and Stacey had ever had a routine. Ryan knew that Tobi had something up her sleeve for the next day, but she hadn't pressed the issue. Whatever it was seemed really important, and she didn't want to ruin it.

Tobi walked around the foot of the bed, and Ryan shivered in anticipation of lying beside her. Tobi climbed in on her hands and knees and dropped down, so she was lying partially on top of Ryan. She folded her hands under her chin and looked into Ryan's eyes with a smile.

"Tired?" Ryan asked.

"Very. What a week. I'm really glad it's Friday and that we have the whole weekend together."

"Me, too...go ahead and shut the light off, and let's get some sleep. I'm getting the feeling that tomorrow is going to be a busy day."

"It could be," Tobi said, leaning down to place a soft lingering kiss against Ryan's lips. Rolling over, Tobi turned the light out and lay on her side with her back to Ryan. Ryan smiled as she scooted up behind her and placed a hand upon Tobi's hip. Tobi took her hand and pulled it across her stomach. She loved sleeping like this because it made her feel safe and warm.

"Night, honey."

"Night, sweetheart," Ryan said, placing a kiss just behind her ear. Snuggling closer, Ryan could hear her muffle a yawn behind her other hand.

Getting out the door was easier than Tobi thought it would be. Ryan never seemed to have problems getting up, but Tobi, on the other hand, took a little longer to get focused and moving. That was not the case this morning. She also figured Ryan would ask a bunch of questions about where they were going and what they were going to do, but she didn't... until they were about thirty-five minutes into the drive.

"Tobi, are you sure you know where you're going?"

"Of course I'm sure."

"Well, it just seems like we've been on the road forever."

Laughing, Tobi replied, "We've only been driving for thirty-five minutes. You are so impatient." Seeing Ryan scowl at her made her laugh even harder. "Oh, lighten up...I promise we're almost there."

"Okay, as long as you promise," Ryan said, pouting.

"Too cute!"

"What?"

"You, that's what..., you and that pout. Does it work on everybody?"

"I have no idea what you're talking about," Ryan said as she pouted some more.

"Yeah, that's what I thought."

Tobi pulled into the drive alongside the barn and turned to look at Ryan, who had a bewildered look on her face. Tobi knew she wouldn't be able to keep the secret much longer, so she got out of the car and walked around to Ryan's side to stand beside her. She took Ryan's hand and tugged her toward the barn.

"Do you like horses, Ryan?"

"I love horses!"

"That's good to know. A couple of days ago, I called a friend of mine to ask if I could bring a special friend out to ride."

"This is what you had to do today, the reason that you wanted me to come along?"

"Yes," Tobi said, grinning. "Have you ever ridden a horse before?"

"It's been awhile, but I used to ride a lot when I was younger. My uncle had several, and we'd go out and ride them all the time. I spent a lot of summers helping him around the farm just so I could spend time with the horses."

Tobi shoved open the large barn door and walked inside. "Shelly?"

"Back here."

She found Shelly in an open stall toward the back of the old barn. She stepped through the door as Shelly turned and smiled. After they embraced, Shelly leaned back with both hands on Tobi's upper arms.

"It's so good to see you, Tobi. How are you? It's been a long time."

"I'm doing well. Shelly, I want you to meet someone very special to me." Taking Ryan's hand and pulling her forward, Tobi said, "This is Ryan. Ryan, this is my dear friend, Shelly."

"Hello, Shelly. It's really nice to meet you. Thank you so much for letting us ride today."

"It's good to meet you, too, Ryan, and you are most welcome," she said with a sincere smile.

Tobi stepped forward to hug Shelly again. "Thanks for letting us come over today. Is everything still where it used to be?"

"Yep, help yourself. I hope this visit means I'll be seeing more of you."

"You will, I promise. I'll talk to you later, okay?"

With a wave of her hand, she said, "Have fun!"

After getting the horses saddled and ready, Tobi went to the car and retrieved the picnic lunch and blanket and placed the items in the saddlebags. She asked Ryan if she was ready to go.

"Ready when you are, cowgirl."

"Very funny," Tobi replied.

Tobi stepped up into the stirrup, threw her leg over, and settled into the saddle. She grabbed the reins, clicked her tongue, and nudged her heels for the horse to start walking. They rode quietly for a long period of time before breaking open into a clearing that surrounded a large lake. Tobi glanced at Ryan and could see that she was pleasantly surprised. Tobi stopped underneath a maple tree and slid down off her horse, then waited for Ryan to do the same.

"You never did say what these beauties' names were."

"Ah, well, that handsome boy you're riding is named Gambler, and this one is Ronica."

"Ronica looks like a quarter horse, but what is Gambler?" Ryan asked.

"Gambler is half quarter horse and half Arabian. He was originally trained for just pleasure riding then for barrels. Now, he's strictly for pleasure."

"They are both so beautiful."

"Shelly bought them from a man who was being very cruel to them. Now, she makes sure that every day is a good day for them." Tobi watched as Ryan caressed Gambler's flank with long, fluid strokes. *God! What I wouldn't give for her to run her hands over my body like that!* Tobi cleared her throat and stepped over to her horse.

"Are you hungry?" Tobi asked, unpacking their lunch. She spread out the blanket and set everything down before sitting down herself.

"Mmm, I could eat. Those sandwiches look great," Ryan said as she sat down beside Tobi.

"I know the typical romantic picnic would be wine, cheese, and grapes, but I'm hungry," Tobi said, laughing. "Actually, I kind of figured you more for a sub sandwich kind of girl than wine and cheese."

"You figured right. I do like all three of those, but not generally as a meal." As Ryan ran her fingers lightly over the blanket, Tobi could tell she had something else on her mind.

"Ryan?"

"Hmm?" she said without looking up.

"Is everything okay?"

Ryan sat with her hands in her lap and looked at Tobi. "It's more than okay. Nobody has ever taken the time to do something like this for me."

Tobi placed her hands on Ryan's. "Well, they should have. You deserve to be pampered. Ryan…I want you to know how much you've come to mean to me. I'm not taking this relationship lightly."

"Thank you," Ryan whispered.

"So, which do you want? Turkey and Swiss on wheat or Swiss and turkey on wheat?"

"That's a tough choice, but I think I'll take turkey and Swiss on wheat."

After lunch, they lay back on the blanket. Tobi rolled to her side to face Ryan and propped her head in her hand. Ryan's eyes were closed and her breathing was soft and even. The slight breeze ruffled Ryan's bangs, dropping a lock of hair low over her brow. Tobi reached up and lifted the dark strands back in place. Tobi's fingers trailed lightly down Ryan's cheek, bringing a relaxed sigh from Ryan. "What are you thinking about?"

Ryan kept her eyes closed as she responded. "I was just thinking how this brought back so many good memories. I really loved being around the horses and the farm. At the end of summer, I always left with a sad heart. There's just something so calming about being around horses."

"I agree. Most are such gentle creatures. What other things do you think about when you think of your childhood?"

"There are so many memories, Tobi. I really had a pretty terrific childhood. I realize I'm very lucky because not too many adults can say that. I do have some really fond memories, though."

"Wanna share?"

"Well, there was this one time when the boys talked me into climbing onto the roof of the barn. They were sliding down the roof and jumping into the water trough underneath. I kept trying to slide, but my jeans wouldn't let me. They failed to mention they were using extra shingles as sleds. When I finally managed to make it to the end, I stood up to jump into the trough. The boys were all doubled over laughing, and I couldn't figure out why. After I jumped into the water, I figured it out. The rough surface of the roof had rubbed holes in the seat of my pants."

The image Tobi got from this story was just too much. She laughed so hard she had tears rolling down her cheeks.

"Are you finished?" Ryan asked with a raised eyebrow.

"I'm sorry, but that was too funny!"

"Yeah, well, the boys didn't think it was too funny when Mom got hold of them. I don't know what she was the angriest about...the jeans being ruined or the fact they had gotten me up on the barn roof."

"Your poor mother. How old were you?"

"I couldn't have been more than seven at the time." Turning her head toward Tobi, Ryan asked, "How about you? What is one of your fondest memories?"

"That one is easy. My sister and I used to have a ton of Barbie dolls. We had all the accessories, too. We'd spend all day making up different stories with them, and, of course, changing their clothes as many times as the stories changed."

"You played with Barbies?"

Tobi punched her lightly in the arm. "Of course I did. We also rode our bikes and pretended we were on secret missions. I can't tell you all the places we visited in our own little minds."

"That sounds more like it. Do you think we would have been friends as little girls?"

"I don't know...RAT...you didn't play with Barbies or cook." Seeing the mischievous glint in Ryan's eye, Tobi knew she wasn't going to let that remark go without some sort of consequence. Before she could move, Ryan had rolled over, so she was straddling Tobi's hips. With Tobi's hands pinned to her sides, Ryan just grinned.

"You just had to go and tease me about my nickname, didn't you?"

"Tease? I wasn't teasing, honey; I was simply being...friendly.

"Friendly? You call that being friendly?" Ryan said as she started tickling her sides.

"Now, Ryan...okay, stop! I give!" Tobi said, laughing and trying to twist out from under her.

"Say mercy!"

"Mercy!" Dropping her hands, Ryan leaned forward and placed her hands next to Tobi's head.

"Promise not to tease anymore?"

"I thought all the people who loved you got to tease you." Realizing what she had just said, Tobi waited to see Ryan's reaction. The smile left Ryan's face as she instantly grasped her lower lip between even white teeth. She pulled back slowly and sat next to Tobi, who also sat up. *Uh-oh, maybe I shouldn't have let that slip.*

"Ryan, I–"

"You–"

While both tried to speak at the same time, Tobi said, "Go ahead."

"Are...are you saying you love me, Tobi?"

"Yes. I know it probably seems too fast, but I know how I feel, Ryan. It's not like anything I have ever experienced."

Tobi wasn't sure what Ryan was thinking since she chose that moment to stand up and walk toward the water's edge. She gave Ryan a few minutes to collect her thoughts before standing up and slowly approaching her. With just inches between them, Tobi placed her hand on Ryan's back and took the last step to stand beside her. Ryan turned toward her, and Tobi could see the unshed tears in her eyes.

"Do you really mean it?"

"Of course I mean it. I wouldn't have said it otherwise."

So quietly that Tobi almost didn't hear her, Ryan said, "Say it again."

"I love you, Ryan," Tobi said, looking directly into her eyes.

As Tobi was folded within her arms, she could feel Ryan trembling. *Stacey must have been a real piece of work for her to be this affected by those simple words. It's almost like she's never heard them before.* Tobi didn't expect her to say it back because she knew what it was taking emotionally for Ryan to accept what she had just revealed. Much to her surprise, Ryan kissed the top of her ear and whispered, "I love you, too, Tobi. I'm sorry that I wasn't strong enough to admit my feelings before now."

Tobi leaned back and placed her fingers lightly over Ryan's lips. "Don't ever be sorry, Ryan. You had to do what felt right for you, and I would never begrudge you that."

As the tears slowly made their way down Ryan's cheeks, she murmured, "But you've been so patient."

"I would have been for as long as it took, honey. I meant what I said; you deserve to be loved and pampered. Luckily for me, I'm the girl you let do it," Tobi said with a smug smile.

Ryan brushed the tears from her face as her lips curved into a grin. "I think I'm the lucky one."

Ryan brought both hands up to cup each side of Tobi's face. She rubbed her thumbs across Tobi's cheeks and then lowered her head to capture Tobi' lips with her own. The kiss that started out softly to convey the love Ryan felt for Tobi quickly turned into a passionate blaze. Ryan couldn't get enough. Her throat felt parched, and Tobi was the only one that could quench her thirst. Ryan quickly tangled her fingers in Tobi's hair and pulled her closer, nipping a path down the sensitive skin of her neck.

Tobi moaned and struggled for control. They were both fighting the inevitable, but now was not the time or place. They were in an open field where the temperature was steadily dropping. Tobi wanted more than a scratchy blanket and the hard ground for their first time together.

Ryan rested her forehead against Tobi's shoulder, trying in vain to catch her breath.

Minutes passed as neither woman wanted to break the spell of unspoken words. The wind picked up and blew a gentle breeze across the water, making Tobi shiver.

"As much as I would rather stay here, I guess we better get ready to go."

Ryan reached up and pulled a couple of stray leaves, acquired during their tussle on the blanket, out of Tobi's hair before letting her hand rest on her shoulder, and nodded in agreement. A crucial moment had just passed in their relationship, and Ryan felt as if there should be something more for her to say. Those three short words said it all though. Instead, she smiled and took Tobi's hand to walk back to the blanket.

"Grab that end, and we'll get this folded up. It's starting to get a little cool out here by the lake."

Repacking the saddlebags, they shared another brief kiss before mounting the horses and heading back to the barn.

While waiting for Tobi to say goodbye to Shelly, Ryan leaned against the side of the car, thinking about what Tobi had said. Ryan wanted to respond and was surprised when the words rolled so easily off her tongue. *She loves me!* She was thrilled by Tobi's proclamation and scared at the same time. She felt incredibly lucky to have this woman in her life. Tobi was someone who seemed to get pure pleasure out of making and seeing Ryan happy. How was she going to make Tobi as happy as she had made her? Watching her hug Shelly and wave goodbye, Ryan didn't have time to consider her options. She waved to Shelly and turned to climb into the car. As they pulled away from the barn, she could see the horses galloping along the back fence.

"I had a really nice time, Tobi. Thank you so much for thinking of this."

"It was my pleasure. I thought we needed some time away, so we could relax."

"Shelly seems really nice."

"She thought the same thing of you. She also found you very attractive," Tobi said with a smirk.

"What's that grin all about?"

"I told her you were taken," she said seriously.

"I am taken."

Tobi looked pleased as she turned the radio up and placed her hand on top of Ryan's. Ryan laced her fingers within Tobi's and relaxed in the seat. They drove home in comfortable silence, each contemplating her own thoughts.

When they arrived back home, Ryan grabbed the blanket and sacks from the car and followed Tobi up the sidewalk. She drew up short when Tobi stopped unexpectedly before the door.

"Tobi? What's wrong?"

"Someone's been in the house."

"What do you mean?"

Tobi pointed to the front door. Ryan looked over her shoulder to see it standing open about an inch. She handed Tobi the items she was carrying and told her to wait there. Ryan approached the door cautiously, stopping long enough to draw her weapon from the ankle holster she always carried, whether on or off duty. She listened for any sounds before slowly pushing the door the rest of the way open. Peering in, she reached for the light switch and flipped it on.

"Holy God!"

Tara Wentz

Chapter Ten

W hat?" Tobi cried.

"Stay there...don't come in," Ryan warned, but hearing a gasp, she knew Tobi had already followed her through the door. Ryan turned back toward her and placed her hand on Tobi's shoulder. She could see the look of utter shock on her face.

"Oh, my..." Tobi stopped in midsentence and looked at Ryan. "Who would do something like this?"

"Baby, I don't know."

The sight in front of them looked like a deliberate act of malice. Someone had taken a knife and sliced the couch almost beyond recognition, there were so many holes and slash marks. The intruder had also pulled fistfuls of stuffing out until there was almost nothing left inside. Ryan glanced around the room and noticed that it didn't appear as though anything else had been disturbed.

"Don't touch anything, honey. Use your cell phone and call 911."

Tobi barely acknowledged her as she pulled her phone out and punched in the number. Hearing a noise in the kitchen, Ryan looked at Tobi and saw the fear in her eyes.

"Stay here; I'm just going to check it out."

"Ryan…"

"Ssshhh," Ryan said as she walked quietly toward the kitchen. As she rounded the corner, she caught a glimpse of a man as he bolted out the back door. "Tobi, call the police, NOW!" Ryan yelled as she ran through the kitchen. She slapped the back door open and took off in pursuit.

"Ryan!"

Ryan knew that by chasing the man, she was scaring Tobi; but she couldn't just let him leave without trying to apprehend him, especially if this was the person who had broken in.

"Stop! Police!" Ryan shouted, hoping to distract him long enough to slow him down a little. Following him down a dark alley was like going through an obstacle course. There were items strewn all over the place. She was either zig-zagging around or leaping over them in her pursuit. Ryan could tell she was gaining on him, and it wouldn't be long before she would have him in her grasp. There was a chain link fence ahead, and she knew this was her chance. She didn't want to fire her weapon because the alley was too dark for her to see him clearly. The man approached the fence, jumped up, and started climbing. As Ryan neared the fence, she grabbed his pant leg and pulled downward. His other leg shot out, his foot connecting with the left side of her forehead. Ryan fell to the ground, and her head smacked against the concrete. For a few moments, she couldn't seem to move. Little white spots were dancing before her eyes. She gradually sat up and rubbed the knot on the back of her head. The lapse of a few seconds was all the man needed to get away; he was nowhere in sight. Ryan holstered her weapon as she slowly got to her feet, placing a hand on the wall as a wave of dizziness washed over her. She swiped a hand across her forehead, and it came away with blood on it.

"Fuck," Ryan growled in anger. *Not only do I take off after the guy, I come back bleeding.* She walked carefully back through the alley and headed to the house. As she neared the back door, Ryan could hear Tobi talking to someone. When she entered the kitchen, Tobi turned and, catching sight of her, rushed to her side.

"Sit down," Tobi said, pulling out a kitchen chair. "What happened?"

"I chased him a couple of blocks down the back alley. We came to a fence, and I thought I had him. I grabbed his pant leg and tried to pull him down. He kicked me and got away."

"You could have been killed. What were you thinking? God, I just can't take this anymore!" Ryan could tell by Tobi's tone that not only was she scared for her, but she was also very angry.

Ryan heard a police radio and some raised voices in the next room and peered around Tobi's shoulder to see Jake entering the kitchen.

"What the hell is the matter with you?"

"Hi, Jake. Nice to see you, too."

"Damn it, Ryan!"

Ryan jumped to her feet as she rushed to defend herself. "I couldn't just stand there and watch him leave without trying to stop him!" As she started pacing, Tobi left. Ryan knew that her actions had upset Tobi, and it was tearing her up inside to see her react the way she was, but she couldn't just let that man leave. She had to try and stop him. It was her job!

"She's really upset, Ryan."

"I know. What are you doing here anyhow?" Ryan asked quietly. It was Jake's day off as well.

"I heard the call go out over the scanner and came over. Listen, I understand why you did what you did. But all Tobi could see was that you were possibly in danger, and it scared her."

Before Ryan could respond, Tobi returned with a first aid kit and gave her a look that required no words. Ryan sat back down in the chair and remained still while Tobi cleaned the wound. She could feel Tobi shaking but didn't know if it was from fear or anger.

"Tobi, we got your statement. As soon as the guys finish taking pictures and dusting for fingerprints, we'll get out of here. Give me a call or let Ryan know if you can think of anything else, okay?" Jake said, moving toward the living room.

105

"Thanks, Jake." As he left, Tobi turned around to look at Ryan. "This cut really needs to have stitches, Ryan," Tobi said, cupping her chin. "Are you hurt anywhere else?"

Ryan knew she was going to get herself in deeper, but she couldn't lie to Tobi even if she wanted to. "When he kicked me, I fell and hit my head."

Tobi slid her hands through Ryan's hair and found the lump on the back of her head.

"For fuck's sake, Ryan," Tobi swore. She took a deep breath before continuing. "Anywhere else?"

Ryan could hear the spark of anger in Tobi's voice and see it in her darkening eyes. Ryan averted her gaze and shook her head. "No. Will the butterfly strips hold it?"

"Probably, as long as you're careful." Tobi continued to clean the wound and finally placed the strips across the cut. She dropped her hands to her sides and stood there looking at Ryan.

"That should do it. I know you're too stubborn to go to the hospital and have this looked at, but will you please tell me if you have any problems?"

Ryan reached out to put her hands on Tobi's waist and was startled when she stepped back.

"Please don't."

Seeing Tobi physically withdraw sent Ryan emotionally over the edge. Her chest ached with fear at the thought of losing Tobi. Ryan didn't know how to ease the tension between them. She wanted to go to Tobi, but her feet were riveted to the floor. She clasped her shaking hands and lowered her head. *I always seem to mess up the things that are really important.*

"You need to let me know if you have vision problems, prolonged headaches, nausea, vomiting…"

"I will, Tobi. I promise. Except for a little headache, I feel fine."

"Can we stay at your place tonight?"

"Sure. I know having him inside the house can leave you feeling violated."

"It's not just that. What he did to the couch," she looked at Ryan now before going on, "was nothing compared to what he did to the bed upstairs. It's a complete loss."

106

Ryan jerked her gaze back to Tobi. She sat surprised, unable to form a complete sentence. "He…to the bed?"

"Yeah. Can we just go?"

After everyone was gone, they grabbed a few things and checked all the locks before climbing into the Jeep to leave.

"I don't know why we bothered to lock the house. It didn't seem to make a difference."

Not knowing what to say, Ryan put the Jeep in gear and pulled away. *I'm so sorry. I wish I had the words right now to make it all better.*

Tobi entered Ryan's house, set her bag on the floor, and just stood there. Ryan taking off after that man had scared her half to death. The couch and the bed could be replaced, but Ryan...there was no replacing her. It didn't seem to faze her that something bad could have happened. She could have been hurt, or even worse, killed. Tobi also knew that Ryan was at a loss for words. She was quiet and chewed nervously at her lip the whole way home. Tobi wished she could just let it go, but when she thought about that lunatic harming Ryan, it made her so damned angry.

"Are you hungry?" Ryan asked.

"Not really. I feel tired more than anything."

Ryan gave a brief nod and picked up Tobi's bag. "I'll show you to your room."

To my room? Could it be that she wanted to be alone tonight? Leading Tobi up the stairs and down the hall, Ryan opened a door on her left. She set Tobi's bag on the bed and waited for her to enter. "The sheets are clean, and there are extra blankets in the closet if you need them. The bathroom is through that door, and there are extra toothbrushes in the cabinet, along with towels and washcloths. My room is right across the hall. If you need anything, let me know." Shuffling her feet a little, Ryan finally turned and walked out.

Tobi sank down onto the bed and listened as Ryan's bedroom door clicked shut. *What the hell just happened?* Reviewing everything that was said, she couldn't identify anything that would make Ryan think she didn't want to be around her. *Maybe she isn't feeling well and doesn't want me to know.* Tobi decided to give her a little time, and then she'd go to her. She walked into the bathroom, shed her clothes, and took a quick shower. After wiping steam from the mirror, Tobi combed the tangles out of her hair. Teeth brushed and moisturizer applied, she headed back to the bedroom. She pulled on some pajamas and crossed over to her door, listening for any noises coming from across the hall in Ryan's room. *Hmm, is she asleep already?* With concern over Ryan looming in the back of her mind, she couldn't even think about going to sleep. Padding across the hall, she stopped briefly outside Ryan's door and, not hearing anything, continued down the steps into the living room.

Tobi roamed around Ryan's house, looking at knickknacks and pictures. Ryan was so close to her family, and it showed in every photograph. There were pictures of her with all her brothers and some of her with just one or two of them at a time. One picture specifically caught Tobi's eye. Ryan was standing next to a tall man with dark hair. He had his arms around her and a big smile on his face. She knew from pictures at Grace's house that this was Ryan's father. She could see the bond between them. Ryan's eyes showed how much she adored him. Tracing Ryan's outline with her fingertips, Tobi smiled affectionately. This room really looked like Ryan; hell, the whole house had Ryan written all over it. The bookshelves were lined with all kinds of books, from mysteries to comedies. She had some of her police handbooks on one shelf, and a set of encyclopedias lined other shelves. The carpet was a rich chocolate color, and the leather couches were soft beige. Across the back of one was an afghan in earth tones. Spying a few magazines on the coffee table, Tobi sat down and started poking through one. After what seemed like just a few minutes, she looked at the clock and realized an hour had passed. Laying the magazine down, Tobi headed back up the stairs.

She stopped outside Ryan's door and raised her hand to knock when she heard a muffled sound come from inside the room. She placed her ear closer to the door but could barely hear a thing. Opening the door a little, she scanned the room for the source of the noise she was hearing. Not seeing anything, Tobi walked farther into the room and noticed another door off to the side. She hesitated for a moment before walking quietly toward it.

What she saw nearly ripped her heart out. Curled on the bathroom floor was Ryan, sobbing uncontrollably.

"G-go...a-away...Tobi...p-please," she said in a ragged whisper.

Tobi, ignoring her plea, rushed to her side, knelt down, and pulled Ryan into her arms.

"Ryan, honey, what's wrong?"

She just shook her head and continued to cry. Tobi rocked her and whispered consoling words in her ear as she rubbed circles on her back. Ryan eventually quieted down.

"Can you talk to me now?"

Not getting an answer, Tobi continued, "Ryan, what's upset you so much?"

She heard a muffled answer and leaned back slightly to look down into Ryan's face. "What?"

"I..." Ryan hesitated.

"What? What is it?" Tobi asked quietly.

"I don't want you to leave me," Ryan said in barely more than a whisper.

"Leave you? Why would...Ryan, look at me, please."

"I can't. It hurts too much."

Tobi placed her hand against the side of Ryan's cheek and let her thumb slide under her chin. Tobi applied a little pressure, and Ryan raised her eyes to meet Tobi's. "I love you, Ryan. Why would you think that I would leave you?"

"Earlier, you said you couldn't take this anymore."

"I guess I need to clarify what I said." Tobi shifted a little on the hard surface and asked, "Do you think we could get off this floor and go somewhere else to talk?"

Ryan pulled herself out of Tobi's arms and slowly stood up. She held a hand out to help Tobi from the floor. Tobi took the proffered hand, and they walked into the bedroom. Tugging Ryan to the large window seat, Tobi sat with her back against the wall. With Ryan sitting between her legs and resting back against her chest, Tobi rubbed her hands up and down Ryan's arms.

"What I meant by that comment was that I couldn't stand all this mystery anymore. Not you, Ryan. It could never be you. I'm happier than I've ever been."

"But—"

"There are no buts on this. I know what your job is, and I accept that. However, it doesn't stop me from worrying, and when you took off after that man, it scared me to death."

"I'm so sorry. I swore I would never do anything to hurt you, and I couldn't even do that."

"There are parts of your job that I have to live with, and I'm more than willing to do that because of how I feel about you. There will be times when you won't be able to keep from hurting me—"

"But I don't ever want to hurt you," Ryan interrupted.

Tobi placed her hand gently across Ryan's mouth to stop her protest and continued, "As I said, there will be times when you won't be able to keep from hurting me because of your job. Eventually, I will find a way to deal with the everyday aspect of it. I have to, Ryan, because I'm not willing to give you up because of it."

Ryan sat up and turned to face Tobi. "I love you so much, Tobi. The thought of losing you...it...I..." Ryan trailed off in a voice still hoarse from all the crying.

Tobi wished she had come to her sooner. She hated knowing that Ryan had been alone and crying for so long.

She put her hands on the back of Ryan's neck, pulled her down and kissed her. "You won't lose me, not because of that. Don't ever think that." Kissing her again, Tobi nipped at her lower lip and slowly let it slip through her teeth. She heard Ryan sigh and placed loving kisses up Ryan's cheek to her ear where she whispered, "I love you." Tobi held Ryan against her and inhaled the fresh scent of her hair. *I can't believe she thought I was going to leave her. Hell, what am I saying? Of course I do. After the number Stacey did on her, I'd believe anything. I hope that I can eventually convince her that not everybody is like her ex.*

"I don't know about you, honey, but I'm exhausted. Let's go to bed, okay?"

"Um...you're not going to sleep in the other room, are you?" Ryan asked hesitantly.

With a small smile, Tobi replied, "Not unless that's where you want me to sleep, which I'm hoping you don't."

"I'd really like you to sleep next to me"

Ryan's red-rimmed eyes pleaded with her. She looked like she was about to fall over. Tobi knew how exhausted Ryan was after the emotional roller coaster she had just experienced. It would not take long for her to collapse. Tobi took her hand and led her to bed. She held Ryan in her arms long after she fell asleep. If there was one thing she vowed to do, it was to make sure that Ryan knew each day that she was here for her. A disagreement here or there could never make her leave.

Tara Wentz

Chapter Eleven

Ryan slipped into a long sleeved, light-blue T-shirt and gray sweatpants, and pulled on a pair of thick, comfy white socks. Tobi wanted to stay home with her, but knowing she was supposed to meet her father for lunch, Ryan refused to let her cancel. Besides, it was only for a couple of hours. She walked down the stairs to the living room where Tobi had already made a nice little nest on the couch for her. With strict instructions to stay as inactive as possible, Ryan curled up on the sofa with blankets all around and enough pillows for an army.

"Promise to call if you need anything?"

"I promise. I'll be just fine. Have a good lunch with your dad."

"I won't be gone too long," Tobi said, leaning down to kiss her. Touching her fingers to Ryan's forehead, she grimaced. "You're going to have one nasty bruise there. Does it hurt?"

"Not too much. It's tender but not that painful."

Tobi ran a finger down Ryan's nose before tapping it lightly. "Be good and please do as I asked."

"I will. Now, will you get out of here already?"

"Okay, okay, I'm going," Tobi said as she walked to the front door. As she opened it to leave, she hesitated. "I love you, Ryan."

"I love you, too. Be careful."

With a wave, she closed the door and was gone.

That was almost thirty minutes ago, and Ryan was still lying in the same spot. Three simple words—it's amazing how they could make everything seem so perfect. She should have been embarrassed after her display the previous night, but the only thing she felt was gratitude. Ryan was so grateful that Tobi didn't just go to bed last night; she wasn't even sure what brought Tobi to her room in the first place. She could also tell that Tobi was going out of her way to make sure Ryan knew she meant every word she said.

Why can't you accept that she isn't another Stacey?

I never said she was.

Come on, you know that's exactly what was going through your mind last night.

No, that is not what was going through my mind.

Well then, Sergeant Smarty Pants, why don't you enlighten me?

For your information, I was just concerned that I always seem to mess things up.

And you based this on…what? One person who did a number on you?

Listen, you don't understand—

Oh, I think I understand perfectly. You're afraid to completely open yourself up to Tobi because you know it will hurt like a son of a bitch if she were to leave you.

It's just…what I feel for her is so different from anything I've ever felt before.

That's a good thing.

But it's scarier than hell!

Of course it is; but don't shortchange Tobi because of something Stacey did. That's not fair to you and certainly not fair to her.

How is it that you're so knowledgeable?

Could it be because I'm not hiding behind hurt feelings?

Ryan scrambled to her feet when she heard a knock at the door. "Jake, what a nice surprise. Did Tobi put you up to this?" Ryan said as she opened the door for him.

"What are you talking about?"

"Uh, nothing...sorry. What are you doing over in this neighborhood?"

"Is it wrong for me to want to check up on you? I just wanted to make sure you were doing all right."

"I'm fine, really."

"Aside from the fact that I was worried, Tim would skin me alive if I didn't stop by, and we both know it."

Smiling, Ryan said, "True. Come on over and have a seat."

"I also went by Tobi's house this morning and looked around."

"And?"

"Nothing, not one single thing I could get some kind of clue from."

"Damn!"

Jake took a breath before continuing. "He got into the house through the front door. There were tool marks in the jamb where he jimmied the lock. The striations are consistent with those of a flathead screwdriver."

"Great, that narrows things down."

"We also ran the fingerprints that were pulled off through AFIS and came up empty on that, too."

Ryan grunted. "Imagine that."

Jake knew that Ryan's sarcasm was not directed toward him. He was just as frustrated and wished they had something to work from. He sat silently, watching Ryan mull things over, before speaking up.

"Ryan, this is all so weird. We have no idea why this man is doing what he's doing. That's assuming that the break-in and the calls are all the same person."

"Exactly. I'm at a loss. I don't even know where to go from here. It was too dark to get any kind of description last night."

"Maybe you need to give Lauren a call. There's got to be something somewhere that ties this guy to Tobi. If anyone can find it, Lauren can."

"I think you may be right. It certainly can't hurt, and who knows what she might be able to come up with? I'll give her a call tomorrow."

"Are you going to be at work tomorrow?"

"Of course, why wouldn't I?"

"Don't be so mule-headed, Ryan. You know why."

"I already told you that I'm fine. Besides, I don't think I'm going to get very far from the couch today if Tobi has anything to say about it."

"Ah, I see who's boss," he said, laughing.

Tossing a pillow at him, Ryan said, "There is no boss. I'm simply appeasing her by following her wishes."

"It's that way, is it?" he said with a wiggle of his eyebrows and a smirk.

"Jake…shut up!"

Jake gasped in mock surprise as he placed a hand over his mouth. "Rude!"

Ryan smiled with mild humor. "Thanks for caring. I don't know what I would do without you and Tim."

"Don't thank me. You know how we feel about you. That will never change. Just take care of yourself because it's not just about you anymore."

"I know."

"It's very evident how she feels about you. Seeing the two of you together is so incredibly awesome. I just can't think of a better word for it. Without flaunting it, you two ooze more love and compassion and sexual heat than any couple I've ever met. Aside from Tim and me, that is," he said with a grin.

"I don't think I've ever heard a nicer compliment come out of your mouth. Thank you, and I truly mean that."

"You, my dear friend, are more than welcome." He stood and walked over to stand beside her. Laying his large hand against the side of her head, he smiled. "Take care, okay? I'll see you tomorrow." With a warm caress to her cheek, he chucked her under the chin and left.

Ryan, realizing how tired she felt, scooted down to a reclining position and closed her eyes.

When she entered the house, Tobi saw Ryan lying on the couch with her eyes closed. She quietly pushed the door shut and engaged the lock. Crouching beside the couch, she examined Ryan's face. The laceration above her left brow was a little swollen under the Steri-Strips, but otherwise it looked good. There was a fair amount of bruising already, and it would become quite colorful over the next few days. She placed her hand against Ryan's cheek, rubbed her thumb gently across the surface, and watched as Ryan's eyelids fluttered open. She appeared to be somewhat disoriented for a moment before she looked into Tobi's eyes and smiled.

"Hi," she said groggily.

"Hi. Looks like you got a little rest while I was gone."

Ryan moved her hips back into the couch and patted the cushion beside her. Sitting down, Tobi felt Ryan's warm hand enclose her forearm. "I slept a little. Jake came by for a visit; he can assure you I stayed on the couch the whole time he was here."

"I'm sure you did, honey. Are you hungry?"

"Mmm, I could eat," she said, scrubbing her closed lids with her fingertips.

"I'll go fix you something. Do you want to watch TV? We could put a movie on if you want."

"TV sounds good."

Tobi handed her the remote and headed to the kitchen. "Okay, you find something to watch, and I'll be right back."

Ryan could hear cabinets opening and dishes clinking as Tobi rummaged around in the kitchen. The sounds of domesticity brought a smile to her face. When Tobi returned, she handed Ryan her plate and set her drink on the coffee table.

"Here ya go."

"Thanks. You didn't have to go to all this trouble, but I do appreciate it."

"You're welcome, and it wasn't any trouble at all. So, what did you find to watch?"

Pulling her feet up closer to her body, Ryan made room for Tobi to sit on the couch with her. "Doesn't seem to be much on this time of day," she said between bites of her sandwich. "Why don't you see if there is a movie on you'd like to watch?"

Tobi flipped through the channels until she came across a Jackie Chan movie. "Have you seen this one?"

"Ummph," she mumbled while swallowing her bite and taking a drink. "No, this looks good."

Part way through the movie, Tobi glanced over and saw Ryan's eyelids drooping. Tugging at Ryan's sock, she said, "Why don't you stretch out here," she patted her legs, "and get comfortable." Ryan unfolded her legs and lay down. Tobi could hear her sigh as she started kneading the muscles in Ryan's calves. Within minutes Ryan's breathing had become deeper. Satisfied, Tobi turned to finish watching the movie.

After she had awakened from a three-hour nap, she and Tobi talked more about everything that had happened.

"Ryan, I know that this is your job, and I respect what the job entails. I was just really scared." Tobi dropped a hand on Ryan's arm before continuing. "Please understand and know that I love you, regardless of your job."

"I'm trying; it's just that my own insecurities get the better of me sometimes." Ryan gave a shy smile and placed her hand over Tobi's. She ran her thumb lightly over the smooth surface and licked her dry lips.

Tobi squeezed Ryan's hand, giving a firm reassurance. She tilted her head to capture Ryan's gaze and smiled in return.

Tobi's eyes sparkled, and the longer Ryan peered into them the more she understood. *Sometimes, actions really do speak louder than words.* Ryan nodded, but said nothing.

"Let's get something to eat, then we can get our showers and get to bed," Tobi said, climbing up off the couch.

Ryan took a shower before the last of her energy was expended. Careful to avoid the knot on her head while washing her hair, Ryan gently kneaded her fingers across her sore scalp. She toweled off and slipped into a T-shirt and boxers. Having brushed her teeth, she opened the door to find Tobi waiting on the other side.

"I wanted to be here in case you needed something."

Ryan leaned down and kissed her softly before releasing her lips and smiling. "Thank you."

Ryan dropped Tobi off at the hospital and drove to the station. She figured she'd make that call to Lauren before she and Jake had to go on duty. She climbed the steps to the precinct and then glanced at her watch before going in. *A little over an hour, that should be plenty of time.* She made her way through the throng of people, sat down, and pulled the phone closer.

"Hey, Thomas, glad to see your mug."

Ryan glanced up at the portly desk clerk before replying, "Likewise, Likowski."

Clapping her on the shoulder as he walked by, he leaned down. "Really, I'm glad you're okay, colorful but okay," he said with a grin.

"Thanks, Franklin," she said, smiling back.

Ryan cradled the phone to her ear and punched in Lauren's number. Lauren, aside from being her best friend, was one of the premier lawyers in town. Mondays were iffy as to whether she would be available. It usually depended on what happened over the weekend. Hopefully, it was a quiet weekend, at least for her.

"Bassett and Jones, Attorneys at Law, may I help you?"

"Lauren Bassett, please."

"May I tell her who's calling?"

"Ryan Thomas."

"One moment, please."

"Thanks."

Ryan listened patiently to the typical elevator music and was surprised when the phone was picked up again almost instantly. "Ms. Bassett is on another line at the moment. Would you like to hold or leave a message?"

"I'll hold, thank you."

"Certainly, I'll let her know." Before Ryan could respond, she was back on hold. With an elbow on the desk, she leaned the right side of her forehead against an open palm and closed her eyes. The soft sounds of the music quelled her jangled nerves.

Ryan heard the music stop suddenly, so she opened her eyes and sat up straight.

"Ryan?"

"Hi, Lauren. Is this a bad time?"

"No, not at all. I was just on a conference call. Is everything okay?"

"Well, not exactly." Relaying everything that had happened, Ryan waited for her to respond. When Lauren didn't say anything for almost a full minute, Ryan finally said, "Lauren?"

"I'm here, sorry. It took me a little bit to get past the part of your getting hurt. You are okay, right?"

Exasperated, Ryan said, "I'm fine."

"Listen, you, don't take that tone with me. You're my best friend, and I have the right to be concerned." Ryan learned a long time ago that Lauren was not somebody you wanted to argue with, so she kept quiet. Whether you were right or wrong, by the time she finished explaining to you why she was right, you believed wholeheartedly that you were wrong. Ryan would never forget a comment Lauren once made. She said, "You have to finesse things for most judges, so you are not telling them what an idiotic ruling they have made and why they need to correct it. And, of course, juries want to think they have reached their decisions on their own, so you need to lead them to the right decision without making it appear that you have." That's why she was so good at being a trial lawyer.

"Do you want me to look into things? See if I can come up with some sort of explanation for what is going on?"

"I'm at the end of my rope here, Lauren. I can't figure it out and as of yet haven't been able to come up with any type of lead."

"I'll want her approval before I start digging into her personal life and background. After I get her consent, I'll have my PI look into it."

"All right, I'll talk to her tonight. Thanks. I really appreciate this."

"You don't need to thank me; you know I'd do anything for you. So, how are things going with you two anyhow?"

"They're good...actually, they're great. She's a remarkable woman."

"When exactly do you think I'm going to get to meet this remarkable woman in person?"

"Soon, Lauren, very soon…she's different from anybody I have ever been with in a relationship. She's beautiful, intelligent, funny, romantic—"

"I get the picture," she said, laughing. "I'm very happy for you. From the sounds of it, she's perfect."

"I think so." Ryan added wistfully, "I just hope I don't manage to screw it up somehow. It's never mattered as much as it does this time."

"I don't think you have much to worry about. From everything you've told me, she's been there when you needed her, which is more than Stacey ever was. Just relax and let it happen."

"I'm trying. I'm just so damned afraid," Ryan admitted quietly.

"Ryan," Lauren started. She hesitated and then spoke in a firm voice. "Quit thinking so much. You have a lot to offer somebody. It's just a shame that the one time you really opened yourself up, it had to be to that bitch."

Ryan laughed. "You never did like her. I should have taken that as a clue from the start."

"Yeah, well…I need to go now, honey. Discuss it with Tobi and then give me a call. I'll start the ball rolling at looking into things and get back to you as soon as I can."

"Thanks, Lauren. I'll talk to her tonight, and if it's not too late, we'll give you a call afterward."

"Sounds good. I'll chat with you later."

Ryan hung up the phone, hopped up with newfound hope, and headed to the locker room.

Tobi hung up her lab coat and walked over to her chair, collapsing into it. She kicked off her shoes and groaned at the instant tingle of relief. The day had gone nonstop from the moment she walked in the door. Tobi couldn't wait to get back to Ryan's and take a nice, long bath in her large oval tub with massaging jet streams. After the break-in, they both decided it would be better to stay at Ryan's house for a while.

Tobi thought Ryan looked so much better this morning. The circles under her eyes had faded, and aside from the bruising, her color was much better.

Tobi heard the knock at the open door and swiveled around to see Marcy holding some papers.

"I just have a few more reports for you to sign then you can get out of here. Busy day, huh?" she said, walking toward Tobi.

"Busy is putting it mildly. Thanks for all your help, Marcy. You made this day bearable."

Tobi handed back the signed reports, slipped her shoes on, and headed out the door.

"I'll see you tomorrow."

"That you will. Good night, Tobi."

Tobi waved and headed to the elevator. She loved this time of day; the anticipation of seeing Ryan always made her stomach flutter. She stepped off the elevator and headed out the automatic doors toward the Jeep. Every time she saw Ryan's beautiful smile, it never failed to send her heart racing.

Just as she pulled the car door open, she had an odd sense of being watched. She took a step to get into the Jeep and glanced across the hood of the vehicle. There, leaning against a beat-up van, was a man looking in her direction. He had a half-eaten sandwich dangling from one hand and a brown paper sack in the other. She had seen this man on the elevator and in the gift shop and it was making her feel really creepy because he was always staring at her.

"Tobi?"

Startled out of her observation, Tobi slid into the seat and closed the door. "Sorry."

"Everything okay?"

"It is now," Tobi said, smiling.

"Good."

"Hey, Ryan. Have you ever seen that man before?" Tobi asked with a nod of her head toward the man.

"He doesn't look familiar to me. Should he?"

"Not necessarily. I've just noticed him around lately."

"Hmm," Ryan commented while staring out the window at him.

Tobi watched Ryan pull at her lower lip and knew there was something on her mind.

"Spill it, honey."

"What?" Ryan asked surprised.

"I know there's something on your mind, so go ahead and say it."

Darting a quick glance in Tobi's direction, she turned her eyes back to the road before saying, "Tobi, we need to talk."

Tara Wentz

Chapter Twelve

I'm assuming that there's something specific you want to talk about."

Ryan didn't think Tobi would be angry that she talked to somebody else about the calls and break-in; however, she wasn't sure how Tobi felt about that person reviewing her personal affairs.

"I talked to my friend Lauren today. She's an attorney, and I told her everything that has been going on."

"That's great; it can't hurt to have another perspective on things."

"She's going to have her private investigator start searching through the hospital records to see if they can find anything, but first she wants your permission to get involved." *C'mon baby, see this in the same light I do.* Ryan held her breath, waiting for Tobi's answer.

"That's not a problem. I don't mind her looking through things, but you know I can't just hand over any patient files. She'll have to do that part of the digging without my help."

As her breath rushed out, making her a little lightheaded, Ryan nodded and smiled in appreciation.

"Ryan…why were you so worried to tell me that?"

"I didn't want you to think that I went behind your back, that I didn't believe you when you said there was no involvement with a patient on a personal level."

"Oh, honey, I know I reacted poorly that night, and I am truly sorry. I know why you're asking, and I understand. I want this guy as bad as you; even more so."

"I just don't want you to think that I don't trust you, because I do."

Ryan pulled into the garage, turned the Jeep off, and walked around to Tobi's side. She waited until Tobi was out of the vehicle then grasped Tobi's upper arms and gave her a serious look. "I trust you more than anyone, Tobi."

"I never doubted that. I was so frazzled that night. I should never have yelled at you like I did. I'm so sorry for that."

"Don't be sorry; it's in the past."

"Don't ever be afraid to talk to me, Ryan. I may not always like what you have to say, and I may not always agree, but I will listen."

"I'll remember that, and I hope that you'll tell me when you need to talk."

"That won't be a problem because I'm big on communication. It'll probably drive you nuts."

Ryan hugged Tobi close to her and placed her lips against the side of her head. Her hair was so soft, and smelled fresh and clean, her body warm and supple. *I'd love to feel her writhe beneath me and make her even warmer.* Ryan's heart skipped a beat, her pulse rapidly accelerating. *Good God! Get a grip woman!* Ryan barely contained a groan of desire. She took two full breaths then kissed the top of Tobi's head and took her hand.

"You could never drive me nuts, sweetheart…at least not in a bad way."

It took a full five seconds before Tobi raised both eyebrows and glanced in Ryan's direction. "Being coy now, are we?"

Ryan grinned and pulled her into the house, closing the garage door.

When they finished cleaning up after dinner, Ryan called Lauren to tell her it was fine with Tobi if she looked into things. After a brief conversation, Ryan handed the phone to Tobi.

"What?"

"Lauren wants to talk to you."

"Why does she want to talk to me?"

"That's what I asked her, and she said it was none of my business," Ryan said, scowling.

Timidly reaching for the phone, Tobi put it to her ear. "Hello?"

"Hi, Tobi. I know this is going to drive Ryan crazy, but she'll survive," Lauren said, laughing.

Tobi chuckled with her after seeing the scowl still on Ryan's face. "You wouldn't believe the sour look she's pulling right now." Pouting, Ryan turned on her heel and went back into the living room.

"Oh, I'd believe it. I've seen it enough times myself. Listen, I wanted to hear directly from you that you were okay with someone delving through your own personnel files, not to mention all the background info that will come back."

"I'm more than okay with it, Lauren, I want this over with. I don't mind you looking into things; just know that I can't and won't hand over any patient files."

"I understand and don't worry about that. We can work around it."

"Thanks. It's one thing for him to harass me, but for him to hurt Ryan is going too far."

"She is all right, isn't she?"

"Except for a few bumps and bruises, she's fine."

"She's so damned stubborn. I wasn't sure whether to believe her or not. She's not very good about telling people when she's hurting."

Tobi detected a hidden meaning in her statement and knew Lauren was talking about more than just a physical hurt.

"I'm finding that out. I hope that I'm slowly convincing her that she can tell me anything. I don't like to see her in pain."

Lauren was silent for a moment before responding. "She's a good person, Tobi. I'm so glad you two have found each other.

She deserves to be happy, and I know that she will make you just as happy."

"I concur, Counselor."

"I'll let you go for now because I'm sure that after this she will need her feelings soothed. No doubt she is still pouting," she said, laughing.

"Thanks, Lauren, for everything."

"No problem, kiddo. I'll give you a call in a couple of days. Take care of yourselves."

Tobi set the phone down and leaned heavily against the counter, pondering what Lauren had said. She knew Ryan held things inside, but she wanted to unlock that part of her, and given enough time, she had no doubt that would happen. Question is, would Ryan give them that time or would she pull away in fear? Speculating wasn't going to bring about the solution; she would just have to show Ryan that she didn't have to be afraid. With a determined push away from the counter, she went in search of her little pouter.

After three days, Lauren called Ryan at the precinct with some information.

"First off, I'm not even going to tell you how my informant got all this information, so don't even ask."

Ryan would have laughed except that she knew Lauren was completely serious.

"There's nothing specifically pertaining to Tobi. Just typical malpractice lawsuits. We looked through court dockets, hospital records, Tobi's personnel file, and even checked with the State Department of Professional Registration for any complaints," Lauren explained. "Out of everything, there's just one incident that jumps out at me."

"What's that?" Ryan asked.

"Well, among the documents pertaining to the death of that pregnant woman, there's a statement from her husband claiming that there had to be a mistake. His wife could not have been pregnant because he'd had a vasectomy two years prior."

Ryan mulled this over, but said nothing.

"There are also several documented follow-up attempts on the hospitals end, but no other correspondence came from the husband."

"Hmm, wonder why that is?" Ryan asked.

"Your guess is as good as mine."

"Well, anyhow, thanks for looking into this for me, Lauren."

"No problem. Take care and give me a call me sometime, okay?"

"Will do, Counselor."

Ryan strummed her fingers lightly on the desk before rolling her chair over and retrieving the husband's address from the computer. *Think I'll stop by and have a chat with Mr. David Hyde.* Grabbing her jacket and keys, she headed out the door.

Following a winding road into the heart of an older subdivision, Ryan found the street she was looking for and stopped in front of a red brick house. She saw a car in the driveway and took a deep breath before heading to the front door.

The door opened to reveal a middle-aged man of average height with short red hair and wire-rimmed glasses. "Can I help you with something?"

"Are you David Hyde?"

"Yes, what can I do for you?"

"Mr. Hyde, my name is Sergeant Ryan Thomas," she said showing her badge. "I have a few questions I'd like to ask you about the death of your wife."

He stepped out of the house, pulled the door closed, and crossed his arms. "What exactly do you want to know?"

"It seems that you submitted a statement saying your wife could not be pregnant. I've read the autopsy report, and there was no question that she was. The hospital tried on several occasions to follow up with you, but there was no further contact from your end."

"Sergeant, I found out shortly after I sent that statement that my wife had been having an affair. With that new knowledge, I didn't see the point in pursuing things any further."

"I'm sorry."

"Yeah, well…is there anything else you need?" he asked in a tone that indicated she was being more than bothersome. Ryan knew she was pushing her luck but had to ask the one question she was sure Mr. Hyde could have done without.

"Do you happen to know who she was having the affair with?"

"No. One of her friends, Cindy, told me about the affair but said she never knew who the man was. Apparently, my wife would never tell her anything about him." Stepping back to the door, he said, "If that's all, I have things to do." When Ryan nodded, he disappeared inside.

Once in the Jeep, Ryan deliberated over what Mr. Hyde had revealed. If his wife, in fact, had been having an affair, then who was this other man? Could he be the one causing all the problems? If so, what exactly was his vendetta against Tobi? *I think I need to do a little more investigating.* Opening her cell phone, Ryan punched in a familiar number.

"Dr. Drexler's office, Marcy speaking. May I help you?"

"Hi, Marcy."

"Hello there, how are you feeling?"

"I'm doing great; thank you for asking."

"Let me guess; you'd like to speak with Tobi."

"Please, if she's not too busy."

"Glad to hear you're doing better, Ryan. Hang on just a second."

"Thanks, Marcy." Ryan listened to the soft beat of music as she ran her hand down the smooth surface of the steering wheel and back up. This was an annoying little habit that reared its ugly head when she had too much pent-up nervous energy.

"Hey, honey."

Instantly grinning, Ryan's hand stopped in mid-motion, "Hi."

"To what do I owe this pleasure?"

"I was wondering if you were free for lunch today."

"It just so happens that I am. Does this mean you're going to spend some of your day off in my presence?"

"If that's okay with you, I thought I might."

"I'd love it. Why don't you meet me in the cafeteria, say in an hour?"

"Sounds good, I'll see you then, sweetheart."

Tobi set the last of the signed reports on Marcy's desk and waited for her to finish her phone call.

"I'm going to meet Ryan in the cafeteria for lunch today, if you should need me."

"Aren't you lucky? What's the occasion?"

"Yes, very lucky," Tobi said, grinning. "She's off today and wanted to spend some time with little ol' me."

"Well, I'll walk down with you. I need to grab a couple of things myself."

After closing the office door, they headed to the elevator. They had just entered the cafeteria when Tobi felt the vibration from her pager against her hip. She checked the number and grabbed Marcy's arm.

"I need to answer this page real quick. Can you do me a favor?"

"Sure. What's up?"

"Can you just watch for Ryan, and if she gets here before I return, tell her I'll be right back?"

"Okay, no problem."

"Thanks." Walking to the bank of phones, Tobi punched in the number. "This is Dr. Drexler. Did someone page?" She jotted down a few notes as she listened. "Okay, I'll be right there." Tobi pocketed her beeper and headed back to Marcy. "Damn, so much for lunch."

Finding Marcy where she left her, Tobi rushed to explain, "Marcy, I really hate to ask this, but can you wait for Ryan to get here and tell her that I'm sorry I couldn't make lunch? The ER just called and needs someone to scan a rigid belly on a trauma that just came in."

"Not a problem; get on over there. I'll let Ryan know what's up."

"Thanks, I owe you one."

Tobi descended the back steps to the entrance of the tunnel that led to the emergency room. Walking through the tunnel always reminded her of those scary movies where the lights were dim, and she could almost imagine a water puddle here and there, making it seem cold. With each step, the sound of the soles of her shoes hitting the concrete floor was the only thing she could hear. As she rounded the corner to the last section before the steps to the ER, Tobi stopped. She thought she had heard someone running toward her. Not hearing anything, she continued on. A few steps more and she heard the noise again. This time, she knew someone was behind her. As if in slow motion, Tobi turned and barely saw the flash of a white-clad arm and dark eyes before taking a blow to the side of her head. Falling back against the wall, she slid down and everything faded to black.

"Hey, Ryan," Marcy said as she approached with a tray in her hands.

"Hi. You mean the boss actually lets you get away to eat?"

"Sometimes," Marcy said, laughing. "Listen, Tobi got called away on an emergency."

"Ah, okay, thanks for sticking around to tell me." With a slight hesitation, Ryan continued, "Would you like to eat lunch since you're already here?"

"I'd like that. I'll go get a table while you get your tray."

Ryan picked up some food, fixed a drink, and went to pay. She found Marcy sitting toward the back wall.

"So, it's your day off, huh?"

Ryan took a sip of iced tea and nodded. "The department does the schedule so that every two weeks, you end up with a day off during the week."

"That sounds like a great schedule. I bet–"

"Dr. Drexler, 5-0 ...Dr. Drexler, 5-0."

Ryan saw a frown form on Marcy's forehead. "What? Why did they page her?"

"They're paging her to the ER, but she should have been there by now."

"How long ago did she leave?"

"It's been at least ten minutes."

"Is that long enough to get there?" Ryan asked, worried.

"It should be, but maybe she stopped off at the desk before going to the exam room."

"Hmm, that could be."

"What was I saying? Oh, I bet that schedule gives you time to get things done during the week that you normally can't."

"Exactly. It's nice to have a day to do errands at places that normally aren't open after regular business hours. How has today been?"

"Not too bad actually. Steady, but nothing like the other day when you were here. Seems Dr. Drexler doesn't spend every night at work anymore," she said, smirking.

"Dr. Drexler to the emergency room, STAT...Dr. Drexler to the ER, STAT."

"Ryan, she should have been there by now; something's wrong."

Ryan stood up. "I'm going to head that way, and I'll let you know what I find out."

Before she even took two steps, Marcy stopped her. "She went through the tunnel when they called her."

"The tunnel?"

"Yeah, take those stairs down," she said, pointing, "and you'll see the tunnel. It will take you to another set of steps that lead right into the emergency room. I'll go back up the other way just in case and meet you in the ER."

"Thanks," Ryan said, running toward the stairs. Taking them two at a time, she came to the tunnel and started at a full run down it. As she came to a corner, she slowed down. Before she got all the way around it, she could see Tobi's form crumpled on the ground. Racing to her side, Ryan dropped to her knees and cradled Tobi's head in her lap.

Ryan's hands shook as she touched Tobi's face. She could see a laceration on the side of Tobi's head where her hair was matted by the steady flow of blood. Ryan caressed her cheek and tried calling her name.

"Tobi? C'mon, honey, open your eyes. Let me see those baby blues. Tobi, open your eyes, sweetheart."

It was at times like this that Ryan appreciated her training in the police academy, not to mention her inherent ability to remain calm when it was most important. Ryan gently picked Tobi up in her arms and quickly made her way to the ER.

Tara Wentz

Chapter Thirteen

Bursting through the ER doors with Tobi in her arms, Ryan shouted for help. A nurse immediately grabbed a stretcher and Ryan gently laid Tobi down. She followed as the nurse rushed Tobi into a private exam room.

"What happened?" the nurse asked while checking Tobi's vitals.

"I don't really know. I was in the cafeteria when she kept getting paged. Her secretary said she had gone through the tunnel to head this way," Ryan explained.

"You didn't see the injury being sustained?"

"No, I…" Ryan faltered momentarily when another nurse and a doctor entered the room and immediately began working on Tobi. "I found her lying on the ground unconscious."

The nurse nodded and passed the information on to the doctor that was examining Tobi. Ryan moved out of the way but stayed as close to the head of the bed as possible.

"Pupils are reactive…three-inch laceration left temple…no other obvious signs of injury." As the doctor examined Tobi, a nurse started an IV in her arm.

Ryan heard Tobi moan again and looked down at her face. She watched her eyelids flutter open briefly before closing just as fast.

"Tobi, open your eyes for me," the doctor said while leaning over her.

"Hurts…" she croaked.

"I know the light makes them hurt, but I need you to look at me for just a minute."

When she opened her eyes, tears slowly trickled down the side of her face as she winced in pain.

Ryan's heart hammered in her chest as she watched Tobi lying there, obviously hurting. Her stomach threatened to revolt at any minute, and she felt so helpless. She now knew exactly what Tobi had gone through the night she had chased that man and was injured.

After doing a thorough exam, including a CT scan of the head, the chief trauma surgeon, Tom Asher, cleaned and placed stitches in the wound. Tobi was awake and alert by this point, but she chose to keep her eyes closed. She held tightly to Ryan's hand while the doctor worked on her.

"Tobi, I'd like to keep you overnight just for observation. That was a nasty blow you took to the head. If everything still looks good in the morning, I'll release you."

"'kay, Tom. Thanks."

"Also, your friend Ryan has agreed to get the police report taken care of after you're released tomorrow. I can't tell you how sorry I am that this happened. I've already talked to your superior and explained everything. He said to take the next few days off, and if you feel up to it, return on Monday."

Tom Asher pulled his gloves off and tossed them on the open tray before standing up. He patted her arm as he looked down at her with affection. "Take care of yourself, and I'll see you in the morning. I've given you something that should help that headache. Someone will be down soon to take you to your room."

"Thanks," she said, opening her eyes and smiling.

Ryan watched him leave the room then turned back to Tobi when she felt a hand squeeze hers. As she gazed into Tobi's eyes,

Ryan again felt the twinge in her chest. Tobi's eyes were clouded with pain, and she was still very pale.

Ryan caressed her cheek lightly. "How are you doing, sweetheart?"

"Other than this headache, I'm not too shabby," she said with a slow smile. "I'm sorry about lunch."

"You're kidding me, right?"

"No, I really wanted to eat lunch with you today."

Ryan stood there dumbfounded. She couldn't believe that Tobi was lying in the emergency room with a gash in her head, and all she was concerned about was missing lunch. On top of that, she looked as if she was pouting about it. If it weren't such a serious situation, it would have been comical.

Before she could comment, an orderly bustled into the room. "They've got your room ready, Dr. Drexler," he said while raising the rails on the stretcher. "If you'll follow me, ma'am, we'll get this pretty lady to her room."

Ryan glanced at his nametag. "Lead on, Jerome."

With a toothy grin, he wheeled the stretcher down the hall and into an open elevator. Ryan reached through the railing to lay her hand on Tobi's arm. Tobi took Ryan's hand in both of hers and with a tug pulled Ryan down to within inches of her.

"I think you're the most beautiful woman," she said in a loud whisper.

Jerome smirked and looked away to study the control panel. *Now what the hell do I do?* Ryan thought. She saw Tobi's eyes close and figured she had fallen asleep. She placed her hand on the rail and started to straighten up when Tobi's hands tightened around hers.

"Don't leave," Tobi mumbled.

"I'm not going anywhere. I'll be right here."

"I love you."

"I love you too, honey."

"Of course you do," Tobi said matter-of-factly.

Jerome chuckled next to her as Ryan smiled when Tobi's hands loosened and dropped to her chest. Her whole body seemed to relax. It appeared that she had, indeed, fallen asleep. *Even in this condition, she's absolutely adorable.*

When the doors opened, Jerome guided the stretcher off and down the hall to Tobi's room. Once she was settled in her bed, Ryan tucked the blanket snugly around her and placed a kiss on her forehead. Seeing how vulnerable she looked brought a surge of anger that made Ryan's body tremble. She tried to regain some control by closing her eyes and taking a couple of deep breaths. If this maniac got this close to her once, he could do it again. *No, it will not happen again, no matter what I have to do to keep her safe.* Ryan pulled a chair close to the bed and settled down for what was sure to be a long night. With the lights down low, she rested her head against the back of the chair. As the blankets shrouding Tobi's body rose and fell with each breath she took, a peaceful tranquility settled within Ryan. Tobi was going to be all right and that's what was important. The only sounds in the room were the gentle hiss of the thermostat and the clicking of the IV pump. Listening to the rhythmic noises, Ryan's eyes grew heavy. As her tension ebbed, she finally gave in to her body's need for rest.

The swirl of the patterned ceiling tiles was the first thing to come into focus as Tobi slowly opened her eyes and blinked. She rolled her head from one side to the other, wincing when the left side grazed the pillow. Reaching up, she barely touched the bandage covering the stitches before remembering what had happened. With a sigh, she dropped her arm, then glanced to the side of the bed and saw the tall form that appeared to be fast asleep. In repose, Ryan looked so relaxed and peaceful. Tobi was relieved to know that Ryan was getting some sleep. She watched the rise and fall of Ryan's chest for a moment before her gaze swept back up to Ryan's eyes. She was startled to see them open and fixed upon her.

"Hi."

"Hi, honey. How are you feeling?" Ryan asked, sitting up straighter.

"I'm a little sore and have a slight headache but not too bad. Nice shirt, by the way," Tobi said with a nod of her head.

Ryan glanced down at the light blue scrub top she had been given after Tobi fell asleep. It had "Truman University Medical

Center" stamped all over it in bold black letters. "Your nurse thought I might want to change since my shirt…" Ryan trailed off. One look at Tobi made her realize she didn't have to explain that her shirt had gotten blood all over it; understanding was written in the small sympathetic smile from Tobi.

Ryan cleared her throat. "Do you need anything?"

"I could use a drink. My mouth and throat feel so dry."

Ryan poured her a cup of water and placed a straw inside before setting the cup down on the tray table. She raised the head of the bed so Tobi was sitting upright.

"Is that okay?"

"That's fine, honey. Thank you."

Ryan responded with a smile as she picked up the cup and held the straw to Tobi's lips.

"You don't have to hold it; I can do it," Tobi said, leaning back slightly.

"I don't mind…humor me?"

"I will but only if you'll sit down beside me."

"Where?"

Tobi moved over and patted the bed. "Right here."

"Um, Tobi, I'm not sure I'm supposed to be doing that."

"It's okay. C'mon, have a seat." Seeing Ryan glance at the door skeptically, Tobi continued, "Trust me; I'm a doctor," she said with a wink.

Ryan tried to hide a smile as she sat down. She took Tobi's hands in hers and debated whether to bring up what happened in the tunnel. She knew what had to be going through Tobi's mind.

"Do you have any idea who did this?" Tobi asked as if reading her thoughts.

Ryan shook her head. "I didn't see anyone. By the time I found you, you were already unconscious. Do you remember anything?"

"Very little. I remember being paged to the emergency room and entering the tunnel. The last thing I remember is hearing someone running up behind me."

"I really think—"

Hearing the knock on the door, she stopped in midsentence. As Tom Asher entered the room, Ryan leaned forward and whispered, "We'll talk about this later, okay?" before standing up and moving aside. Tobi nodded and smiled at the doctor.

"Hello, Tom."

"Hello there, yourself. How are you feeling this morning?"

"Pretty good, all things considered."

Taking the spot Ryan had just vacated, he pulled out a penlight and checked Tobi's pupils. "No blurred vision, nausea, vomiting, dizziness..." he trailed off as she shook her head to each question. "Well, I don't see any reason why you can't go home. I'll leave a prescription for some Tylenol with codeine with your discharge papers in case you need it. Call me if you have any problems." He patted her leg, stood up, and with a wink at Ryan, walked out of the room.

"He has got to be one of the nicest men," Ryan said.

"He is. He's got four daughters of his own and still treats me like I'm one. He's been a terrific mentor."

There was another knock on the door, and it opened again. This time, a nurse came in carrying a chart.

"Looks like you're out of here, Dr. Drexler. I'll just get this IV out then you can sign your papers and be discharged."

"That sounds like a terrific idea. Not that you aren't nice and all, but home sounds really good right about now."

The nurse pulled the tape off Tobi's arm and removed the IV catheter. She glanced up at Ryan and then back at Tobi. "Looks like you'll have someone to watch over you, as well," she said with a nod of her head toward Ryan.

Seeing the weak attempt at a scowl from Ryan, Tobi laughed. "I think you're right."

"She didn't leave the entire time, in case you didn't know," she said in a mock whisper.

As Ryan fidgeted, Tobi quietly replied, "Thanks, I didn't know, although I kind of figured."

"I'll be right back. Go ahead and get dressed, then we'll get you discharged."

The nurse left the room, but Tobi's gaze never left Ryan's face. She could tell that Ryan was embarrassed by the nurse's comments. All Tobi wanted at this moment was to be home, curled up in bed with her arms and body wrapped around Ryan.

"I love you. Thank you so much for staying with me last night."

"You don't have to thank me. There is nowhere else I'd rather be than by your side, Tobi."

Tobi swung her legs off the bed and sat up straight. "C'mere," she said while beckoning with her finger. As Ryan stepped closer, Tobi grabbed the waistband of her jeans and pulled her to stand between her legs. With arms wrapped around Ryan's waist, she rested her head against her and placed a kiss on the hard plane of her stomach.

"Help me get dressed so we can get out of here?"

"Absolutely," Ryan replied while leaning down and kissing Tobi fully on the lips.

When Tobi had dressed, the nurse returned with the discharge papers and a wheelchair. Knowing this was the only way she was leaving the hospital, Tobi complied without an argument. *It won't be long before I can hold Ryan in my arms.*

Ryan had barely closed the front door and turned when Tobi threw herself into her arms. Ryan automatically tightened her arms and hugged Tobi close. She felt Tobi's fingers glide up the back of her head, sending shivers up her spine, the gentle pressure on her neck bringing her face closer to Tobi's. Ryan caught the barest glimpse of moistened lips before they were nipping gently at her own. An insistent tongue begged for entrance, making Ryan shiver in anticipation. Her legs trembled as the kiss continued and the possessive nature of it deepened. Hands against Ryan's chest pushed her back against the kitchen wall. She gasped in surprise as Tobi leaned fully against her, her thigh between Ryan's parted legs and her hands on her shoulders.

While Tobi's teeth nibbled at her neck and ear, Ryan's arms encircled her, pulling her closer. The heat racing through Ryan's body burned even into her toes and fingertips. *Fuck! I don't know how much more of this I can take.* Ryan bent her knees slightly, cupped her hands under Tobi's hips and lifted. Tobi immediately wrapped her legs around Ryan's waist.

"You are driving me crazy," Ryan whispered as she walked forward and deposited Tobi on the kitchen table. She stood between Tobi's legs and continued to kiss her with such fervor that it left them both gasping for air.

Tobi tangled her fingers in Ryan's shirt, pulled her down, and licked the outer edge of her ear. "I can't seem to get enough of you."

As they started to fall back, Ryan dropped her hands onto the table beside Tobi's thighs, bringing her precariously closer to Tobi's full, inviting lips.

Tobi placed her hands around Ryan's hips, letting her thumbs rest intimately next to the spot that she knew could send Ryan over the edge.

Tobi traced Ryan's lips with her tongue and purred. "You taste so good, honey."

"I need you, baby," Ryan whimpered.

Tobi smiled and pulled Ryan closer. "And I need you, so very much.

Ryan groaned in raw desperation. She yearned to take Tobi right where she stood. Ryan felt the intensity of the moment rising as Tobi's hands worked their way up under her shirt. Her hands roamed across Ryan's stomach and sides before coming to rest on her breasts. Tobi's palms raked across Ryan's hard nipples. Ryan gasped and pulled back slightly.

"Tobi…"

"Uh-huh," she said without stopping.

"Tobi…please, honey…we have to stop."

"I don't want to stop."

"I know, sweetheart, but we need to for right now. You just got out of the hospital."

"I don't give a damn; I feel fine."

"You do right now, but you may not be saying that later."

Sighing, she let her head drop back to look into Ryan's eyes. "You," she said pointing at Ryan's chest, "are driving me insane."

"I'm—"

Interrupting, she said, "Yes...driving me insane."

Ryan had no idea what to say. As she stood there with her mouth open, Tobi reached up and gently closed it.

"Ryan, I want you so bad."

Ryan leaned her forehead against Tobi's and responded with a simple kiss to her lips. She drifted back a little and looked earnestly into Tobi's eyes. "I want you, too, honey, more than you know."

Tobi raised an eyebrow. "Well then…"

"I just don't want to hurt you. You just got out of the hospital with a head injury and…well, that really scared me," Ryan admitted, quietly.

Tobi's eyes welled with tears. "I'm so sorry I put you through that, Ryan."

"Hey," Ryan started, using her thumb to wipe away a tear. "You didn't put me through anything. This wasn't your fault."

Tobi nodded in agreement. "I know. It's just that…" Tobi took a deep breath and then continued. "I guess we have some things to talk about, huh?"

"Yes, I guess we do," Ryan responded with a smiled.

Tobi thought about what she said and finally asked, "Okay, which do you want to do first?"

Tara Wentz

Chapter Fourteen

Tobi watched the glazed over, lust-filled look enter Ryan's eyes and knew that she was ready for their relationship to go further. Ryan actually appeared to be struggling over her choices. Tobi ran her nails up and down the length of Ryan's arm, teasing her, tempting her, begging her.

Something inside Ryan snapped and she grabbed Tobi's hand, yanking her forward, against her chest. Ryan captured her lips and slipped her tongue between Tobi's teeth. She moaned into Tobi's mouth as their tongues tangled, each demanding more from the other.

Tobi knew that if she didn't stop this soon their first time was going to be on top of the kitchen table; not that it would be such a bad thing, but she wanted the talking out of the way. Once they started making love, she didn't plan on stopping. *But God is the waiting going to kill me!*

"Ryan," Tobi said against her mouth.

"What?"

"You're going to think I've lost my mind, but we should stop."

Ryan snapped her head back to glare at her, and Tobi couldn't help but laugh. Ryan narrowed her eyes even more. Tobi knew she shouldn't laugh, but some of Ryan's expressions were downright adorable.

"You're not serious, are you?"

"I am, but let me explain," Tobi said, holding up a hand before Ryan could interject. "I want to talk first because once we start making love, I don't want to talk. Understand?"

Ryan nodded instead of speaking for fear her vulnerability would show in her voice. *Vulnerability? Hell yes! Her every move and every moan makes me vulnerable to her. I'd give her anything she wanted right this minute!* She leaned her forehead against Tobi's chest, valiantly trying to slow her breathing.

Tobi grabbed fists full of Ryan's dark silky hair and placed a kiss on the crown of her head. *You are so damn sexy, and I can't wait to get my hands all over your body.* Tobi's stomach tightened at the mere thought of being naked with Ryan.

Ryan straightened and held out her hands for Tobi. She pulled her to the edge of the table until her feet touched the floor, and they left the kitchen hand in hand.

As they sat on the couch, Ryan took a deep breath and stared at Tobi before chuckling and shaking her head.

"What?"

"You want to talk about who is driving whom insane here?"

Tobi laughed with her but could only shrug. "What can I say? I love to share."

"Okay, so let's talk. We already discussed the tunnel and the fact that neither of us saw anything."

"Right, but I think we can assume it was our guy."

"Exactly. I talked to Lauren about the pregnant woman yesterday, as well." Ryan relayed the information Lauren had given her and waited for it to sink in before continuing. "So, I looked up his address and drove out to talk to him. He said his wife had been having an affair, and he knew nothing about it. Apparently, one of her friends told him, so he didn't feel the need to continue contacting the hospital about the baby."

"Do you think that whomever she was having the affair with has something to do with what is going on?"

"That certainly crossed my mind. Nothing else makes sense, Tobi. The only problem is, we don't know who this man is. Mr. Hyde said his wife's friend didn't know who he was either."

"Do you think she's telling the truth, or is she just trying to hide it?"

"I thought about that, and I really don't see why she would hide it. At this point, she has no motive for keeping it to herself."

"What do we do now?"

"Well, I'm going to do a little more digging where Mrs. Hyde is concerned and see what I can come up with. I'm also going to get her home and cell phone records; maybe there will be something in those that can help."

Tobi rubbed her left temple with her fingertips, suddenly aware of the headache that had returned in full force. The throbbing made her stomach queasy, and the lights appeared to be too bright. She placed a hand over her stomach and closed her eyes. Flinching at the touch to her shoulder, Tobi glanced at Ryan a little too fast, causing her head to spin. She groaned quietly and leaned her head back against the couch and shut her eyes.

"Headache?"

"Yeah," Tobi whispered.

"I'll go get your pain meds; be right back, sweetheart."

Tobi let her thoughts drift in hope of distracting herself from her rebelling body. She could hear sounds from the kitchen and felt a sense of peace wash over her. It was so nice having someone to care for her and be there when she needed it. Smiling, Tobi turned her head away from the light and took some deep breaths to calm her roiling stomach.

"What are you smiling about?"

Without opening her eyes, Tobi replied, "You."

"Me? Why me?"

"It's just really nice having you here, Ryan. I think back to before I met you, and I just can't imagine not having you in my life now."

"The feeling is mutual, sweetheart. Now, sit up and take these."

Tobi took the glass of water and pills from Ryan's hand and swallowed them down. She took a few more sips before setting the glass on the coffee table.

"Stand up for just a second."

Without bothering to ask what Ryan had in mind, Tobi did as she was told. Ryan sat with her back to the arm of the couch, splaying her legs, and patted the space between them. Tobi snuggled in and leaned back against her chest. Once comfortable, Ryan spread a throw blanket over the both of them. With her left arm around Tobi's waist, Ryan raised her right hand to caress the hair back and away from Tobi's face. She ran her fingers through Tobi's hair and let her nails lightly scratch her skull. Tobi's eyes grew heavy as she slipped into a deep sleep. Ryan pressed her lips lightly to her head, murmuring words of comfort over and over.

Long after Tobi had fallen asleep, Ryan was still holding and caressing her. She hoped this rest would give Tobi a chance to heal. Physically, she would be fine in a few days, but mentally, Ryan wasn't sure how much more Tobi could take. She was going to strongly suggest Tobi spend some time with her mother in the following days when Ryan had to work. At least then she would feel more comfortable leaving her.

Ryan nuzzled her hair and reflected back to the scene in the kitchen when they had first arrived home. She was taken off guard by the intensity of their kisses. Even more surprising, she was ready to go further. The velvety touch of Tobi's lips had awakened an ache that Ryan thought had long since been buried. She hadn't been sure that she would ever be ready to let herself feel again after Stacey had left. It had hurt too much to give so much of herself only to have it thrown back in her face.

With Tobi, the giving and obvious love were different in so many ways. She went out of her way to let Ryan know what she meant to her, and that she knew Ryan's job was important to her. Even with things in such disarray, she took the time to make sure Ryan was okay. The transition from being alone to constantly being with someone should have been more difficult, but with Tobi it wasn't. Ryan should have been frightened, but she wasn't. Hell, she should have been a lot of things that she wasn't.

Wherever this took them, she was more than willing to let it play out to the end. The kisses and touches had ignited a fire within her, and each subsequent touch was like throwing more fuel on the flames.

As she felt Tobi stir and sigh against her, Ryan propped the side of her head against the back of the couch. She wrapped her arms protectively around Tobi and closed her eyes.

After what seemed like only a few minutes, Ryan felt warm soft lips against her chin. Her eyes opened and collided with blue orbs that appeared to be free of pain. She studied Tobi's features and saw the flicker of desire in her eyes. The sensuous curl of her lips as she smiled informed Ryan that this was "later." She leaned forward and placed a tender kiss upon Tobi's uplifted face. Tobi shifted to her knees and deepened the kiss until Ryan was forced to recline against the arm of the couch, pulling Tobi on top of her. Ryan sucked gently on Tobi's lower lip, releasing it to lay a row of butterfly kisses along her cheek and down her neck. She continued to nibble lightly as Tobi groaned and tilted her head back in submission. Ryan bit and licked her way back up Tobi's neck and took an earlobe between her lips.

"No more talking?" Ryan whispered in her ear.

"No more talking," Tobi responded, her voice hoarse with desire.

As Tobi's lips captured Ryan's once again, she gave in to the pleasure Tobi bestowed upon her. Ryan felt Tobi's body move against her, making her heart pound inside her chest. With one hand on her neck and the other moving into her hair, Ryan pulled Tobi into her and deepened the kiss. Ryan gradually became aware of hands pulling her shirt free of her pants. She reached down to help, but her hands were pushed away.

She gazed into Tobi's eyes and could see a sparkle of raw anticipation. Her breathing came in shallow gasps as Tobi's fingers nimbly unbuttoned her shirt, placing a kiss on each new section of skin as it was revealed.

Tobi blew a hot kiss over cotton-covered nipples and moaned at the whimper emitted by Ryan.

A torrent of heat coursed through Ryan when Tobi moved her hips against her. Tobi's lips ravaged her mouth and her hands roamed freely down her abdomen, finally coming to rest on the button of Ryan's pants. Tobi released the button and raked her fingernails down Ryan's thigh and back up before slowly lowering the zipper. *Oh, my God, she's killing me!* Ryan closed her eyes and surrendered to the passion consuming her.

Tobi slid her hand inside the last barrier separating them and rubbed her palm across Ryan's hip, placing soft sensuous kisses on her mouth. Ryan groaned as Tobi moved her hand down through the thatch of curly hair. She slowly entered Ryan's slick folds, moving her fingers up and down each side of her clit.

Ryan couldn't stop her hips from responding and knew it would not be long when Tobi moved her fingers over the hardened bundle of nerves.

"Tobi, honey...Oh, God..."

"That's it, baby; let it go."

Ryan pumped her hips against Tobi a few more times before crying out her release. She sagged back against the couch, only to be brought to the edge again by Tobi's hand. Tobi's hand drifted lower as she pushed two fingers inside Ryan all the while moving her thumb over her clit.

"Jesus Christ," Ryan cried out.

Tobi grinned and kissed her way down Ryan's chest and nuzzled her bra aside to capture a hard nipple in her mouth. She sucked the nipple and moved her fingers inside Ryan, eliciting a gasp of pleasure.

Ryan curled the fingers of one hand in Tobi's hair and clutched the couch cushion with the other, moving her body in sync with Tobi's.

"Oh, my God, please."

"That's it, Ryan," Tobi encouraged, stroking Ryan's nipple with her tongue.

"Yes, Tobi...oh, yes."

"Mmm, come on, honey."

"I'm coming, baby," Ryan shouted.

As Ryan collapsed, Tobi cradled her in her arms. Ryan's heart threatened to beat right out of her chest, and she knew that Tobi could feel it against her.

Raising one hand to stroke Ryan's face, Tobi pulled back to

look at her. She was startled to see tears forming in her eyes.

"Ryan, honey, what's wrong? Why are you crying?"

"I...I'm not...it's just been so long...and honestly, Tobi, I've never felt this way before. It's simply astounding."

"I know. Are you afraid?"

"I've been afraid of a lot of things but mostly of wanting you the way I do."

"I can understand that," she said.

Kissing the tears from Ryan's eyes, Tobi held her for a few moments. "I've got you," she murmured.

Ryan didn't want to be afraid anymore, and with Tobi, her emotions felt safe. She was able to knock down some of those barriers surrounding her heart.

"Tobi?"

"Hmm?"

"I want to make love to you."

Tobi let her eyes wander lovingly over Ryan's face before kissing her and standing up.

Ryan took Tobi's outstretched hand and stood. She buttoned her pants, so she wouldn't trip and followed Tobi up the steps. They made it to the top of the stairs before Ryan started kissing her again. Tongues clashed wildly as the kiss seemed to go on forever. Tobi felt her knees go weak and groaned into Ryan's mouth.

With a sultry moan, Ryan ended the kiss. "Bedroom, now."

Tobi stood in front of the bed and pushed the already unbuttoned shirt from Ryan's shoulders. As the shirt floated to the floor unnoticed, she couldn't take her eyes off Ryan. *My God, she's gorgeous.* The muscles in her arms were well-toned but not large. Her shoulders were average in width and led to a small waist. Tobi ran her fingers over Ryan's chest, but dropped her hands when Ryan grasped the bottom of her cotton shirt and pulled it up and off. Without breaking eye contact with Tobi, Ryan reached around and unhooked her bra. Sliding her hands up Tobi's back to her shoulders, she grasped the straps and lowered them down Tobi's arms. Tobi watched as Ryan's fingers gently caressed the pink scar across her left breast. She placed feather

151

light kisses upon the mark before her eyes slowly rose to meet Tobi's.

"You are absolutely beautiful, Tobi."

Tobi placed a kiss on Ryan's lips, released the button on her pants, and pushed them over her hips. With Tobi's hands on her waist, Ryan kicked her pants to the side.

"So soft," Tobi's purred while her fingers caressed their way up Ryan's sides. She smiled as she reached around to unhook Ryan's bra and slide it off.

Ryan moved her hands between them and unbuttoned Tobi's pants, sliding them and her panties down in one motion. Kneeling, she slipped Tobi's shoes off and lifted each foot clear. Tobi shivered in anticipation as Ryan kissed her way up her thighs. She placed one last kiss on Tobi's hip before standing upright and pulling Tobi into her arms.

"You. Are. Exquisite," Ryan said, emphasizing each word with a kiss.

Tobi yielded completely and moaned as Ryan begged for more with the last kiss. She walked Ryan backward and turned as they neared the bed, pulling Ryan down on top of her. The heat her kiss had evoked was consuming Tobi. She wanted all of Ryan, and she wanted it now.

"You have too many clothes on," Tobi said, reaching for Ryan's panties.

Ryan raised her hips enough so Tobi could slide her panties down. As Ryan pushed them off, her face moved closer to Tobi's chest. The heat of her breath against Tobi's nipple puckered the sensitive skin. Ryan flicked her tongue across the nipple, making her gasp at the intense pleasure. A few more of those, and she would come before Ryan could touch her further. She slid her hands into Ryan's hair and pulled her face up to claim her lips. Tobi raised her knee and pressed into Ryan's moist center. The heat emanating from Ryan made her head spin. She clutched Ryan's hips and moved her leg against her, eliciting a groan from Ryan.

"Uh-uh…not this time. It's my turn," Ryan said.

She moved her lips down Tobi's neck and sucked lightly. Tingles shot through Tobi's toes and fingers; her body felt as if it might explode. Tobi whimpered and grabbed Ryan's shoulders, pulling her even closer. Ryan nuzzled her way down Tobi's chest, stopping long enough to love both breasts appreciatively before continuing lower to swirl her tongue around her navel. Tobi didn't think she could take much more; unconsciously she opened her legs wider and gave Ryan permission to explore further. The moment she felt Ryan's lips wander lightly over her hip, she clutched the sheets tightly.

"Ryan, honey, you're killing me here."

Tobi squirmed beneath her, silently pleading for more. Ryan moved to her inner thigh before lightly blowing against her heated center. Spreading Tobi's lips gently with her fingers, Ryan ran her tongue the full length of Tobi's velvety folds before sucking her clit into her mouth.

"Oh," Tobi gasped at the contact of Ryan's warm, wet tongue.

"Mmm, you like that, baby?"

"God, yes. Please don't stop."

Tobi moved her hips against Ryan's mouth, her fingers clenching and unclenching around the sheets, Ryan's moans of pleasure making her body scream for more. The pressure of her impending orgasm was almost more than Tobi could take...almost. Ryan's tongue was eliciting incredible sensations, and within seconds, Tobi arched up off the bed as her whole body exploded. Shuddering with aftershocks from the orgasm, Tobi threaded her fingers through Ryan's hair.

"Come here."

Ryan slid up next to Tobi and wrapped her in her arms. Tobi wanted to tell her exactly how she felt, but she couldn't find the words to convey what was in her head and her heart.

"I love you, Ryan."

"I love you, too, honey."

"You completely stun me. I've never felt what I do when I'm with you. Before now, I'm not sure I really knew what it was to be in love with someone."

Ryan shifted and rose up on one elbow, letting her eyes roam across Tobi's face before coming to rest upon her eyes. With a smile, she traced Tobi's lips with her finger.

"I know what you're feeling because I feel the same way.

Never have I felt so totally loved, and I'm not just talking about today, Tobi."

Rolling Ryan over onto her back, Tobi kissed her with every intention of letting her know just how important she was to her. Heated kisses, tender touches, and whispered words of love took them deep into the night. Wrapped tightly within each other's arms, they drifted into an exhausted slumber.

Chapter Fifteen

Ryan watched as Tobi slept in her arms. She was enraptured. To let go last night had felt so incredibly amazing. *Tobi was breathtaking.* The fervor of their lovemaking caught her totally by surprise. It had never been that way with anyone, and she certainly never thought that it could go on as long as it did. Even as they fell asleep, Ryan still wanted her.

Is it possible to be more in love with her than I already am?

A-ha!

Not you again.

So, you admit that you're in love with her?

I never denied that.

But you never outright admitted it either, did you?

Of course I did.

You said you love her, but you have never believed in that all-encompassing love that could shake a person to the core.

Go away!

Don't want to admit it exists? Or is it that you don't want to admit that you're shaken by how much you love her?

155

As she lay there arguing with herself, Ryan realized that Tobi's breathing had changed and glanced down. She was startled to see Tobi's eyes open and studying her.

Tobi smiled, leaned up on an elbow, and kissed her.

"Good morning."

"Mmm, good morning," Ryan said with a languid stretch.

"How did you sleep?"

"Like a baby…after you let me go to sleep."

"Me? I believe you were the one who couldn't keep her hands to herself," Tobi said with a laugh.

"I don't know what you're talking about."

With lightning speed, Tobi jumped up and straddled her hips. She grasped Ryan's wrists and held them above her head, grinning wickedly. Ryan knew she was in trouble as she tried to pull her arms away. She realized that Tobi was a lot stronger than she looked. Ryan raised an eyebrow but continued to smile. *I'll just try a different approach.*

"Tobi, baby, I love you."

When Tobi threw her head back to laugh, Ryan lunged forward, knocking Tobi onto her back and effectively reversing their positions. Her fingers curled around Tobi's as she leaned down and kissed her parted lips. She deepened the kiss and uncurled her fingers, lightly running them across Tobi's open palms and down her arms. Ryan released a ragged moan when Tobi's legs encircled her hips, pulling her closer.

Tobi slid a hand to the back of Ryan's neck, ran her nails down her chest making Ryan's nipples harden instantly. She circled a nipple with her fingertip before taking it into her mouth and sucking it.

"Oh," Ryan gasped. Her head dropped in submission as Tobi's pelvis started rocking against her own.

"You are so incredibly sexy, Ryan."

"You're making me crazy. God, I need you so bad."

"You have me…let it go, baby," she whispered.

Ryan moved her hips faster against Tobi's, knowing that the much-needed release she craved was almost there.

"That's it honey." Tobi licked her earlobe and nibbled gently as she whispered, "Come for me, Ryan."

With one last fervent thrust against Tobi, an orgasm ripped through Ryan's body, draining what energy she had left. She felt Tobi stiffen beneath her and knew she had followed right behind. Ryan kept an arm across Tobi's waist and a leg thrown between hers as she rolled off and to the side. Tobi raised her hand and swiped a bead of sweat from Ryan's brow with her thumb. She rested her fingers against Ryan's cheek and peered into her eyes with an intense look of love.

"I've never felt what I feel with you, Tobi...never." Ryan looked away before continuing. "I really didn't think I'd find this kind of love. I've always wanted the type of relationship my parents had, but gave up on it after putting so much into Stacey and me."

"I'm glad it didn't keep you from giving us a chance, Ryan. I love you so much."

"I love you, too."

As Ryan worked her lower lip, she wondered if now was a good time to talk to Tobi about going to her mother's.

"Tobi, there's something I wanted to discuss with you."

"What is it, honey?"

"Well, since you're going to be off the rest of the week, I was wondering if you'd consider going to my mom's while I'm at work."

"I'm fine. The headache has subsided, and there don't seem to be any other side effects."

"It's not that. It's just that I'm concerned about your being alone with this psycho still out there. I'd worry constantly."

Tobi stared at Ryan for a moment before responding. "If it would make you feel better, then I'll do it. The last thing I want is to worry you while you're working because then you wouldn't be concentrating, and I don't want you getting hurt again."

The myriad emotions swirling within Ryan made speaking difficult, and as a single tear fell, she knew it might convey the wrong message.

"I don't know what I did to deserve you, but I thank God everyday. I love you more than I can say, Tobi."

"I love you, too, baby."

Trying to lighten the mood, Ryan leaned back and said, "So, are you going to let me out of bed today?"

Tobi pretended to contemplate the question as she tapped a finger to her chin. "Hmm, well, if I have to."

"There is nothing I'd like better than to spend the entire day in bed with you; however, duty calls."

"Okay, why don't you go take your shower, and I'll start the coffee."

"That's an offer I can't refuse. As much as I'd like you to join me, I know you can't get those stitches wet. Some other time?"

"Absolutely. I'll hold you to it."

Untangling limbs, they both crawled out of bed. Ryan felt somewhat self-conscious as she looked around for her robe. Before she could reach for it, Tobi's hand grasped her arm.

"Don't," she said, pausing, "You're beautiful, Ryan, don't hide it."

Ryan looked into her eyes for endless seconds before nodding her head. With a huge grin, Tobi squeezed her arm before grabbing a T-shirt and padding out the door and down the hall. That one simple statement disclosed so much. More than anything, though, it said, "Don't be afraid." Ryan almost skipped into the bathroom.

As the aroma of the brewing coffee filled her senses, Tobi's thoughts meandered. She hadn't expected Ryan to let go so much, and the thought of someone breaking her heart made Tobi angry. How could someone take something so precious and taint it the way Stacey had done? Just the fraction of what Ryan had already given Tobi made her realize what a fool Stacey was for letting Ryan go. Shaking her head, she went to the cabinet and pulled down two mugs. Ryan exuded strength and integrity; one would never have guessed she had such a soft side. She was sweet and thoughtful, very loving, and one of the strongest people Tobi had ever known. *Stacey is an ass!*

"Hey there," a husky voice whispered in her ear. As Ryan's arms came around her, Tobi leaned into her and seized the roaming hands. She pressed them against her lips before kissing her knuckles. Tobi slowly turned in Ryan's arms to face her.

"Hey there yourself. Looks as if you had a nice shower," she said. She smiled while tucking a strand of hair behind Ryan's ear. "Your skin is nice and pink, and you smell delectable."

"Delectable, huh?" Ryan said with a wiggle of her eyebrows. Smacking Ryan's stomach with the back of her hand, Tobi picked up a cup and passed it to her. Ryan leaned against the counter and took a careful sip before glancing in Tobi's direction and grinning.

"What is that look for?"

"No reason. Having you here just makes me happy, happier than I've been in a very long time."

"Then, I look forward to an abundance of these happy mornings," Tobi replied, kissing her cheek. She left a hand against Ryan's cheek and whispered in her ear, "I love you."

Tobi wrapped her arms around Ryan and felt her tremble. She hoped her comment about more happy mornings was making Ryan shake in a good way. With Ryan's cheek resting against hers, Tobi could hear her breathing and knew that she was trying to calm herself. Knowing Ryan and the things she had shared about her past, Tobi was almost certain the intensity of the night before and this morning must have surprised her. As she leaned back in the circle of Ryan's arms, Tobi finally noticed the chilly morning air.

"Why don't we get dressed and you can call your mom," Tobi said.

"What, you don't like what I'm wearing?" Ryan asked, mischievously

Tobi ran a hand over Ryan's skimpy T-shirt before responding. "Oh, I like it all right. That's the problem. If you don't get dressed soon we'll never make it out of here."

"Okay, okay, I see your point."

"Ryan, you don't think she'll mind my coming over and camping out for the day, do you?"

Laughing, Ryan replied, "Mom? No, she won't mind at all. She'll probably welcome the chance to quiz you for more details."

"Details?"

"About us, honey."

"I see, and what exactly would you like me to tell her?"

"Anything you want. I trust you."

Tobi regarded her silently. *I trust you.* Those three little words conveyed more than Ryan would ever know. They went from taking small steps to giant leaps; it felt a little overwhelming, but it was a welcome feeling nonetheless.

"C'mon, honey, let's get dressed," Tobi said, taking her by the hand.

"I'll give Mom a call and then—," Ryan stopped abruptly when she entered the bathroom and caught Tobi's reflection in the mirror. Tobi was completely naked except for the flirtatious grin on her face.

"And then?" Tobi teased without turning around.

Ryan couldn't look away from her image even if she had tried. She stepped forward and wrapped her arms around Tobi, cupping a breast in each hand. She rolled puckered nipples between her fingers and pressed her body into Tobi's.

Tobi gasped and fell back against Ryan. "And then what, Ryan?"

Ryan swung her around and then lifted her onto the vanity. She moved between Tobi's thighs, pulling her hips closer at the same time. She leaned forward and licked a path up Tobi's neck to her ear.

"And then this," she whispered and proceeded to show Tobi the affect that saucy smile had on her. The delay was more than worth it.

Ryan glanced at the clock, knowing she didn't have much time before she needed to head into the precinct. She grabbed the phone and sat in the recliner, curled one leg under the other, and placed the call to her mom.

"Hello?"

"Hi, Mom."

"Well, hello, honey. What a pleasant surprise hearing from you today. What's up?"

"Can't a girl just call and talk to her mother?" Ryan asked indignantly.

Grace laughed as she replied, "Ryan, as long as you've been old enough to talk, I've never known you to make small talk on the telephone. You just aren't a phone person. So, as I said, what's up?"

"That's spooky, Mom. You know me too well."

After Ryan filled her in on the details of Tobi's attack, the break-in, and phone calls, Grace readily agreed to have Tobi stay with her as often as she wanted or needed.

"Thanks, Mom. We'll be over shortly."

"You're welcome, honey. I'll see you soon."

Ryan clicked the phone off, laid it on the end table, and relaxed against the chair. She used her free foot to set the chair rocking and sighed, as she thought about all that had transpired in the last few months. What a wild ride it had been, but she wouldn't change a thing, except for this psycho stalking Tobi. She wouldn't have believed it possible to be in love with someone and feel the way she did about Tobi in such a short time.

Ryan peered up as she felt a hand caress the top of her head and met her lover's eyes. With a smile, Tobi walked around the chair and perched herself on Ryan's lap. Ryan wrapped her hands around Tobi's waist and smiled in return.

"Is your mom all right with me coming over?"

"Of course. I told you she wouldn't mind. Matter of fact, she's looking forward to it."

"Should I be worried?"

"Hmm, maybe." Seeing the startled look on Tobi's face, Ryan grinned. "No, my mom really likes you, Tobi. I think she's looking forward to getting to know you a little better."

"Ah, so I should turn on the charm a little, huh?"

"Honey, you don't have to do anything differently; she likes you just the way you are."

"You think?"

"I know."

Ryan leaned forward and took Tobi's lips in a slow passionate kiss. Nibbling her bottom lip, Ryan coaxed her mouth open, and their tongues met. Tobi slid her hands up Ryan's arms and around her neck and pulled her closer so their chests were touching. Ryan could feel her nipples become taut, and her body was on fire. Tobi ended the kiss and took a deep breath, resting her forehead against Ryan's chin. Ryan placed a kiss on her forehead, and began rocking again. With Tobi's head resting against her chest, she closed her eyes and let her head fall back against the chair.

"I can feel your heart beating," Tobi said, breaking the silence.

"I'm sure you can; it tends to beat a little faster and harder whenever you're around."

"Good to know, Sergeant, good to know." She kissed Ryan's chin and stood up. "We'd better get ready. You have to get to work, and I have a date with your mother," Tobi said flippantly while heading up the stairs. Ryan laughed and pulled herself up to follow.

"Remember, if there's anything you need, don't hesitate to call."

"Ryan..." Tobi and Grace said in unison.

"Okay, okay...I'm going."

Almost shyly, she leaned in and kissed Tobi. Folding Tobi within her arms, Ryan whispered, "I love you," in her ear before releasing her.

Tobi whispered back, "I love you, too."

Ryan hugged her mother, turned, and with a wave was gone. Grace closed the door and turned to fix her gaze on Tobi.

"Tobi, please make yourself at home. I've got to do some things in the kitchen, so you can visit with me if you want, or you can just watch TV. There are some books on the shelf there. Help yourself if you'd like."

"That's very kind of you, Grace. I really appreciate everything. Would you mind if I sat in the kitchen with you?"

"Not at all, honey. C'mon."

Tobi followed her into the kitchen where Grace motioned for her to have a seat. "Would you like something to drink?"

"You don't have to wait on me."

"All right, sweetie, the glasses are there," Grace said, pointing, "and you can help yourself to anything in the refrigerator. I also have a fresh pot of coffee."

Traffic Stop

Tobi took a cup down and fixed some coffee before settling into a chair at the counter. As she sipped her coffee, Tobi watched Grace place various spices in a crock pot.

"How are you feeling?" Grace asked, glancing briefly over her shoulder at Tobi.

"I'm really not too bad, a little tired and a headache that comes and goes, but overall, I feel much better."

"If you need to lie down, please do," Grace said, turning around completely. "It won't bother me a bit, honey."

"Thank you, Grace."

"Oh, you don't have to thank me. You're important and special to Ryan, and that makes you important and special to me." After wiping her hands on a dishtowel, Grace tossed it back on the counter before moving to Tobi's side. "I've never seen Ryan take so quickly to someone as she has to you. I've always worried about her because she's my baby but even more so after her last breakup."

"With Stacey," Tobi said, nodding her head.

"You know about her, huh?"

"Ryan told me what happened, yes."

"I never liked that girl. She never wanted to spend time with our family, and when she did, she acted so put out. George kept telling me I wasn't giving her a chance, but a mother can just sense these things." George was Ryan's father, and from what she had heard of him, he was the fairest man a person could ever meet.

"Seems like you were more than justified in the way you felt."

"I wish I hadn't been. To see my baby hurt that way…" Grace blinked her eyes rapidly, and Tobi knew she was fighting off tears.

"I understand, Grace, believe me. I've had some purely evil thoughts where that woman is concerned."

Grace patted Tobi's hand as she smiled tremulously. "I'm so happy you're in her life. Please take care of her; she's so very important to me."

"I will do my absolute best."

"Now then, do you like chicken and noodles?"

"Mmm, I love chicken and noodles," Tobi said, practically drooling.

"It's one of Ryan's favorites, that and–"

163

Tara Wentz

"Mint chocolate chip ice cream," they said at the same time.

Laughing, Grace walked around the counter and wrapped Tobi in a motherly hug. "I really like you, Tobi. I can see that you're going to be very good for my daughter." After placing a kiss on the top of her head, Grace took Tobi's face between her hands and looked into her eyes.

"You look tired, sweetie. Why don't you go lie down on the couch and rest for a while?"

"I am a little. I also have a slight headache," Tobi admitted.

"Do you have something you can take?"

"Yes, Mom, I do," Tobi said, smiling gently.

Grace chuckled as she rubbed her thumb lightly against Tobi's cheek before motioning with her hand, "Well, get to it then."

Tobi took a pain pill from her pocket and swallowed it with a sip of coffee. Grace waited for her to hop down from the chair before showing her into the living room.

"Go ahead and lie down, sweetie. After Ryan called earlier, I brought a pillow and blanket out for you in case you wanted to rest."

Tobi curled up on the couch and shifted the pillow more comfortably under her head. Grace pulled a blanket over her and tucked it around her shoulders before reaching under the blanket to slip her shoes off and tuck her feet in.

"Sleep well, Tobi," Grace said with a fond caress to Tobi's hair.

"Thank you," Tobi murmured before falling fast asleep.

As Grace stood there watching for a few more moments, she slowly smiled to herself. *Oh, Ryan, did you ever hit the jackpot with this charming young woman.* Moving toward the doorway, she looked one last time at the sleeping form on the couch before disappearing into the kitchen.

Chapter Sixteen

R yan, why don't you just call her? You know it's going to drive you nuts if you don't," Jake said as they pulled to a stop at a red light.

Ryan tapped her foot and shifted in her seat. "Jake, if I keep calling, my mother is going to think I've lost it. I've called twice already, and everything is fine."

Jake turned the police radio down a notch before turning his attention to Ryan. "Then, why are you so damned fidgety?"

"I can't help it," she said, glancing out the car window. "This whole thing is starting to grate on my nerves something fierce. I don't like knowing that psycho son of a bitch is still out there." Ryan turned back to look at Jake, threw her hand out in exasperation and said, "What's more, I don't even know who the hell he is."

"I know, but just calm down. We're going to get him."

"When, Jake? When it's too damned late to do anything about it?" Frustrated, Ryan ran her hand over her hair and stared out the side window of the patrol car. She knew Jake was right but damned if she could help what was going on inside her head. Ryan wanted this bastard, and she wanted him now. "I'm sorry. I'm just scared for Tobi. It's getting too dangerous, and I feel so helpless."

Jake patted her leg before taking the wheel again to move through the green light. "I do understand. I know it's difficult sitting back and not being able to control any of this right now, but we will get him. We've sent in the request for the phone records; now, we just have to wait."

"I know," Ryan sighed. She needed to take her mind off the situation. Changing the subject, she asked, "How is Tim doing?"

"He's doing great. The flower shop has been booming with business. He hired another lady to help him out during the day since he's gotten so busy. She's in her seventies, but he swears she runs circles around him," he said, laughing.

"Now, that I find hard to believe. I've never met a person with more energy than Tim. He wears me out just watching him."

"He thinks the sun rises and sets around her. She is very good, though. Her bouquets are absolutely beautiful. Speaking of which, you should send something to Tobi."

"That's not a bad idea, Jakey," Ryan said, lightly punching him in the arm.

Two hours later, after dealing with a drunk and disorderly who decided to puke in the back of the car, Jake decided it was time for lunch.

"Jake, how can you eat after the smell in that car?"

"I'm hungry, what can I say?"

As they slid into a booth, a waitress appeared to take their order.

"I'll have the cheeseburger platter and a large Coke, please," Jake replied. Ryan was completely shocked because Jake was always so fanatical about eating healthy. It took a few seconds of prodding from the waitress before she gave her order.

"Uh, just a chicken Caesar salad and an iced tea, thanks," she said, handing the waitress the menu. She waited for her to leave before starting in on Jake.

"What the hell? You never order food like that. What's going on?"

"Ryan, you don't eat every meal with me. Besides, I'm happy and I'm starving."

"Yeah, but...are you sure nothing is wrong?"

"I'm positive. Look, I'm just in a peaceful stage in my life right now. I'm with the man of my dreams, and one of my best friends has finally found the woman of her dreams. I'll pay for it later, but right now, I'm going to enjoy it."

"She is pretty amazing, isn't she?" Ryan said with a huge smile.

"You just beam whenever you talk about her, and it's even worse when you're around each other. It's sickeningly sweet. I love it."

A blushing Ryan reached for the phone vibrating at her hip. Seeing the number, she glanced up at Jake just as he rolled his eyes and gestured with his hand to hurry up and answer it.

"Hello," Ryan responded.

"Hi, baby. How is your day going?"

"It's much better now. How's yours?"

"It's going great. Your mother is a blast. We've been playing cards, but I'm starting to think she cheats." When Ryan burst out laughing, she asked, "What's so funny?"

"Tobi, my mother is a card shark. No matter what game she's playing, she always wins. Don't ask me how she does it because I have no idea."

"Figures," she said with a chuckle. "Not much going on, huh?"

"Nope, just a drunk who decided to use the cruiser as his personal puke pan."

"That's disgusting, Ryan. Whatcha doing now?"

"Jake and I stopped for a late lunch. We're waiting for the food to get here. Have you been taking it easy?"

"Would your mother have it any other way?"

As the waitress set their lunch and drinks down, Ryan took a sip of her tea. "Mmm, not likely, honey. I'm glad to hear it, though; the rest is good for you."

"I won't keep you. I just wanted to tell you that I'm thinking about you and I love you."

"I love you, too. Tell Mom I said hello."

167

Ryan heard her relay the slightly muffled message. "She said hello back, honey, and not to spoil your dinner because she made your favorite."

"Oh, chicken and noodles?"

"Yes," Tobi said, laughing. "Be careful. I'll see you later."

"You got it, sweetheart."

Ryan closed the phone and looked to an amused Jake. "Don't even think about it," she said with a raised eyebrow. She knew Jake well enough to know that if she let him get started, she would never hear the end of it. He loved to tease her, and it didn't matter what it was about.

They finished lunch, dropped some money on the table, and headed back out. The last couple of shifts had been relatively quiet, so they both expected all hell to break loose at some point. What they didn't expect was for it to happen with only forty-five minutes left to their shift. They had been making regular rounds through the river bottoms after several reports of suspicious activity in the area. For over a week, they hadn't noticed anything out of the ordinary, but on this day, they saw two unfamiliar cars in front of one of the warehouses. As they pulled around back, Ryan called in their location.

"I haven't noticed these cars down here before, have you?" Jake inquired.

"No. I've not seen either of them this past week. I'll go around the left side."

"I'll meet you around front," he said, heading toward the right.

Ryan kept her back to the wall and her weapon braced between both hands, and quietly made her way toward the front. A quick glance around the edge of the building showed that Jake was already in position. She scanned the perimeter and noticed there were three men, two of whom were in a heated discussion. As their hands gestured at each other, Ryan could see one of the men holding a gun. She glanced back at Jake, and he acknowledged that he saw the weapon, as well. Ryan thumbed her walkie-talkie, calling for backup. She and Jake kept surveillance on the situation while waiting for backup to arrive. Ryan couldn't hear the conversation between the men, but the aggressive nature of those hand gestures and the raised voices put her on edge.

Fuck! We can't wait any longer or this situation is going to get out of control really fast.

She looked at Jake and circled her finger in the air. He nodded his agreement and stepped forward to announce their presence. They would subdue first and ask questions later.

"Police! Drop the gun and put your hands on your head!"

The two men immediately quit arguing and turned to Jake. He stood with his weapon trained on them as the man with the gun threw it to the ground and raised his hands in the air.

"Shit!" he exclaimed, as Jake got closer to him.

"Turn around and put your hands on the car." Seeing the other hesitate, Jake replied, "That means both of you." As he patted them down and placed them in cuffs, Ryan knew Jake had not seen the third man stooped behind the car.

Ryan kept him in her sights as she walked closer to the car. He was standing on the other side, so she could not see his hands, but from his body language, she could tell he was becoming impatient. She got as close as she could without exposing herself when he swiveled his head toward her and glared.

"Put your hands where I can see them!"

As if in slow motion, the man jumped across the hood of the car, putting Jake between himself and Ryan. Seeing no other option, he took off toward the back of the building.

"Damn!" Ryan mumbled as she holstered her weapon and ran past Jake. She rounded the corner in pursuit and could hear Jake talking to Dispatch asking where backup was. She caught a glimpse of the man turning left and knew he was headed toward the docks. If she didn't cover some ground fast, he would be lost among the crates scattered about. She increased her stride and arrived on the docks a few seconds behind him as he darted behind the first large crate and disappeared from sight.

Ryan drew her weapon and crouched behind the same crate before slowly making her way around it. Pivoting, she swung into a squatted stance and took aim. The man was nowhere in sight, so she skimmed the area before moving ahead. Without making a sound, Ryan weaved around the various crates and barrels, eventually coming upon a large metal container where she stopped and listened. What sounded like a light scratching noise was coming from the other side. Ryan slid along the side and peered around the edge to see a cord hanging loosely from a tarp that was gently blowing in the breeze and rubbing against the crate. She barely had time to react as she turned and a large shoulder hit the right side of her chest, knocking her to the wooden floor and sending her gun clattering. Casting a glance over her shoulder, Ryan could see the rippling water of the river below. *Shit!* She scrambled to her feet as the attacker tried to wrap his arms around her shoulders, but a well-placed elbow to his gut and the back of a fist to his nose sent him sprawling.

"C'mon man, you don't wanna do this," Ryan said, holding a hand out to ward him off.

"How do you know what I want, bitch?"

Climbing back to his knees, he jumped at her. Ryan stood stock still, catching Jake out of the corner of her eye, hurling himself toward the man. In the process of intercepting him, Jake stumbled into Ryan. Her feet lost purchase on the dock, and her arms flailed as she tumbled into the ice cold depths of the water below. She gasped and inhaled a mouthful of water before sinking below the surface. As she drifted toward the bottom, Ryan kicked her feet to propel herself back toward the surface. Lungs burning, her head finally emerged. She felt several pairs of hands grab and pull her to the dock. Ryan coughed and hacked until eventually she rolled to her knees and vomited. She remained hunched down on her knees and rested her forehead against the wooden planks. Trying to take deep breaths, Ryan felt a warm hand against her back and one on her arm.

"You okay, Thomas?"

"Yeah," Ryan rasped.

"Let's get you up then."

With Jake's help, she got to her feet, wincing at the ache in her ribs and chest. While they watched the man being led away from the dock in cuffs, Jake placed a blanket around her shoulders. She brought her left arm across her chest to hold her sore right ribs, then walked carefully back to the patrol car with him. Jake held the door for her as she gingerly eased her aching body down onto the seat. Jake helped her buckle her seat belt, shut the door, and climbed into the driver's side.

"Do you need to go to the hospital?"

"I'm okay, just a little sore and cold," Ryan said, shivering.

"Are you sure?"

"I'm positive."

"Okay then, I'm going to take you home. I'll go in, do the reports, and you can check them tomorrow."

"My car is at the station, and Tobi is at Mom's, so I need to pick her up. Why don't you just take me to the station, and I'll go home from there."

"You gonna be all right to drive?"

Ryan rolled her head to the side and looked at him. "I'll be fine." She held his gaze a few moments before he finally nodded.

"I'm really sorry about that. I never meant to knock you into the water."

Ryan placed her hand over his and squeezed gently before turning her head back and closing her eyes. "I know that, Jake. I'm just glad you were there. He'd already gotten in a good shot to my ribs. Thanks for saving my butt."

"That's what partners are for," he said as he handed Ryan her retrieved weapon.

Jake started the car and headed toward the precinct.

Tobi knew Ryan was supposed to be home almost an hour ago and began to worry. She glanced at the clock for the umpteenth time when she noticed Grace quietly observing her.

"She'll be home soon, honey."

"I know. It's just that with everything going on, I guess I'm a little more anxious than usual."

"I understand. Would you like another cup of coffee?"

"Actually, that sounds really good."

Tobi followed her into the kitchen and watched as she finished filling their cups before speaking. "I really appreciate your letting me spend the day here. I've enjoyed it, and I know Ryan felt better."

"It was my pleasure, Tobi. I liked having the opportunity to spend time with you. I happen to think you are a delightful young woman, and my daughter is lucky to have you in her life."

Tobi demurely replied, "I feel like the lucky one, Grace. Your daughter is an amazing woman."

"I happen to think so, but then, I'm her mother," she said, smiling. "I hope you'll always feel welcome in my home whether it's with Ryan in tow or not."

"I already do."

They heard a car and made their way to the front of the house. Tobi stood off to the side and waited while Grace opened the door.

"Good Lord, Ryan, what happened to you?" Grace asked with concern.

Soaking wet from head to toe and shivering, Ryan made her way into the house. Tobi scrutinized her closely but didn't see any visible signs of injury. She noticed, however, that Ryan was moving rather gingerly.

"Are you okay, honey?"

"Yeah, I'm just freezing."

"What happened?" Ryan's mother asked.

"Well, we came across some unusual activity down at the river bottoms and while we were taking the men responsible into custody, one took off. I ran after him and followed him down to the docks. To make a long story short, Jake took him down but not before knocking me over the edge of the dock and into the water."

With a sigh of relief, Grace replied, "Well, I'm glad you're all right. Raef still has some clothes upstairs. Why don't you go on up and take a hot shower before dinner?"

"Thanks, Mom. I'll be right back down."

Tobi watched as she made her way up the stairs before looking back to Grace. Taking her eyes off her daughter, Grace glanced at Tobi, and with a gesture of her head, said, "Go ahead. I'll holler when dinner's ready."

"Thanks," Tobi said, hurrying up the steps. She met Ryan coming out of one of the bedrooms. Sweats and socks in hand, Ryan stopped and regarded her silently.

Tobi took her hand and said, "C'mon." Walking into the bathroom, Ryan set the clothes on the counter and with shaking fingers attempted to unbutton her shirt.

"Here, let me." Tobi moved Ryan's hands aside, unbuttoned her shirt, and pulled it from her shoulders. As she tugged the shirt off, Tobi noticed Ryan's white T-shirt clinging to her, revealing her well-defined torso. Tobi grasped the edge of the shirt and pulled it up and over Ryan's head. She felt a quick stab of desire that was immediately extinguished when Ryan whimpered. Dropping her eyes to Ryan's chest, she could see a large mottled bruise already forming from just under her arm all the way down the side of her ribs and under her right breast.

"Is this where he got you?" Tobi asked as her fingers lightly moved across Ryan's skin.

"Yeah," Ryan said, kicking off her shoes and undoing her belt. With some effort, she attempted to push her wet pants down her hips. Tobi watched her struggle, then knelt and peeled off Ryan's pants. She removed her socks and took a cold foot between her hands.

"Let's get you into the shower. You're like ice."

Tobi helped her out of her bra and panties then stepped aside so she could enter the shower. Ryan adjusted the water and stepped beneath the spray.

Tobi pulled the curtain. "I'll be right here if you need anything."

"Um, do you think you could help me wash my hair? It pulls too much when I raise my arms."

"Sure."

She slipped out of her clothes and climbed into the shower. "Turn around, sweetheart." Tobi released the band holding Ryan's hair back and poured shampoo into her palm. She used her fingers and nails to massage the clean-smelling gel throughout Ryan's hair before rinsing it out and applying the conditioner. Tobi lathered up a washcloth and gently ran it over Ryan's bruised body.

"You don't have to do that," Ryan murmured.

"I know I don't, but I want to, so just relax."

As the water washed away the remaining soap and conditioner, Tobi leaned in and enclosed Ryan lightly within her arms to place a kiss above her right breast. Ryan wrapped her arms around Tobi and ran the tip of her tongue across Tobi's bottom lip. She nipped lightly at Tobi's top lip before slipping her tongue into her mouth. Heat coursed through Ryan's body as their tongues melded. "I love you," Ryan whispered through the intoxicating kiss. She shifted their positions, so Tobi's head would not get wet then leaned her back against the wall and slid a silky thigh between her open legs. Moaning from the contact, Ryan pulled her lips from Tobi's and nuzzled her way down her neck. She brought her hand up Tobi's side and clasped a nipple between her fingers, gently rolling it.

With the onslaught of Ryan's attentions, it was all Tobi could do to remain standing, much less hold off the impending orgasm. Tobi moved her hips against Ryan's thigh, barely registering the knock on the bathroom door.

"Girls?"

They jumped apart, and Tobi hid her face in her hands as Ryan responded breathlessly, "Yeah, Mom?"

"Dinner's ready."

"Thanks, we'll be right down."

Ryan groaned and pressed her forehead to the wall above Tobi's shoulder. "Don't suppose you'd want to finish what we started, would you?"

"Ryan! Your mother is right outside that door. I most certainly will not finish what you started."

Sighing, Ryan responded, "You're killing me, Tobi."

Tobi smiled with a cocky grin. "Guess it's a good thing there's a doctor in the house then, huh?"

Ryan chuckled, turned off the water, and opened the curtain. She stepped out and handed Tobi a towel. Drying quickly, Tobi pulled on her clothes and helped Ryan with hers. She towel dried Ryan's hair and pulled the comb through it before holding out her hand for Ryan to grasp.

"Let's go eat, honey."

Ryan held Tobi's hand as she grabbed the wet towels to take to the laundry room and flipped the light off on their way out the door.

Chapter Seventeen

As the two women left Grace's house, Victor Santiago slouched down in the seat of the van grumbling to himself.

"Don't think you can hide from me, you stupid bitch, 'cause I know everything there is to know about you. Didn't know that I've been following you for days, did you, little girl?"

He watched them back out of the drive and pull away before sitting up straighter and tossing the burger wrapper behind him. He took a sip of soda and started the van.

"Fuck! Fuck! Fuck!" Victor shouted in anger, slamming his fist against the steering wheel.

He glared at the Jeep a few cars ahead of him as he shook his stinging hand.

"What gives you the right to go about livin' your life and being so happy all the time, huh?"

Rocking from side to side, he continued, "It won't be long before you'll know what it's like to really hurt. There won't be a damned thing you can do about it, either, just like I couldn't."

Victor followed as the Jeep turned onto a residential street and sped past when it turned into a driveway. He glanced in the rearview mirror and saw the vehicle pull into the garage. Turning at the next street, he yanked the van to the side of the road. He was breathing heavily as he extracted a small envelope from his pocket. He shook two pills into his palm, tossed his head back, and swallowed them down dry. Quivering with the rage inside him, he sat planning his next move until the pills took effect. The pills allowed the anger to dissipate, if only minimally, as he put the van in gear and drove away.

Ryan eased into a kitchen chair and rested her arms along the tabletop. Tobi had driven the Jeep home because Ryan's side was hurting, and she was not too proud to admit it.

"I'll be right back, sweetheart," Tobi said and disappeared into the other room.

Tobi stepped back into the kitchen with several items in her hands. She filled a glass from the cabinet with juice before sitting at the table next to Ryan.

"Here, honey, take these then I'll wrap your ribs."

"What are they?" Ryan asked, taking the pills.

"Just a couple of my pain pills. I thought it might help you sleep better tonight."

"Thanks." She washed the pills down with a swallow of juice. She looked at Tobi and smiled as she raised her hand and caressed the side of Tobi's cheek. Ryan pushed a lock of hair behind her ear and rested her hand on Tobi's shoulder.

Tobi stood and bent to kiss Ryan's forehead. "Why don't you go on upstairs? I'll lock up and turn the lights out. C'mon," she said, holding out a hand. "I'll be right behind you."

Ryan took her hand and, with Tobi's help, got to her feet. She kissed her lightly on the lips, turned, and made her way upstairs.

Ryan shuffled into the bedroom and turned the light on beside the bed. Since her shoes had been soaked, she wore home an old pair of Raef's tennis shoes. They were a couple of sizes too big, but at least they were dry. She placed a hand on the dresser to keep her balance and used her toe to kick them off. She pulled open a dresser drawer and grabbed a T-shirt and some panties.

Going commando for a short time was fine but definitely not something she would do on a regular basis. Ryan pushed the sweatpants off her hips and removed them, as well as her socks.

Tobi watched from the doorway and grimaced in sympathetic pain as Ryan slowly stood upright.

"If you weren't hurting so much right now, this would be an incredible turn-on."

"You mean it's not?" Ryan said, taunting her.

"Honey, fully clothed, you are one hot woman. Half-naked is more than I can stand. My fingers are itching to touch you, but you're in no condition to do anything tonight." Holding up her hand to stave off the comment she knew was coming, Tobi added, "Plus, it won't be long before those pain pills kick in, and you'll be out like a light."

"You're probably right," Ryan said, sighing.

Tobi walked over to stand in front of her. She took the clothes from Ryan's hands and knelt down to help slide the satiny cloth up her legs. Tobi kissed her hip before standing up. She helped Ryan remove the sweatshirt and then raised Ryan's right arm.

"Hold that up, and I'll get you trussed up here." Ryan placed her hand behind her head and watched as Tobi wrapped the ACE bandage snugly around her chest.

"Is that too tight?"

"No, it feels about right."

After pulling the T-shirt on, she sat heavily on the edge of the bed. Studying Ryan's features, Tobi could see her eyes blinking rapidly and knew she was fighting the pull of the medicine that was forcing her body to shut down.

"Go ahead and crawl under the covers, honey, and I'll be right back."

She crossed to the bathroom and glanced back over her shoulder. Ryan hadn't moved except to rub her eyes like a sleepy child. Tobi smiled affectionately before stepping in and closing the door. Tobi went about her nightly routine and thought back to how sweet Ryan's mother had been today. She was so attentive but not overly so. Ryan was extremely lucky to have this woman still in her life. Ryan looked a lot like her mother. But the intensity of her eyes was a quality garnered from her father, whose eyes were identical in shape and color. Tobi watched Grace and Ryan together and realized why some of Grace's hand movements and facial expressions seemed so familiar—like mother, like daughter.

Tobi laid the hairbrush down and opened the door, only to stop in her tracks. Ryan was exactly where she had left her, except she was lying on her back with her legs dangling over the edge of the bed, and she was fast asleep.

Tobi sidled up to Ryan and studied her face. She seemed pale but otherwise peaceful. And her breathing was deep, indicating she wasn't seriously hurt. *Now that's a relief!*

"Ryan, honey, come on. Let's get you into bed."

Ryan mumbled, but hardly moved a muscle. Tobi tried again by lightly patting her cheek.

"Ryan…wake up, sweetie."

Ryan begrudgingly opened her eyes and tried to focus. . "What?"

Tobi took her arm and helped her sit up and turn before getting her situated under the covers. She slipped her T-shirt off and crawled into bed herself. After tucking the blankets around Ryan, she turned to shut off the light.

Ryan moved her body closer to Tobi's and draped an arm across her waist. Rubbing her hand up and down Ryan's arm, Tobi turned her head and kissed Ryan's lips.

"I love you," Ryan said sleepily.

"I love you, too, baby."

The pain pills that Tobi gave Ryan had effectively knocked her out. She was still wrapped around Tobi and very groggy when she woke up. Ryan was in no hurry to get up, not that Tobi seemed to mind either. From her resting spot against Tobi's shoulder she had an unobstructed view of smooth creamy breasts and rose-tipped nipples. She slid her hand up over Tobi's warm stomach and cupped a soft breast in her palm.

"Mmm," Tobi moaned and then stretched.

Ryan raised her chin so she could look at Tobi's face. Sparkling blue eyes captured her own. Ryan smiled, but said nothing.

Tobi rubbed a thumb over Ryan's cheek and leaned in to kiss her lips.

She kept the kiss simple and then lay back. "Good morning, sweetheart."

"Good morning, yourself," Ryan replied with a croak. She cleared her throat before continuing. "I guess we better get a move on, huh?"

Tobi took a quick peek at the bedside clock before answering. "Looks like it. How do you feel?"

"Stiff and sore, but I'll live."

"Ahuh. Let's go, tough girl." Tobi untangled herself from Ryan and stood to help her out of bed.

After the slow start to the morning, Tobi and Ryan finally made their way to Grace's but not before stopping at Tobi's place so she could pick up her mail and grab more clothes. When Ryan left, her lover and her mother were engrossed in a conversation over some show on HG-TV.

Ryan arrived at the precinct and was surprised to find she was assigned to desk duty for the next couple of days, the result of the scuffle and impromptu swim of the previous day. Normally, this would have put her in a foul mood, but it gave her the opportunity to investigate Mrs. Sylvia Hyde's background a little more. The search warrant for the phone records should be available, as well. She had convinced the judge to sign for a search warrant based on a reasonable person standard claiming that the phone records might have information in regards to a suspicious activity.

Ryan rolled her chair over to the database computer and typed in her login information. As she waited for the hourglass to fill and tip and fill again, Ryan blew out a breath of frustration when the page came up "Temporarily Unavailable."

"Damn."

She drummed her fingers lightly on the desk patiently waiting before making another attempt. On the second attempt she tapped into the case index to see if Mrs. Hyde had ever made a police report, reported a crime, witnessed a crime, or been arrested by their department. Ryan didn't find anything there so she moved on to the woman's driving record, which showed only one incident, and that was a speeding ticket three years ago. After going through CopLink and the National Crime Information Center with no luck, Ryan leaned back thoughtfully in her chair.

Feeling a light thump to the back of her head, she looked up to see Jake standing beside her.

"Hey, Jake."

"Hey there yourself," he said, hesitating before speaking again.. "I hope you're not upset with having desk duty."

"I'm not angry at all. This just gives me the opportunity to do some more investigating on Sylvia Hyde."

"Did you find anything?"

"Not yet. The only thing I've come up with is a speeding ticket three years ago."

"Did you check CopLink and NCIC already?"

"Yep, came up with zilch."

"That search warrant you wanted came in," he said, handing Ryan the paper. "Maybe those phone records will help."

"Yeah," she said, slapping the paper against her knee. "Do you think the captain would let me pursue this?"

"I don't know why not. It's not like you're out on patrol. He's in his office, so why don't you go talk to him?"

Ryan shifted nervously before standing. She glanced at Jake when he started laughing.

"What are you laughing at?"

"You, that's what. He's not an ogre, Ryan. You avoid him at all costs just because he intimidates the hell out of you."

Ryan glared at him but didn't respond.

"Ryan?"

"What?" Ryan mumbled.

"Just go talk to him."

She nodded and walked over to a doorway, knocking lightly before peeking in. Captain Luther Vitrolli waved her in while he finished his phone conversation. Ryan took a seat in front of his desk and studied the awards and certificates on his wall.

Hanging up, he leaned forward in his chair and regarded Ryan for a minute before speaking. "What can I do for you, Sergeant?"

"I…" she took a deep breath and began again. "I wanted to get your permission to follow up on a search warrant I requested on some phone records."

"Is this concerning the situation involving Dr. Drexler?"

"Yes, sir."

"Thomas, do you think that maybe you're a little too close to this case?"

"Sir?"

"Ryan, don't fuck with me here; you know what I'm talking about."

"I just want to obtain the records and look through them, Captain. There's got to be something in them that will give us some clue as to what was going on with Mrs. Hyde. "

He leaned back in his chair and sighed before responding. "Okay, get the records and you can look them over, but if you find anything, and I mean anything at all, you need to let me know. Do you understand me?"

"Yes, sir. Thank you, sir."

Captain Vitrolli watched her walk away and smiled as he picked up a folder on his desk. He knew she was one of the best cops in his division, smart as hell, too. He tended to be a little harsher with her than most would expect, but it was because Ryan demanded that of him. *"No special treatment. Push me if you think I need to be pushed,"* were her exact words the first day on duty. She was destined for bigger and better things whether she knew it or not, and he would be there to support her the whole way.

After obtaining Sylvia Hyde's cell phone records directly from the service provider, Ryan walked back and sat in the car to look through them. She noticed several numbers that popped up frequently. One Ryan recognized as Sylvia Hyde's own home phone number. The others she would put into the database and see what name they came up with.

Ryan drove back to the station, pushed through the door, and made her way to her desk. She typed in the numbers from the records and waited. As the results displayed, she printed them off and studied them. The first number was a cell phone number for

David Hyde. The second was for a woman named Cynthia Raleigh. *I wonder if that's the Cindy David referred to.* The last number was for a Geraldo Santiago.

Ryan felt the phone vibrate at her hip, grabbed it, and flipped it open in one movement.

"Thomas."

"Oh, don't you sound all butch and sexy?" Tobi purred.

Ryan knew the heat in her chest and neck were working their way to her face, so she turned her back to the rest of the office before responding.

"Stop that," she replied hoarsely. Hearing her in that husky low voice sent tingles down Ryan's spine. "Do you have any idea the hassle I would get if anyone saw me right now?"

Tobi laughed and responded, "Oh, baby, tell me more."

"You are so bad," Ryan exclaimed, giving Tobi a few minutes to quit laughing. "What are you up to?"

"Not a whole lot. Your mom and I watched TV for a while, and now she's puttering around in the kitchen doing something. I was reading and thought I'd take a few minutes to see how you were doing."

"I got assigned to desk duty, so I'm doing fine."

"Desk duty? Is that because of what happened yesterday?"

"Yes."

"I'm sorry, honey."

"Don't be; it gives me time to do more checking on our friend Sylvia Hyde. It also means I'll be home on time tonight."

"That was going to be my next question. So, I guess I'll see you in a little bit then."

"That you will. I should be home in about forty-five minutes."

"Okay, I love you."

"I love you, too, sweetheart."

Ryan hung up and turned back to the computer, keying in a few more numbers before sitting back and waiting. She jerked forward and stared at the screen. She couldn't believe what she saw next to the flashing cursor.

"What the hell?"

Chapter Eighteen

R yan, why aren't you out of here yet?"
"Come take a look at this, Jake."
He stood behind her and glanced over her shoulder.
Pointing at the screen, he asked, "You mean this?"

"Yeah."

"It says he's deceased. What's the big deal?"

"Look at the date."

"January 16, 1997...I still don't get what this is about."

Ryan turned to face him and replied, "Jake, the computer says that this man is dead, but that is the exact name and birth date that comes up when I put in one of the phone numbers from Sylvia Hyde's phone records."

"Maybe Geraldo Santiago needs to be looked into a little further," Jake said, frowning.

"My thoughts exactly. However, I need to get home before Tobi starts wondering where the hell I am."

"C'mon, I'll walk you out."

Ryan and Tobi headed home after a short conversation with Grace. On the way, they decided to just order a pizza for dinner.

They sat curled on the couch together while waiting for the delivery guy to bring their dinner. Sitting side by side with her arm over Tobi's shoulders, Ryan sifted her fingers through Tobi's hair.

"So, you had a good day then, huh?" Ryan asked.

"Yes, your mother is great. She's so easy to talk to, and I love spending time with her. Not to mention all the wonderful pictures she has shown me."

"Pictures? What kind of pictures?"

"Oh, you know, just some of you growing up and of the family." Tobi looked at Ryan since she sounded almost upset. "You okay?"

"Yeah, I'm fine. I was just wondering which pictures she showed you. I was such a gawky girl."

"I thought you were cute. You just finally grew into those long legs of yours." Tobi saw Ryan's teeth pulling on her lower lip and sat up a little straighter.

"Ryan, is something else wrong?"

"No, I was just thinking is all."

"Okay, well, do you want to share what's on your mind?"

Ryan removed her arm and stood up, pacing across the living room. She walked to the bookshelf and ran a finger across it before turning back to face Tobi.

"It's this whole thing with this attacker and the phone calls, Tobi." Ryan threw her arms out in frustration and then swung around to face the bookcase again. She rested her hands against a shelf and dropped her head a little. "It just seems so strange. It's like the pieces are there, but we aren't making the connection."

Tobi moved toward Ryan and wrapped her arms around her waist. "Did something else happen?"

Ryan turned and let her arms relax over the top of Tobi's shoulders. "I got Sylvia Hyde's phone records. There were several numbers that appeared more often than any others. When I plugged them into the computer, one of them came back a little odd."

"What do you mean, a little odd?"

"The name that matches the number was of a man who apparently...isn't alive."

"How can that be?"

"I don't know. It's one of the things that Jake and I are going to check into. It's got me curious, though."

"I can see why. Just be careful, okay?"

Ryan leaned down and kissed Tobi on the lips. "Always." Tobi returned Ryan's kiss and felt arms enclose her and pull her tight. Ryan nibbled on her lip, waiting for Tobi's mouth to open before sliding her tongue inside. As the kiss heated up, Ryan could feel Tobi's nipples harden against her. Ryan rubbed her palm across Tobi's breast and gently squeezed. Tobi moaned and walked her backward toward the couch. Just as Ryan felt the back of her knees bump against it, the doorbell rang.

"His timing is impeccable," Ryan said.

"Absolutely." Kissing Ryan one last time, Tobi stepped around her to get the door. She heard a thump and turned back to see Ryan face down on the couch and groaning. Laughing, Tobi opened the door to fetch their pizza.

While Ryan cleaned up the pizza mess, Tobi squatted down before the stereo and turned on a soft, slow tune. She stood back up and walked over to Ryan, who was leaning against the wall watching. Tobi turned down the lights, took her hand, and pulled her to the center of the room.

"Dance with me?"

"Um, Tobi, I really don't dance very well."

"Put your arms around me and just move with me," Tobi said, positioning her arms across Ryan's shoulders and sliding her fingers into the hair on the back of her neck.

Ryan nodded and placed her hands on Tobi's waist. As Tobi's hips started moving, Ryan watched her feet and slowly moved with her.

Tobi slid her hands down Ryan's chest and wrapped her arms around her. She smiled and laid her head on Ryan's shoulder. They danced for some time before the words of the song started sinking in, making Tobi's feet slow down until they were almost standing still. She could feel Ryan's heartbeat beneath her ear as they listened. The lyrics spoke so strongly of the heartache Ryan had been through; the moments of crying and of needing a friend to comfort her from the hurt. Tobi wanted to be there to always kiss away Ryan's tears.

Tobi looked intently into Ryan's eyes and could see the emotion mirrored in them.

Ryan leaned in and kissed Tobi with all the heat and passion that she was feeling as the last verse played.

Tobi hummed with the music and whispered in Ryan's ear as the song ended. "I'm going to stand by your side, so you'll never feel alone."

Tobi took Ryan's hand and tugged her to the carpet. She knelt in front of Ryan and took her face between her hands and sent a searing kiss across her lips. Tobi tangled her hands in Ryan's hair, tilted her head back, and bit her chin softly before moving to nuzzle her neck. Tobi heard the moan deep in Ryan's throat as she took an earlobe between her teeth and gently blew in her ear. *Mother of God! Ryan is going to send me over the edge without even touching me!*

Ryan yanked Tobi into her arms, and they tumbled back until Tobi came to rest fully on top of her. Ryan groaned quietly, and Tobi shifted her body, so she was lying mostly next to her, realizing they had forgotten about her sore ribs.

"Sorry, sweetheart," Tobi said, moving a tress of hair behind her ear.

Ryan's head was resting in the crook of Tobi's arm as she caressed Ryan's mouth with her own. Tobi moved a hand gradually up her thigh, dipping her fingers underneath Ryan's shirt to stroke the hard, yet smooth surface of her abdomen. Ryan trembled slightly below her and Tobi could feel the ridges of goose bumps forming on her skin.

"Cold?"

"No," Ryan rasped. "I love you, Tobi."

"I love you, too, baby."

"Make love to me?"

"I thought you'd never ask," Tobi said, grinning.

Tobi helped her sit up and stripped her shirt and bra off. Ryan laid back down as Tobi nuzzled her chest, taking in the scent that was distinctly Ryan.

Ryan's nipples were hard, and she was breathing heavily. Tobi curled her hands inside the waistband of Ryan's jeans, popped the button, and slid the zipper down. Each click from the teeth on the zipper sent Ryan's libido into overdrive.

"Raise your hips, honey."

Ryan lifted her hips and Tobi slid the jeans and panties down inch by agonizing inch. Tobi brushed each knee with her lips before stopping at Ryan's ankles to remove her shoes. She tugged each sock slowly from Ryan's feet and grinned while tossing them aside. Tobi nipped at her toes then grasped the legs of her jeans and pulled them off. Tobi ran her hands back up over Ryan's ankles and gathered the silky panties in her fingers. She removed them with ease and laid them aside.

Tobi caressed the soft skin around Ryan's ankles and shifted to enclose strong calf muscles within her palms. She squeezed gently before sliding her hands up and over Ryan's knees to the inside of her smooth, warm thighs.

Ryan whimpered as Tobi's hands moved up and over her pelvis without making contact with the part of her that needed it most.

Tobi supported herself above Ryan's hips and leaned down to run her tongue across Ryan's navel. Ryan quivered as Tobi's tongue traced a path around her navel, up her abdomen, and into the valley between her breasts.

Ryan drew her breath in sharply when Tobi moistened one nipple and then the other with her tongue. Tobi rolled a nipple between her fingers and gently bit down on the other.

"Please," Ryan said in a voice hoarse with desire.

Tobi slowly kissed her way down to the thatch of soft curly hair between Ryan's legs. The scent of Ryan's arousal spurred Tobi along. The smell was driving her insane, and Tobi couldn't wait another minute to taste her. Tobi ran her tongue the full length of Ryan's moist folds and gently flicked the hardened nub.

Sweet Jesus! Tobi's own heart rate skyrocketed after one delicious sample of Ryan.

Ryan arched her back and groaned at the sweet torture Tobi was wreaking on her.

"Baby," Ryan rasped. "Please, I need you."

Ryan bent her knees and gave Tobi her complete trust by dropping her legs wide open and exposing herself. Tobi kissed each thigh before returning to Ryan's heated center. She slid a finger then two slowly inside while sucking on the bundle of nerves, threatening to send Ryan over the edge.

"Oh, God, Tobi…honey, that feels so good."

Tobi twisted her fingers a little and again stroked her tongue across Ryan's hard clit as she felt the inner walls enclosing her fingers tighten. Ryan threaded her fingers through Tobi's hair and pulled her closer as the orgasm tore through her, and she cried out.

As Ryan's body relaxed around her, Tobi moved up next to her and cradled Ryan in her arms. Tobi looked down into closed eyes and waited for her breathing to slow before speaking. Ryan opened her eyes as Tobi's fingers brushed across her cheek.

"You are so beautiful, Ryan," Tobi said as she leaned down to kiss her lips. "I love you."

Unfocused eyes settled upon Tobi's as Ryan's mouth opened slightly. "I love you, too."

Ryan rolled them over and looked down at her. "Your turn," she said as her hands went to Tobi's clothing.

Several hours and a few rug burns later, they fell into bed, completely satiated.

A call to David Hyde confirmed that Cynthia Raleigh was indeed the same Cindy he was referring to. Now to figure out exactly how Geraldo Santiago figured into the picture. Ryan logged into the computer and typed in Mr. Santiago's information. She was slowly reading through it when one particular item jumped out at her. She glanced back over the details she had written down the day before, and noted a discrepancy in the addresses. One was what came up from the phone check, and the other was the last reported address that was showing up today. Ryan wrote the other address down and browsed through the rest of the information. According to this spreadsheet, Mr. Santiago died from several gunshot wounds; one to his head had ultimately claimed his life.

"This just doesn't make sense," Ryan said quietly before clicking a few more keys. There were statements in the report that the death appeared to be a hunting accident. "What kind of accident has *multiple* gunshot wounds?"

"Keep talking to yourself, and soon they'll think you've really lost it."

Ryan looked up and saw a smirking Jake standing next to her. "Hey," she said, slapping his leg.

"Hey yourself. Whatcha got there?"

"It's the information on Geraldo Santiago. It says he died from multiple gunshot wounds during a hunting trip."

"Multiple?" Jake asked.

Ryan only nodded in response. "Jake, do you think it's just a coincidence that his name appears on a phone bill that belonged to a woman who is now dead, too?"

"Anything is possible at this point. Did you get an address?"

"As a matter of fact, I got two."

"Two?" Ryan held up the paper showing two addresses and Jake continued, "Well, we've got time, why don't we go check out at least one of them?"

"Sounds good," Ryan said as she grabbed her jacket to follow him.

"Turn here," Ryan said as the street came into view. "It should be down on the left." They had decided to check the address that coincided with the phone bill first and see what they came up with. They stopped and looked across the street at the front of the house. It appeared badly in need of repair. Shutters dangled off their hinges, and the screen door had a large rip through the center. The house itself needed a paint job. Various bags of detritus sat in the yard, and layers of trash were strewn across the porch.

"You ready?"

"Whenever you are," Ryan said.

They got out of the car and approached the house cautiously. Ryan stayed behind as Jake made his way up the rotting steps. Jake stepped over a bunch of old milk cartons and empty boxes and knocked solidly on the door with his nightstick. He waited for a minute before knocking again; they were both surprised to see a small child answer.

The little boy stared at them in surprise and seemed almost scared.

Jake crouched down to put himself at the boy's level before asking, "Hi, is your mommy or daddy home?"

The little boy continued to stare but didn't say a word. Just as Jake got ready to ask him again, he slammed the door in his face.

Raising both eyebrows when Jake looked at her, Ryan shrugged her shoulders. He stood back up and knocked again. This time when the door opened, a woman was standing there.

"Yes, what do you want?"

"Ma'am, we're looking for a Geraldo Santiago. Do you know who this man is?"

"No," she said as she started to close the door again.

"Wait..." Jake said, holding out his hand. "You've never heard of this man before?"

"I told you no, why you gotta keep bothering me?"

"Ma'am, your address came up in our database when we were checking cell phone records."

"I ain't got a cell phone, and there's been no man here in years."

"Thank you, ma'am. We'll lea–" he started to say as the door was closed in his face for a second time. Making his way back down the steps, he shook his head as they walked to the car. "I guess she's a little bitter about that, huh?"

"I guess so," Ryan said, chuckling.

Jake closed the door and glanced at his watch before looking at Ryan. "We really don't have time to check out the other address. Why don't we save it for tomorrow, and we'll do it first thing?"

"Okay." Ryan really didn't want to wait another day, but she knew their shift was almost up, and Jake had plans with Tim tonight, so she conceded.

Ryan sat in her Jeep after saying goodbye to Jake, thinking about the last address. She knew it was on the way home because the street name looked familiar. As she sat there sliding her hands up and down the steering wheel, she made the decision to check the address out on her own.

What are you doing, Ryan?
What do you mean?
Don't play that innocent game with me. You know that what you're thinking of doing is against standard operating procedures. *I know, but damn it, this is about Tobi! I made a vow to protect her. I can't do that if I'm sitting and waiting for this psycho son of a bitch to come to me.*
What about the trouble you could get into from work?
I'll have to cross that bridge when I get to it.
You have no backup! What about your own safety?
I refuse to sit back and let him get close enough to harm Tobi again.
This is not like you, Ryan. You don't go off half-cocked like some type of rogue agent.
Well, I've never felt this way about anyone before, and I won't let her be taken from me now.
But-
No buts, end of discussion.
She grabbed her cell phone and punched in Tobi's number.
"Ryan?" Tobi responded after a couple of rings.
"Hi, honey."
"What's wrong?"
"Nothing's wrong. I just wanted to let you know I'm on my way home, but I need to make a stop first. I shouldn't be too long, okay?"
"Okay, be careful, and I'll see you soon."
"Love you, baby."
"I love you, too," Tobi said before hanging up.
Ryan placed the phone back in its holder, started the car, and headed to the address on the piece of paper. Ryan took the exit off the highway and followed the street around as she glanced at the numbers on the buildings. She slowed to a stop in front of a house, checked the numbers to make sure they matched, and put the Jeep in park. Several lights were on in the house, so she figured someone was probably home. Ryan took a deep breath, climbed from the vehicle, and walked steadily to the front door. She looked around then knocked. As the door opened, she saw a

man who was a little taller than she was, but approximately the same age.

"Yes, may I help you, officer?" he said, opening the door a little farther.

"Yes, I'm looking for a Geraldo Santiago. Do you know where I can find him?"

He hesitated briefly then nodded before gesturing for Ryan to enter. "Please, come in. I was wondering how long it would be before someone caught on to him."

Ryan stepped into the house and felt the hairs on the back of her neck rise as he closed the door.

Chapter Nineteen

Ryan followed the man down a short narrow hallway to a living room. He rushed to pick up a few items lying on the couch.

"Have a seat," he said, tossing the papers onto a tiny table next to the recliner.

"Thank you," Ryan responded, sitting on the edge of the couch. "What did you mean when you said you wondered how long it was going to be before someone caught on to him?"

The man sat in the recliner bouncing his knees in a nervous gesture before raking his hand across his face. He blew out a mouthful of air, stood once again and clasped his hands under his arms.

"Listen, I just don't think you'd understand."

"What? What exactly am I supposed to understand here?"

"It's not so simple to explain," he said, raising his voice.

Ryan held her hands up. "Hold on. Why don't we just take it slow and you can try to explain it?"

He chewed on a thumbnail, but didn't respond; instead, he continued to stare at the coffee table.

"Sir?"

He dropped his hand and looked at Ryan as though he hadn't seen her before. "I'm kinda thirsty. Would you like something to drink?"

"No, thank you."

Nodding his head, he said, "I'll be right back."

Ryan watched him leave the room then let her eyes survey the walls. There were many pictures scattered about in various sizes. She walked over to peer more closely at a couple of them. Some of the smaller pictures contained a man and two young boys. As she stepped sideways following the pictures along the wall, she looked closely at each one. The last one was of an older man with someone she couldn't quite make out. She leaned closer to get a better look and bumped into a table, knocking a stack of papers to the floor. She kneeled to gather them up and stood. As she started to lay them back on the table, a sparkle caught her eye. Ryan reached down and picked up a bracelet that strongly resembled one that Tobi owned. She turned it over and noticed an inscription on the back. It read, *"To Sylvia, the love of my life, now and forever."*

"It's all makin' sense to you now, isn't it?"

Ryan jerked her head around and found herself looking down the barrel of a very large gun.

"Ya know, I couldn't have planned this better if I'd tried," he said with a leer.

"Who are you?"

"I'm your worst nightmare, lady." Motioning with the gun, he said, "Sit down."

She edged her way past him to the couch and sat.

"Go ahead and slide that piece I know you got over here."

Ryan slowly removed the gun from her holster and did as she was told. He picked it up and stuffed it into the waistband of his pants.

"Are you going to tell me who you are?"

"I'm exactly who you were looking for...well, almost. It won't hurt to tell you who I am now because soon it won't matter."

Ryan remained quiet while he continued to glare at her. Finally, he leaned back in his chair.

"I'm Geraldo Santiago, just not the one you think. Geraldo was my father, who happened to have a very…how should I say…untimely death." He narrowed his eyes at her, and Ryan got the feeling that his father's death was not an accident at all. With a wicked grin, he stood up and stepped closer to her. Yanking the bracelet from her fingers, he swung his arm back and smashed the butt of the gun against the right side of her head. He grabbed a fistful of Ryan's hair and pulled her face closer to his.

"You can call me Victor," he said through clenched teeth.

As he shoved her away from him, Ryan fell back against the couch, fighting the temptation to close her eyes. She reached up with her fingertips and lightly touched her head where Victor had hit her. Searing pain brought little white stars dancing before her eyes.

"Why are you doing this, Victor?"

"Why? Why?" he nearly screamed. "I'll tell you why. I was in the hallway that day, waitin' to see pictures of my baby. I heard Sylvia yellin' and then that bitch let the only woman I ever loved die. Now, she's gonna lose what's most precious to her."

Ryan watched as he pulled a little white envelope from his pocket, opened it, and looked inside. With almost a growl, he tipped it up and swallowed its contents. He crushed the paper between his fingers and threw it to the floor.

"You wanna know what that happens to be, Miss High and Mighty Cop?"

Not answering him was the wrong thing to do as he grabbed her by the front of her shirt. He jerked her forward, making her head pound even harder.

"Do you?"

"What?" Ryan rasped.

"You." He released her shirt and stepped back to the recliner. Turning, he said, "The best part is that she's gonna be here watchin'. I wanna see the look on her face when you die, and when I'm done with you, she's next."

"You don't have to do this, Victor. We can help."

"Help? What kind of fucking help do you think I need?" Appearing to grow even angrier, he spun back around. "Fuck that!"

Ryan had to think of some way to get to him. She had no doubt that if he got Tobi here, he'd follow through on his threats. The longer he paced around, the angrier he became.

"Victor, why don't you tell me about Sylvia?"

He stopped and looked at her. "What do you wanna know? She was an incredible woman. So full of love, and she was givin' me a child. Don't you see what that bitch took from us?"

"What else?"

"That bastard husband of hers didn't deserve her. He didn't know how to treat her. I was good to her. I gave her all the things he didn't."

"Why do you think that Dr. Drexler was the one who took all that from you?"

"She didn't try hard enough. She gave up and let my Sylvia die."

"Victor, what happened wasn't Dr. Drexler's fault."

"Shut up."

Continuing, Ryan said, "Don't you see? She just happened to be in the wrong place at the wrong time."

"I told you to shut up, bitch!"

She knew she was pressing her luck, but Ryan stood up and tried one more time. "She tried to save her, Victor. There was nothing she could do."

When Victor whirled around, she had no time to react as he slammed the gun into Ryan's already sore ribs, causing her to double over and fall to her hands and knees. As she felt the blow to the back of her head, Ryan collapsed onto the floor. The last thing she remembered before fading out was the smell of the musty carpet and the dark soles of the shoes standing before her.

"Where the heck is she, Tobi? She should have been here by now, shouldn't she?" Grace asked, peering at her watch.

"That's what I thought. She said she had to make a stop first but that she wouldn't be too long."

"That was almost two hours ago. Have you tried to call her?"

Nodding her head, Tobi responded, "Yes, I've tried twice with no answer. I'm getting a really bad feeling about this, Grace."

"This isn't like her at all. We should give Jake a call and see if he knows where she might be."

"I'll page him now."

Tobi opened her cell phone, found Jake's pager number in the contacts list, and waited for the beep. She entered Grace's home phone number and hung up.

"I put in your number, Grace, just in case Ryan tries to call."

"Okay, honey," she said, patting Tobi's hand. "I'm sure there's a good explanation for this."

"I hope so, but with everything that has been going on, I'm really worried."

Tobi jumped at the sound of the ringing phone. She clasped her hands nervously while Grace answered it.

"Yes, hello, Jake. I'm really sorry to bother you, but Ryan hasn't made it home yet, and I was wondering if you knew where she might be."

Tobi stood and listened to Grace's end of the conversation. Not being able to contain her nervous energy, she paced around the living room.

"Okay, yes, we'll see you in just a bit." Grace hung up the phone and turned toward Tobi. "Jake said Ryan left the same time he did, and as far as he knew, she was heading home."

Tobi felt almost dizzy as her heart rate quickened. Whatever stop Ryan had to make was the reason she wasn't home.

"Honey, sit down. You're white as a ghost. Jake is on his way over." Grace led her to the couch where Tobi sat down heavily.

"Thanks."

"I'm going to go fix us some coffee. I'll be right back, honey." Turning on her heel, Grace disappeared into the kitchen.

Where are you, Ryan? The sinking feeling Tobi felt in her stomach did nothing to alleviate her fears. She just prayed that Jake had some idea of what was going on, or where Ryan might be.

"Can you get that, Tobi?" Grace asked, hearing the knock at the front door. Tobi opened the door to see Jake standing there with Tim in tow.

"Hi, Jake, come on in. Hi, Tim."

"Hey kiddo," Jake said as he walked in and closed the door. Tim was as tall as Jake was but not as muscular. They were a striking couple together, and standing between them, Tobi felt small, yet very safe.

Tim wrapped his arm around Tobi and pulled her close. "How are you doing, honey?"

Close to tears, she hugged Tim and replied, "I'm okay. I just wish I knew what was going on."

Jake took a seat on the couch. "How long ago did she call?"

Grace walked back into the living room and handed Jake and Tim a mug before sitting down next to Tobi and handing her one.

"It's been over two hours."

Tobi relayed Ryan's exact words to Jake, and he sat there for a few minutes before saying anything.

"The only thing I can possibly think of that she would have done was to go check out that other address. She's stubborn enough that I don't think she wanted to wait another day to follow up on it."

"Do you know where this other address is?"

"Not right offhand, but I can get it. It'll just take a little time." Climbing to his feet, he gestured toward the phone, "May I?"

"Please...let us know if there's anything we can do," Grace said.

While Jake called the station, Tim, Grace, and Tobi talked quietly among themselves. He hung up the phone and sat back down.

"They're going to call me when they get the addresses. In the meantime, Tobi, is there anything at all you can remember about this guy?"

"No, I never saw him. The one time he got close enough, he hit me before I knew what was happening."

Before Jake could say anything else, Tobi's cell phone vibrated on the table. She quickly grabbed it and glanced at the number. Smiling at Jake, she stood up and answered.

"Hey, where are you, honey?"

Silence greeted her from the other end.

"Ryan?"

Tobi looked at Jake and shrugged her shoulders.

"Honey, are you there? Ryan?" Tobi asked, raising her voice.

"Well, isn't that sweet?" The voice sent chills down Tobi's spine. It was the same voice from the calls she had received in her office.

"Who are you? Where is Ryan?"

"Oh, we'll get to that, but first you're gonna listen to me, bitch."

Trembling slightly, Tobi sat back down. "I'm listening."

"If you ever want to see her alive again, you'll do exactly as I say."

Tobi stifled a sob and bit down hard on her lower lip before responding. "What do you want?"

"Before I answer any more of your questions, you're gonna meet me. After that, I'll tell you whatever you wanna know."

"Tell me where."

Tobi motioned for a pen, and Grace handed it and a piece of paper to her.

"How do I know she's still alive?" Tobi asked after writing down his instructions.

"Don't fuck with me, lady, or I'll kill her now."

"Wait. If you want me to show up there, you have to give me some indication that she's all right."

After a slight hesitation, he said, "Hang on."

Tobi listened intently and could hear a low moan and a rustling noise coming from the phone. Flinching at the sound of flesh hitting flesh and a cry of pain, Tobi put her hand over her mouth as her lips quivered. She kept quiet as she overheard him talking to someone.

"Come on, bitch, say something. I got your little girlfriend on the phone here."

"Tobi?" she heard faintly before more rustling and a loud crash occurred.

"Is that good enough for you?" he asked, breathing heavily.

"Please, don't hurt her. I'll be there. Just tell me when."

"You got one hour, lady. Come alone, and if you don't show, she's dead," he said.

"How will I find you?"

"You know what I look like; you've seen me around the hospital enough times," he said as he hung up.

"Oh, my God."

Tobi closed the phone and looked up to the expectant faces of Grace, Jake, and Tim. "He's got her and he's hurt her," she said as tears coursed down her cheeks.

Jake moved closer to her. "What exactly did he say?"

Tobi repeated the conversation, and also described what she heard just before the man hung up. "It was her, Jake. She said my name. I've got to get to her." Tobi stood and started to make her way around them.

Jake grabbed Tobi's arm to stop her. "You can't go to him alone, Tobi. It's not safe, and what happens if he gets you, too?"

"I have to do something, Jake. I just can't sit here and wait. He'll kill her!"

Taking her by her upper arms, he shook her gently. "I'm not asking you to sit here and wait. I'm just saying you can't go alone. I know the area where he wants to meet you. It's heavily populated. I'll go with you and keep back far enough so that he won't see me."

"I'll go, too," Grace said.

"Me, too," Tim added.

"Now, wait a minute. I can't expect you all to put yourself in danger for me," Tobi said.

Grace walked up to Tobi and placed her palm against her cheek. "I can and will, Tobi. That's my daughter we're talking about. Furthermore, I consider you my daughter, as well. What kind of mother would I be if I didn't do everything in my power to protect the ones I love?"

Tobi sobbed and threw herself into Grace's arms. Grace rubbed her back and held her close until the tears slowed.

"Now, let's all work together and bring Ryan home."

Tobi leaned back and nodded as she wiped her eyes with the tissue Tim handed her. "I'm sorry."

"Don't be sorry," Jake said. "We understand; but Grace, I need you and Tim to stay here in case they call back with that address." Glancing at Tim and seeing his nod of understanding, he looked at Grace and saw that she was about to argue. He placed a hand on her arm. "Please?"

Grace had a moment of indecision before finally agreeing. "Okay. Bring my girls back home to me, Jake."

"I'll do my best." Turning toward Tobi, he said, "To do that, Tobi, I need to call in some backup help."

"Jake, you can't do that. You know what he said. If I don't go alone, he'll kill her."

"I'll make sure he can't recognize them. We do this all the time."

Tobi saw the sincerity in his eyes and knew he wanted what was best for her and ultimately for Ryan. "Okay," she said with a resigned sigh.

Jake patted her knee and stood up. "I'll be right back," he said, heading toward the kitchen.

Jake returned after a few minutes and sat back down. "I've arranged for two squads to help. Let me show you how this is going to work." He grabbed the pen and paper and diagrammed the area. After marking the spot where Tobi was going to be, he placed Xs where the rest of them could find cover.

"Just try to keep some distance between the two of you at all times, okay?"

"Okay," Tobi said, standing.

Jake looked pointedly at each one of them before saying, "Let's do it."

Tara Wentz

Chapter Twenty

Victor yanked the cop upright and tightened the rope around her, effectively securing her to the chair. He grabbed a handful of her hair and jerked her head up to peer into eyes glazed over with pain. Even with the split lip and bruise forming on the side of her face, she was beautiful. If this had been anyone else, he would have found her extremely attractive, but knowing who she fucked infuriated him.

"Too bad your girlfriend had to go and screw everything up for you," he mumbled. "It'll be the last damned time she does. I'm gonna make sure of that."

He kicked her foot as he walked by and threw himself into the recliner. Running his hand along the side of the gun, he leaned forward.

"In less than an hour, that bitch will be standin' in front of me. I'll make her understand, then she'll really be sorry."

He grabbed a roll of duct tape and tore a long piece off. He placed it over Ryan's mouth, then tore off another piece and put it over the first.

"Don't want you gettin' any ideas while I'm gone."

He left the room to grab his coat and came back. He turned the television on and turned the volume up before walking to the doorway and taking one last look at the bruised cop. He tugged his coat on and strolled down the hall and out the door.

Ryan heard the door close and slumped in relief. Every part of her body ached. The last blow of his fist connecting with her jaw was almost more than she could handle. Whether she was quiet or not, it didn't seem to make much difference. Victor hated her, and nothing she could do would change that. Looking into the dark depths of his eyes, Ryan sensed that she was peering into the soul of a cold-blooded killer, and she and Tobi were his next victims. If only she could get these ropes loose.

After hearing his conversation with Tobi, Ryan knew she had to do something, and fast. She jerked against the tight restraints holding her to the chair, but they wouldn't budge. She looked down at the ropes holding her wrists and pulled to see if they were even the slightest bit loose. She lurched against the bonds again and again, but they remained fast. As she pulled one last time it made them tighter and the ropes dug into her ribs. Ryan's chest heaved as she tried to catch her breath. She closed her eyes in dejection as a single tear slipped down her cheek. *I'm so sorry, Tobi.*

Ryan opened her eyes. She realized she must have dozed off or passed out. It was a little darker outside, and the glow from the television provided the only illumination in the room. She glanced down at the table next to her where old and yellowed newspaper clippings were scattered about. One particular headline caught her eye. It read, *"Death of Young Boy a Mystery to County Examiners."* Narrowing her eyes, Ryan tried to make out what the article said but could only make out the name Santiago. As she pursed her lips, Ryan looked back to the pictures. *Is it possible that Victor was responsible for the other boy's death, as well as his father's?* The throbbing in her head was making it almost impossible to think. Images and thoughts floated around with no real meaning.

Ryan felt the bile rise in her throat and pushed her tongue against the tape, hoping to loosen it. Feeling it pull against her skin, it finally gave a little where the blood from her lip didn't allow it to adhere. She took deep breaths through the small opening, praying her stomach would settle.

Ryan heard voices outside the window and started yelling as much as the opening in the tape allowed. She continued screaming until her voice went hoarse, knowing there was only a slight chance of being heard. Feeling lightheaded, she listened for a response. The only thing her ears registered was the roar in her head. Ryan couldn't keep her eyes open any longer, so she let them close and willed the pain to subside. She thought about Tobi and all that she had come to mean to her.

Tobi rode with Jake to the open access mall and listened while he talked on his phone, relaying what had happened to this point.

"Yes, sir, I understand, sir." Nodding his head as if agreeing to something, he continued, "We'll meet you there, sir, and please remember what I said. There are to be absolutely no uniforms and no cruisers, marked or unmarked." Pausing, he said, "Copy that, sir."

He hung the phone up and looked at Tobi. "Are you hanging in there?"

"I am. I have to for Ryan."

"The captain has five officers, including himself, who will meet us there, and before you say anything, they will all be out of uniform. Also, he has another backup squad that will provide support."

"I hope this works, Jake."

"It's one of our own, Tobi, not to mention that Ryan's a pretty special lady."

With a sad smile, Tobi patted his arm. "Tell me what to expect when we get there."

As he drove, Jake outlined where the others would be in comparison to where she would be standing. The open access mall was similar to a big open courtyard with all of the store entrances being outside. All those entrances were facing the courtyard. He explained that once Tobi was in place, she could be seen from every direction.

"Just remember, keep as much distance as possible between the two of you, and whatever you do, do not leave the area with him."

"When will you get Ryan?"

"Assuming he's got her with him, we'll get her; don't worry about that."

"What do you mean, 'assuming he's got her with him'?"

"Tobi, I would be very surprised if he brings her along. For one, if he's harmed her, it would be visible and draw attention. Two, she's a cop, and the last thing he needs is for someone to recognize her."

"I..." Tobi swallowed, "I hadn't thought of that. Jake, I don't think I could stand to see...to see—"

"Tobi," he said before she could finish, "I'm going to tell you what I once told Ryan. You need to be strong. I know it's hard, but she needs you thinking as clearly as possible right now. You need to pay attention and listen for any kind of clues he may unintentionally drop."

Tobi took a few deep breaths and thought about what Jake was saying. Nodding her head, she responded, "Okay, you're right. We're almost there, so talk to me. What do I need to listen for?"

"Listen for anything...any kind of indication of where he might have her. Highways, roads, street names, color of a building, type of building, his car, and any names he might be using. Open your mind because it could be absolutely anything."

Jake pulled onto a side street and put the car in park. "This is where I get out; just in case he's watching you from the minute you arrive." He got out as Tobi slid behind the wheel. "You won't see me, but I'll be there. Just play it cool, and everything will be fine."

"Thanks, Jake."

He patted her shoulder and closed the door. Tobi buckled the seat belt, put the car in drive, and pulled away. She glanced in the rearview mirror and watched as Jake disappeared into the bushes. As she pulled into the lot two blocks later, she parked and shut off the engine.

Tobi exited the car and locked the door. She tucked the car keys into her jacket pocket, took a deep breath and turned to walk through the parking lot. She followed a sidewalk around the side to where it opened into the courtyard. Instantly spotting the large inflated balloons marking the spot where she was supposed to go, Tobi continued walking. As she did, she looked all around, taking in the multitude of shops and the even broader spectrum of people. *How on earth will they be able to keep me in their sight at all times?* Even with all the lights on, there were still some dark areas to lurk in. There were so many people just milling around outside the stores.

Tobi arrived at the specified bench and sat down. She continued watching as people passed back and forth through her line of vision. The noise and bustle around the courtyard should have made her more nervous; instead it faded into the back of her subconscious. Her eyes scanned the crowd urgently, looking for familiarity in the faces of complete strangers…in reality, looking for Ryan. She should have remembered her gloves, Tobi thought, as she rubbed her hands together to keep them warm. She glanced at her watch and realized there were still seven minutes until he was supposed to show. Tobi kept the same mantra running through her head. *Keep calm and think smart!* She would pump him for any information she could, and maybe they would get Ryan home before the night was over.

The small crowd in front of her dispersed, and there stood a man with the most diabolical smile on his face. Tobi swallowed hard, feeling her hands tremble and her heart racing. This was the eerie man from the elevator that day, and the same man she saw in the parking lot afterward. He'd been watching her all along. Tobi felt anger well up within her, and had to remind herself why she was here. *Ryan, this is for Ryan.*

He sat down next to her and remained silent. Tobi started to fidget as she waited for him to say something. Not being able to stand it any longer, Tobi broke the silence.

"Where is she?"

"What, you don't wanna know how I am or how my day has been?" he asked, feigning a hurt posture. "How's the head feelin'?"

Tobi saw the cocky grin on his face and faltered momentarily as understanding dawned on her. This was the man also responsible for the incident in the tunnel. Instinct told her she needed to get as far away from him as quickly as possible, but she was more concerned at this point about Ryan.

Tobi's muscles tensed and her palms became damp as she raised her chin defiantly. "Cut the sarcasm; you know why we're here."

"Tsk, tsk, Dr. Drexler. You don't need to be rude."

"Please, can you just tell me where she is?"

"In due time. Isn't it a lovely night out?"

"Why are you doing this to me?" Tobi asked with a slightly raised voice.

He leaned toward her. "Listen, bitch, we do this at my pace and no faster. You ever wanna see her alive again, you'll shut your fuckin' mouth and do what I say, you got that?" Swiping a hand across his face, he smeared a line of saliva that had slipped out during his tirade.

"Yes."

He sat back and replied, "Good."

Tobi chose to remain quiet and looked around to see if she could pick out any of Jake's men or Jake himself. She wanted to appear nonchalant, but if her heart beat any louder, it would give her away.

"You don't have a fuckin' clue what this is all 'bout, do you?"

"No, I really don't."

"Well, you will before it's all done and over with."

"Is it something Ryan did?"

With a snort, he stood up and started walking away. Tobi thought he was going to leave when he turned back and walked toward her. He stopped directly in front of her and bent at the waist so his face was within inches of her own.

"That your bitch's name?"

"That's my girlfriend's name, yes."

He waited a few seconds before saying anything more. "I bet you love her a lot, don't you?"

Unsure of how to answer, Tobi spoke from the heart. "Yes, I love her very much. I'd do anything for her."

"That's good to know, Doc, because you just may have to."

He sat back down and leaned in close. "Do you take me for a fool, Doc?"

"I…I don't know what you're talking about."

"Do you think that I would just assume you came here without any kind of help?"

"I came alone, just like you asked."

Laughing, he grabbed her arm, digging his nails in through her coat, and hissed, "She's a cop, you stupid bitch." With a jerk to her arm, he let go and leaned back.

She rubbed her arm to alleviate some of the pain but had no idea what to say. Luckily, she didn't have to talk because he started speaking before she got the chance.

"Here's what we're gonna do. You're gonna follow me, and we're gonna lose your tails. If I'm satisfied with what I see, I'll take you to her. If not, you're both dead. Understand?"

"Yes." *I'm sorry, Jake, please forgive me. I have to take a chance for Ryan's sake.*

Victor took her arm and jerked Tobi away from the direction she had entered. He knew that all the main entrances and alleys would probably be monitored, so he'd already made plans for their escape another way. Going into one of the shops, he said, "You'll have to hurry to keep up with me." They ran down some back stairs that opened into an underground passage, past several overflowing trash bins, and boxes upon boxes piled high. This appeared to be the place where all the stores dumped their trash for pickup. Victor pulled her through a dark and damp tunnel where the stench was so strong that Tobi felt bile rising in her throat. Just when she thought she couldn't stand it any longer, they came to the end of the tunnel, which opened into another underground passage. He opened one of the large steel doors and pushed her up the stairs. At the top, they went through another door that led directly into an alley. Looking around, Tobi realized they were across the street from the mall. "Over here," he said, yanking her arm toward a beat-up old van. He opened the door and motioned for her to get in. When she hesitated, he gave her a hard shove in the back.

"It's her funeral."

She climbed into the van and winced as he slammed the door. He hopped behind the wheel, started the van, and put it in gear all in one motion before quickly pulling away from the curb at high speed. Tobi wasn't able to retain much about where they were going. Not knowing what else to do, she reached into her pocket, opened her cell phone, and pushed a couple of random buttons. She wasn't sure what number was being speed dialed. She quickly pulled her hand back out because she didn't want to draw his attention to what she was doing. He darted in and out of traffic before exiting off the highway onto a residential street. Several blocks later, he pulled into a driveway, jumped out, and slammed the door. Yanking Tobi's door open, he roughly pulled her out. Tobi almost fell to her knees, but caught herself on the door and stood up.

She followed him up some worn steps and waited while he unlocked the door. He pushed it open and shoved her through as he stepped in. After he closed and locked the door, he looked at her.

"You did good. I had my doubts, but you must really love her."

Tobi ignored his remarks and just stood there. He wrenched her arm and pulled her down the hall and shoved her into a dimly lit room. Tobi stumbled over something on the floor and fell to her knees. As she stood back up, the lighting in the room intensified.

"Time to wake up, bitch. You've got company."

Tobi froze after hearing those words. Tied to a chair was a bruised and battered Ryan. She had a large mark on the side of her cheek that was partially obscured by a piece of tape covering her mouth. The side of her head appeared damp but from what Tobi wasn't sure.

Tobi's entire chest ached, and it took every ounce of her willpower not to run to Ryan immediately.

He grabbed Ryan by the hair and Tobi could hear her whimper. He pulled her head up and jerked it around before yelling, "I said, wake up!"

Slowly, Ryan's eyes opened, and Tobi could see the glazed and dilated look. She definitely had some kind of head injury, but Tobi was unsure of its extent.

"Stop!" Tobi knew she was taking a huge chance but walked over and shoved his arm away from Ryan. Glaring, he backed away and leaned against the wall.

"Ryan?" Tobi reached for the edge of the tape and gently pulled it off. Seeing Ryan's split lip and the blood on the tape made her blood boil. She was trying hard not to completely lose her temper now because she knew it would do neither of them any good. First chance she had, though, Tobi was going to make sure this bastard paid for every bump and bruise on Ryan's body.

Tobi put her fingers under Ryan's chin and raised her head. *God baby, what has he done to you?* Tobi could see tears and reached up with her thumbs to wipe them away.

"I'm sorry," Ryan whispered.

Tara Wentz

Chapter Twenty-one

Where the hell did they go?" Jake shouted.

"They just disappeared, Jake. I don't know what happened."

"Damn! Now, he's got them both. Whatever her reason for leaving with him, it had to be pretty important. I drilled it into her to stay away from him!"

He opened his phone and punched in Grace's number. As he waited for her to answer, he paced in front of the bench. How the hell was he going to explain to her what happened?

"Hello?"

"Grace, it's Jake."

"What's going on?"

"Well, I don't even know how to say this, so I'll just spit it out. Tobi went with him, and they disappeared. I have no idea where they went or even what direction to check. Did the station call back yet with that address?"

"No. What do you mean she went with him? She knew that was too dangerous."

"I know," he said, sighing. "Whatever the reason, Grace, I'm sure she felt she had to."

"Dear Lord, Jake, what are we going to do?"

"Just hang tight. I'm going to try one other thing. I'll call you back, okay?"

"Yes, all right."

He disconnected the call and immediately dialed another number. After the first ring, it went to voice mail. If Tobi had her cell phone on, that could mean a couple of things. Either she was using it or she was thinking along the same lines he was and turned it on so there was the possibility she could be tracked.

"Captain, I think we should call the phone company and find out what cell tower she's closest to. If we can narrow it down, among all of us we should be able to cover that area pretty fast."

"Good idea. You get on that, and I'm going to try and get those guys to pull their heads out of their asses and get me that fucking address!"

Jake watched as the captain stalked back to his car. He then placed a call to the cell phone company's corporate office.

"This is Sergeant Jake Smith, Badge Number 994, and I have a life and death emergency."

Jake patiently explained the situation and was told that if he went to the company's nearest cell phone dealer with proper identification, they would fax him the information he needed. If Tobi's phone had been a newer model they could have given him her exact location with the advancement of technology. After relaying this information to the captain, Jake headed to a nearby phone dealer. He obtained a map of the general area the signal was coming from and called the captain.

Agreeing that they'd all meet in a central location, Jake hung up and placed a call back to Grace.

"We have the general area she's in. We're all headed that way. I'll keep you updated as to what's going on."

"Thank you."

Grace hung up the phone and turned to Tim, visibly shaken. Tim pulled her to him in a comforting hug. "Keep your chin up, Grace. Ryan's smart, and you know she won't let anything happen to Tobi." At her tentative nod, he said, "C'mon, let's go play some cards. It'll take our minds off it a little."

She smiled and followed him into the kitchen, all the while saying a silent prayer. *Please watch over my girls.*

"Sweetheart, you have nothing to be sorry for," Tobi said, looking lovingly into Ryan's eyes. She knew Ryan was in a lot of pain because her normally vibrant eyes looked so dull. Tobi tilted Ryan's head so she could see the side of it; there was a nasty gash that appeared to have bled quite a bit but was dry at the moment.

"Get away from her!"

Tobi almost forgot the man was still standing there and jumped when he yelled. She backed away from Ryan and looked at him.

"Still haven't gotten any nicer, huh, Victor?" Ryan said.

Tobi bit her lip as he walked over to Ryan. She flinched when he grabbed Ryan by the face. "You're in no position to be smartin' off to me, you little bitch, so keep your mouth shut."

He shoved her face away from him, and Tobi could see white marks on Ryan's skin where his fingers had been. Ryan looked at Tobi and winked. Tobi wasn't sure what Ryan was up to, but watching him physically attack her was almost more than she could tolerate.

"Sit down."

Taking a seat on the farthest end of the couch allowed Tobi to keep Ryan in her sight, as well as Victor.

"Are you going to tell me what this is about?"

He looked at Ryan and asked, "You wanna tell her, or should I do the honors?" Seeing that she was going to keep quiet, he turned back to Tobi.

"Where to even start..." he said, pausing. "How 'bout the day you completely destroyed my life?"

"Me? What is it that I supposedly did to you?"

"You took the love of my life and my child from me."

"Victor, I don't know what you're talking about," Tobi said completely confused.

"Sylvia—do you remember her, or are they all just a blank face to you?"

Tobi glanced toward Ryan briefly then looked back. "I remember her, but what do I have to do with all this?"

"It's your fault that she's dead. You let her die," he said, pointing the gun at her. "Why didn't you save her? Answer me that!"

"I did everything in my power to help her, Victor. She had taken some kind of drug, and that's what ultimately killed her."

"She didn't take drugs. Why are you sayin' that 'bout her?"

As he paced around the room, Tobi could tell he was getting angrier and angrier.

"Why do you think she didn't take drugs?"

"Because she was always on my case 'bout them. I promised her I would get off the drugs, but it was so hard."

"I understand, Victor."

"You don't understand nothin,' bitch, but you will."

He walked over to the recliner and sat down. "You'll understand soon enough what losin' someone you love feels like."

With sudden clarity, Tobi realized that no matter what happened, he was going to kill Ryan. Glancing in her direction, Tobi knew that she would do whatever she had to for Ryan to survive this.

"Why don't you just let her go and take me? I'm the one you really want."

"Oh, don't worry about that 'cause when I'm done with her, you're next. You think I'm gonna let you just walk right out of here after watchin' me off your girlfriend?"

"Why don't you tell us about your brother, Victor? Did you kill him, too?" Ryan asked.

He stood up, walked over, and backhanded her, causing her split lip to bleed again. "Shut up! You don't have a fuckin' clue what you're talking about." Striding back to the wall, he clenched his fists before turning back around. "It was an accident. I tried to save him."

"Just like Dr. Drexler tried to save Sylvia?"

The bottom of Tobi's stomach was raw. A ball of fear worked its way up and threatened to choke her. *What the hell are you doing, Ryan?*

With a look of pure rage falling over his features, Victor stalked back over and grabbed Ryan with both hands. Shaking her and the chair, he yelled, "Shut up. Just shut up," through gritted teeth as he slammed her back down with such force that the chair teetered before settling.

"Let me guess; you tried to save him like you tried to save your father?" Ryan replied, breathing heavily.

Tobi stared wide-eyed at Ryan. She couldn't believe Ryan was purposefully provoking him.

"You just wanna die, don't you, bitch?" Nostrils flaring, he continued, "Keep it up, and I'll kill her before I ever get to you," he said, pointing in Tobi's direction.

Giving Ryan a look that said, "Please, be quiet," Tobi saw a small grin turn up the corner of her mouth. Puzzled, Tobi shook her head at Ryan, silently begging for her not to make him any angrier. Tobi raised an eyebrow at Ryan and concentrated on what she was trying to tell her.

Jake turned down each street, keeping his eyes peeled. They had been searching the remote area for almost an hour now and had yet to come up with anything.

"They have got to be here somewhere," he mumbled to himself.

He reached for the microphone and asked the captain if he had found anything yet.

"Nothing yet, but they should have that address for us real soon."

"What's taking so damned long?"

"They had to get the records again, Smith. Then, they need to cross-reference the name again to find what Thomas found."

"Figures. She always was smarter than all of us put together."

"That she is…we'll find her."

"I know. I just hope we're not too late." He ended the conversation and picked up his cell to call Grace.

"Hello."

"Hi, Grace. I just wanted to touch base. We're in the area of transmission, but we haven't found anything yet."

Jake heard her deep sigh and knew she was feeling as nervous as the rest of them. Ryan was her only daughter, and the bond they shared was amazing. Grace was not only Ryan's mother, she was also her friend, and she'd fight tooth and nail with the rest of them until Ryan was found.

"We'll find them, Grace. That's a promise I will keep."

"Be careful, Jake. Tim would like to talk to you."

After some rustling, he heard Tim's strong voice. "Hey, how's it going?"

"Not too good. I can't find a damn thing out here in the dark. Honestly, we could be missing a lot of things, but we're doing everything we can."

"That's all you can do, honey."

"I know. How's she holding up, Tim?"

"She's doing remarkably well. I admire her strength and courage. I'm not sure I'd be doing as well as she has been."

"If there's one thing I know about Grace, it's that she's a fighter. You'll never meet another woman with as much tenacity."

"I agree completely," Tim said, hesitating before continuing. "I love you, Jake. Please be careful."

"Love you, too. I'll call when I know something."

Jake had no more than hung up when his radio crackled. Grasping the microphone, he responded, "This is Charlie Nine, go ahead."

"Charlie Nine, we have that address you were holding for, over."

"Go ahead, Dispatch, over."

Writing down the address, Jake replied, "Copy, over."

"Captain?"

"What have you got, Smith?"

After giving him the address, Jake turned the car around and sped in that direction. He rounded the corner and pulled up next to the unmarked police vehicles before hopping out and running over to where the other officers were standing.

"Listen up," the captain said. "Here's what we're going to do."

The captain explained the procedure twice. "Does anyone have any questions?" Waiting for a few seconds, he continued, "Nobody moves or fires unless I give the word, understand?"

With a round of "yes, sirs," the men spread out and surrounded the house. Just as Jake was getting ready to peer through a window, he heard a gunshot ring out.

Giving the order, the captain shouted, "Go!"

Over the pounding in her head and face, Ryan could see that Victor was getting extremely pissed off and unpredictable. He was pacing back and forth, casting furtive glances at her and Tobi, and his hands kept tightening around the gun. She hoped that if she kept him off balance, she would get him confused enough for Tobi to make a move. At first, she wasn't sure if Tobi had understood what she was doing, but before long, Tobi also was making comments to him.

"So, are you saying that you tried to save your brother but not your father?" Tobi asked.

Swinging back toward Tobi, he stomped over and got in her face. He had one foot on the floor and the other resting on the couch, straddling her hips as he leaned into her. "Shut your fuckin' mouth, bitch." He stared at her for a long time before moving away. "What is the matter with you two? Are you wantin' me to just shoot you sooner than I had planned?"

With his back briefly turned to them, Ryan looked at Tobi and nodded her head. Ryan knew that Tobi understood as she nodded in reply and grinned. *Yes! This could work, just play it cool, Ryan, and you both might get out of here alive.* With any luck, she'd find an opening and could act upon it. Ryan just hoped that it didn't get them both killed in the process. Even though that's what he had in mind, they would die trying to fight back instead of letting him just do what he wanted.

"So, how exactly did you kill your brother, Victor?"

As his control snapped, he turned toward Ryan with his back to Tobi. Raising his gun, he said, "I've had it with you, bitch. Your time is up."

Eyes wide, Ryan watched as everything happened in slow motion. Upon hearing his words, Tobi jumped up, yelling, "No!"

Tobi wrapped her arms around his and yanked down, and he pulled the trigger. Ryan felt a white hot searing pain pierce her left side just before the chair tipped and fell sideways. Moments after the gun went off, there was yelling, and Ryan could hear wood splintering. She looked up from the floor and saw Victor turn the gun on Tobi. Just as he tried to pull the trigger again, several bullets ripped through his body and threw him against the wall. As he slid down, his blood smeared the wall. He slumped to the side and stared at Ryan as his ominous dark eyes lost all signs of life.

The bonds holding Ryan to the chair were released, and she fell to the floor in a heap. Groaning, she closed her eyes to the intense pain wracking her body. Ryan knew he had shot her, but didn't know how bad the wound was. She felt her body being lifted slightly and opened her eyes to see Tobi cradling her in her arms and Jake standing beside her.

"Get an ambulance now!"

Tobi heard none of the commotion going on around her as she stared down into her lover's eyes. The pain coursing through Ryan dulled her normally bright eyes.

"Just hang in there, honey. Help is on the way," Tobi said as the tears flowed freely down her cheeks. She held Ryan tenderly while trying to hide the panic and fear threatening to shatter what was left of her already crumbling composure.

Ryan reached up then moaned before dropping her arm to her side again. "I love you, Tobi."

"I love you, too, baby." *Please, not now, not when I just found you!*

Ryan closed her eyes and tried to fight the lethargy that crept into her.

"Ryan, hang in there, kiddo. The ambulance is almost here," Jake said. Ryan could hear the fear in his voice and knew that things were worse than either was admitting. Looking at them both again, she smiled. Tobi was alive, and that's what was important.

"Jake," Ryan whispered. He leaned closer to her ear and she continued, "Thanks for being a friend when I needed one so badly. I'll never be able to repay you."

"Stop talking like that, Ryan. You know we love you, and I'm going to remind you of it when this is all over."

As the burning in her side seemed to subside, she felt fatigued and very cold. Ryan couldn't keep her eyes open any longer and let them close. She felt Tobi shift and cradle her closer.

"Ryan, you're going to be okay. I need you. Please open your eyes, honey," she desperately begged.

Forcing her eyes open again, Ryan looked into hers. "Tobi…"

"I'm right here, baby," Tobi said while rocking her gently.

"Tobi," Ryan rasped, "I don't even know your middle name."

Letting her eyes close one last time, Ryan could feel Tobi squeezing her tighter. She heard Tobi screaming, but the only word that seemed to make sense was "no," then nothing made sense at all. Her body completely relaxed, and Ryan felt as if she were floating.

Tara Wentz

Chapter Twenty-two

Tobi felt Ryan's body relax in her arms and knew that the life was seeping out of her. Frantically she ripped her jacket off and pressed it against Ryan's side, but the wound was still bleeding profusely, and the injuries to her head were making her condition even worse. The heavy ache invading Tobi's heart was more than she could bear.

"Ryan! Don't you leave me, baby. Don't you die on me!"

As Jake leaned down to take Ryan out of her arms, Tobi's body reacted of its own accord. She swung her arms at him and screamed, "No!" over and over.

She sobbed, frantically pleading with Jake not to take Ryan from her. "Please, I can't lose her, Jake."

Jake squatted down in front of Tobi and took hold of her arms. "Tobi, honey, the paramedics are here. You need to step out of the way so they can do their job."

Tobi put a hand to her mouth and nodded her head in acknowledgment. She moved back and stood up so the medical team could take over. Tobi watched as they ripped Ryan's shirt open, and she gasped at the wound in Ryan's side. She felt her knees go weak and would have fallen if not for Jake's arms around her. While one paramedic put compresses over Ryan's side, the other checked her vitals.

"She's got a weak pulse; she doesn't appear to be breathing on her own."

The paramedic started rescue breathing for her as the other put layers of gauze against Ryan's head and wrapped it to stop the flow of blood. He then positioned her head to put a mask over her face to continue forcing air into her lungs. Ryan never moved the entire time this was going on, including when the IVs were started in her arms. The paramedics hooked her up to the monitors, moved her onto a backboard, and lifted her to the gurney. Following them out, Tobi glanced at Victor and saw one paramedic shake his head at another as he covered the body with a sheet.

They wouldn't allow Tobi to ride in the ambulance with them to the hospital. Ryan's condition was critical and they needed all the room they had to try and stabilize her on the way to the hospital. Jake promised to follow right behind them. Sirens blaring, they pulled away from the scene.

"We need to call Grace, so she can meet us there," Tobi said emotionless.

"Do you want me to do it?"

Reaching for the phone, Tobi responded, "No, I'll call her, but thanks." She dialed the number and listened to each ring before Grace finally answered.

"Grace?"

"Tobi? Is that you, honey?"

"It's me. I'm okay."

"Oh, thank God! How about Ryan?"

Tobi hesitated, not realizing this would be so hard. "She...she's," she faltered, fighting back the tears, and Jake took the phone from her shaking fingers.

"Grace?"

"Jake," Grace said with a catch in her voice, "is my baby dead?"

"No, no, she's alive, but she was shot. They're taking her to Truman University Medical Center. We should be there in about ten minutes."

"I'm on the way, Jake."

"Okay, can I speak to Tim real quick?"

Without an answer, the next thing Jake heard was Tim's voice. "Hi, I'm assuming from what I heard on Grace's end that Ryan's hurt."

"She was shot, Tim, and it's pretty serious. Don't let Grace drive, please."

"I won't. I'll call Patrick, Morgan, and Lauren. We'll be there as soon as possible."

"Be careful."

Handing the phone back, Jake grasped Tobi's hand and squeezed. "She's going to be okay, Tobi. She's a strong person."

"She has to be," she murmured quietly.

Tobi glanced out the car window, not noticing the scenery going by; instead, her mind kept replaying the events of the last hour. Was there something she could have done differently to prevent Ryan's injury? Would Grace forgive her for putting her daughter in the middle of this whole fiasco? Would she be able to forgive herself?

Jake pulled into the emergency drive and had barely parked before Tobi jumped out. She rushed through the doors and followed as they wheeled Ryan into one of the trauma rooms. Tobi listened while they evaluated Ryan until a nurse approached her.

"Dr. Drexler, I know you want to be here, but I have to ask you to step out while they assess her status. I'm sorry."

"Please..."

"Let them help her, Tobi," she pleaded.

With a short nod of understanding, Tobi opened the door and, with one last look, walked out and into the waiting room. Jake stood up as she approached and encircled her in his arms.

"How are you doing?"

"I don't know, Jake. I—," Tobi faltered momentarily. "I feel like the best part of me is lying in that room and there isn't a damned thing I can do to help."

"I know, sweetie, I know."

Tobi burrowed into the warmth Jake's arms provided, failing to notice someone else approaching until she felt a hand at her back. Tobi looked up into the face of the one person she wasn't prepared to see.

As her eyes teared up, Tobi whispered, "I'm so sorry."

"Oh, baby," Grace said, wrapping her arms around Tobi.

Tobi held on tightly to Grace and was unable to control the tears that flowed freely down her face.

Whispering in Tobi's ear, Grace assured her, "It's going to be all right. Ryan's a fighter, and she's got something to fight for standing right here."

With a tremulous smile, Tobi replied, "Thank you."

Time passed slowly as they waited for word about Ryan's condition. Finally, Tom Asher came through the emergency room doors and approached Grace and Tobi.

"Tobi," he said, acknowledging her.

"Hi, Tom. I'd like you to meet Grace Thomas, Ryan's mother."

"Hello, Mrs. Thomas. I wish we were meeting under better circumstances."

"I wish we were, too, and please, it's Grace."

He nodded and continued. "Sorry to keep you all waiting out here so long, but we were doing some diagnostic tests. Since there was a blunt trauma to her head, we did a CT scan, which confirmed what's called an intracranial hemorrhage or bleed. Essentially that's bleeding within the skull that occurs when a blood vessel in the head is ruptured or leaking. The bleed is causing some increased intracranial pressure. We had already called the neurosurgeon when we found out that Ryan had a significant head injury and was in route to the hospital. He's here and has gone over the findings on the CT of her head. We also did a CT scan of her abdomen and pelvis. She has some internal bleeding, which appears to be coming from a lacerated spleen. She's being prepped for surgery as we speak, so we'll know more once we get her in there and take a better look."

"Tom, was she awake at any time?" Tobi asked.

"No. As soon as she arrived, they intubated her." Turning toward Grace, he said, "Right now, we are more concerned with the swelling around her brain, so we have put her into a medically induced coma. The neurosurgeon, Dr. Timothy Stafford, is going to be in the operating room at the same time we are, so when he's done, he can come out and brief you. Are there any more questions?"

Tobi looked at the others and waited until they all had an opportunity to ask questions before speaking. "Thanks, Tom. We'll be in the surgery waiting room."

Tom placed his hand on her shoulder and patted it gently before leaving. As he disappeared through the double doors, Tobi blew out a deep breath and turned to the others.

"I guess we just wait now."

"Why don't you show us where the waiting room is, Tobi? We may as well get settled because I think we're going to be here awhile," Grace said.

They made their way through the halls in silence, and Tobi couldn't prevent the one thought that kept pressing on her mind. She felt so responsible for what was happening to Ryan, and the guilt was consuming her. They entered the waiting room, and she found a chair in the back and out of the way. Sitting down, Tobi leaned her head against the wall and closed her eyes. She listened to the sounds around her and valiantly tried not to think.

Tobi heard voices coming their way, so she opened her eyes and raised her head. Patrick, Morgan, and a group of police officers walked into the waiting room and approached Grace. Tobi watched as Ryan's brothers hugged their mother, and the guilt she felt threatened to overwhelm her. She stood and paced in front of the large window overlooking the hospital parking lot. Tobi stopped and leaned her forehead against the glass and clasped her arms around her torso. She closed her eyes once again and prayed that Ryan would come out of this without any complications.

Tobi felt hands on her shoulders and looked up into Grace's reflection. Raising a hand to cover one of Grace's, Tobi looked down at her feet.

"Tobi, I know what you're over here thinking, and you can stop it right now. None of this is your fault. That man was very sick, and you are not responsible for his actions." She turned Tobi around to face her and looked directly into her eyes. "There is not one person here who blames you for what happened. If you don't believe me, take a look for yourself."

Tobi glanced over Grace's shoulder and encountered sympathetic smiles and nods of agreement. Grace pulled Tobi against her and hugged her before saying, "I love you like you were my own daughter, Tobi. Please quit beating yourself up about this, honey."

"I'll try," Tobi said as fresh tears fell from her eyes.

Reaching up to wipe them away, Grace said, "No more tears now. It's time for us to be strong because Ryan is going to need both of us when she gets out of surgery."

"Okay."

Grace took her hand and pulled her over to the rest of the group. Just as she was about to sit down, Tobi heard someone say Grace's name. Walking toward them was a tall and very beautiful blonde woman.

"I'm sorry I couldn't get here any sooner, Grace. Do you know anything yet?" she asked while hugging Ryan's mother.

"Not yet, sweetie," Grace said, pulling out of the embrace. Grace took the woman's hand and turned toward Tobi. "Have you met—"

"Tobi?" the blonde woman interrupted.

Tobi looked nervously between the two women before nodding her head. "Yes, I'm Tobi."

The woman took Tobi's hand with one of her own. . "It is so nice to finally meet you. I'm Lauren Bassett; we spoke on the phone."

Tobi smiled and relaxed visibly. "Lauren, it's great to meet you. I just wish it were for a different reason."

"It's the nature of her job, Tobi, whether it was you or someone else. I hope you understand that."

"I'm learning," Tobi said, looking at Grace.

The OR doors opened, and the crowd all turned to watch as a man in scrubs walked toward them. "Hello, I'm Dr. Stafford. Are you all with Ryan Thomas?"

Grace, flanked by Patrick and Morgan, stepped forward and shook his hand. "Yes, Doctor, we're her family."

"Let me tell you what I found and what we've done. As expected, we encountered a bleed within her skull, which caused some swelling. We placed a tube inside to help it drain and take away some of that pressure. It's just a matter of time at this point. We'll keep her monitored, and over the next twenty-four hours, we should know a little more about how this will affect her, if at all."

"You're saying that she may not have any complications from this, Dr. Stafford?" Grace asked.

"I won't know for sure until she wakes up and we can evaluate her, but she appears to be very healthy, and my hope is that she will recover with no side effects."

"Thank you, Doctor," Grace replied. *I hope so, too, for Tobi's sake as much as Ryan's.*

"I'm going to go back and get her transferred from surgery to the recovery room, but Dr. Asher should be out to talk with you shortly."

As he left, Grace turned to Tobi with a smile and pulled her into an embrace. "See? She's going to be all right, Tobi."

Tobi sighed in relief, but said nothing. Grace's support meant more to her than she'd ever be able to express in words. Actions definitely speak louder than words.

A short time later, Tom came out to talk to them, as well.

"Well, I've got good news. It seems the bullet did minimal damage. We had to remove her spleen because we couldn't stop the bleeding. Other than that, she has a couple of broken ribs. My guess is that the bullet ricocheted off the ribs and into her spleen. She'll be sore from the incision for a few days, but from my standpoint, things look really good."

"Thank you, Tom," Tobi said, taking her first full breath since she saw her lover shot.

"I'll be around. If you have any questions, please don't hesitate to have me paged." Pulling the surgery cap off his head, he walked away, turning back briefly to wave before disappearing through the operating suite doors.

After hearing the news, there were audible sighs of relief. Everyone sat and chatted among themselves and slowly the number of officers waiting started to dwindle down. As they said goodbye to Grace, they included Jake and Tobi in their parting thoughts and well-wishes. Jake was upset and very worried, as any partner would be. The other officers understood that bond and offered him support and encouragement. Lauren and Tim had stayed and made several trips during their wait to get coffee for everyone. Two hours later, a nurse told them that Ryan had been moved to the Intensive Care Unit for observation.

When they arrived at the ICU waiting room, they let the desk clerk know they were there. "Hello, Dr. Drexler. Ms. Thomas's nurse tonight is Andi, and she should be out shortly to talk with you all."

"Thank you," Tobi replied with a smile.

Andi arrived fifteen minutes later and told Grace and Tobi that they could see Ryan. As they entered Ryan's room, Grace took Tobi's hand. Being on this end of the hospital environment gave Tobi a whole different view of how things appeared to her patients. The room was sterile-looking even with the mauve and light blue accent colors. The hissing of the respirator and beeping of the monitors were the only sounds and added to the room's cold and morose feel.

Tobi stood beside the bed and looked down upon the woman who had come to mean so much to her. They had taken great care not to tape the tube near Ryan's split lip. Aside from the bruise marring her skin, she looked to be sleeping peacefully. Her head, which was wrapped in a large white bandage, had a drainage tube coming out of it. Tobi took Ryan's hand in hers and continued to lovingly gaze down at her. Ryan's skin was cold to the touch, but the warming blanket covering her would soon remedy that. She leaned down and placed a kiss on Ryan's cheek and whispered in her ear.

"I love you, Ryan. Come back to me soon, darling."

Tobi stood back up and watched as Grace took Ryan's other hand in hers. She was not crying, but there were tears visible on the edges of her eyelids. Tobi left the room to give Grace some time alone with Ryan, and went directly to a staff phone to place a call requesting a leave of absence. This time of year was when she typically took time off anyhow, so there wouldn't be a problem. Ryan needed her now more than the radiology department did.

Through the night, Grace and Tobi took turns staying with Ryan. The others had taken their leave after Grace promised to call if there were any changes. Each time her turn came about, Tobi stood or sat keeping a vigilant watch over Ryan. She was surprised seventeen hours later when Ryan opened her eyes.

"Hello there, beautiful."

Ryan turned her head slightly to look at Tobi and felt a moment of panic at her inability to speak because of the tube down her throat. She automatically reached for the tube before Tobi grabbed her hand. "Leave that alone, honey, its helping you breathe. I know it's uncomfortable. I'll have the nurse call your doctor, and we should be able to have it removed."

Tobi pushed the call button for Ryan's nurse as she continued to look into her eyes. When the nurse came in, she told her Ryan was awake and asked her to call Dr. Stafford. As the nurse left, Tobi reached over the railing and ran her fingers gently across Ryan's cheek.

Smiling, she said, "I love you, Ryan." She ran her fingers over Ryan's brow and leaned down, kissing where her fingers had just been.

When Dr. Stafford arrived, Tobi went to tell Grace that Ryan was awake. They both returned to the room just as he finished a brief assessment and was ready to take the tube out. Having the endotracheal tube removed from her throat made Ryan cough. The coughing jarred her side and she moaned. They had hooked up a second IV line that contained pain medication, so Tobi pushed the button to release a dose.

"I just gave you some pain medication through your IV, Ryan." Placing the button in Ryan's hand, Tobi said, "As long as it's not too soon, you should be able to push this when you feel you need something to take the edge off."

Ryan nodded her head and tried to talk. "My throat..." she whispered.

"I'll be right back, honey." Tobi left the room to get a cup of ice. Returning, she took a spoon and scooped some up. "Here you go." Tobi held the spoon close to her lips and Ryan took a couple of pieces in her mouth and sighed before closing her eyes.

Ryan slept off and on for the next several hours, and talked briefly when she was awake. During one of her waking moments, she asked for the details of what had happened at Victor's house. Tobi described the events as she remembered them, which seemed to satisfy Ryan.

Ryan felt a wave of relief wash over her knowing that Tobi was safe. There was a period of time at Victor's house when Ryan had experienced a fear she had never felt before.

"I love you so much, Tobi. I don't know what I would have done if I'd lost you. I was so afraid that everything I was doing wasn't enough."

"Honey, it was more than enough," Tobi started to say, reaching over to caress Ryan's cheek. "I can't imagine my life without you."

Ryan took Tobi's hand and gave her as big a grin as her healing split lip would allow.

"There's just one more thing I want to know," Ryan said.

Tobi laughed softly. "It's Elizabeth. My middle name is Elizabeth."

About the author

Born in 1969 and a lifelong Missouri resident, Tara Wentz shares her home with her life partner, Chris, her son, Conner, and their four dogs. Tara has been in the medical field for 17 years, a job she truly loves. Her hobbies include reading, photography, and writing.

If you have questions or comments please feel free to email her at twentz67@yahoo.com.

OTHER TITLES FROM INTAGLIO

A Nice Clean Murder
by Kate Sweeney; ISBN: 978-1-933113-78-4

Accidental Love
by B. L. Miller; ISBN: 1-933113-11-1

Assignment Sunrise
by I Christie; ISBN: 978-1-933113-40-1

Code Blue
by KatLyn; ISBN: 1-933113-09-X

Compensation
by S. Anne Gardner; ISBN: 978-1-933113-57-9

Crystal's Heart
by B. L. Miller & Verda Foster; ISBN: 1-933113-24-3

Define Destiny
by J. M. Dragon; ISBN: 1-933113-56-1

Gloria's Inn
by Robin Alexander; ISBN: 1-933113-01-4

Graceful Waters
by B. L. Miller & Verda Foster; ISBN: 1-933113-08-1

Halls Of Temptation
by Katie P. Moore; ISBN: 978-1-933113-42-5

Incommunicado
by N. M. Hill & J. P. Mercer; ISBN: 1-933113-10-3

Journey's Of Discoveries
by Ellis Paris Ramsay; ISBN: 978-1-933113-43-2

Josie & Rebecca: The Western Chronicles
by Vada Foster & BL Miller; ISBN: 1-933113-38-3

Misplaced People
by C. G. Devize; ISBN: 1-933113-30-8

Murky Waters
by Robin Alexander; ISBN: 1-933113-33-2

None So Blind
by LJ Maas; ISBN: 978-1-933113-44-9

Picking Up The Pace
by Kimberly LaFontaine; ISBN: 1-933113-41-3

Private Dancer
by T. J. Vertigo; ISBN: 978-1-933113-58-6

She Waits
By Kate Sweeney; ISBN: 978-1-933113-40-1

Southern Hearts
by Katie P Moore; ISBN: 1-933113-28-6

Storm Surge
by KatLyn; ISBN: 1-933113-06-5

These Dreams
by Verda Foster; ISBN: 1-933113-12-X

The Chosen
by Verda H Foster; ISBN: 978-1-933113-25-8

The Cost Of Commitment
by Lynn Ames; ISBN: 1-933113-02-2

The Flip Side of Desire
By Lynn Ames; ISBN: 978-1-933113-60-9

The Gift
by Verda Foster; ISBN: 1-933113-03-0

The Illusionist
by Fran Heckrotte; ISBN: 978-1-933113-31-9

The Last Train Home
by Blayne Cooper; ISBN: 1-933113-26-X

The Price of Fame
by Lynn Ames; ISBN: 1-933113-04-9

The Taking of Eden
by Robin Alexander; ISBN: 978-1-933113-53-1

The Value of Valor
by Lynn Ames; ISBN: 1-933113-04-9

The War Between The Hearts
by Nann Dunne; ISBN: 1-933113-27-8

With Every Breath
by Alex Alexander; ISBN: 1-933113-39-1

Forthcoming Releases

Bloodlust
By Fran Heckrotte

Contents Under Pressure
By Alison Nichol

Preying on Generosity
By Kimberly LaFontaine

Revelations
By Erin O'Reilly

You can purchase other Intaglio Publications
books online at StarCrossed Productions, Inc.
www.scp-inc.biz or at your local bookstore.

Published by
Intaglio Publications
Walker, LA

Visit us on the web:
www.intagliopub.com

Printed in the United States
76135LV00002B/269

9 781933 113739